INTERNATIONAL BESTSELLING AUTHOR
seven rue

SCAN THIS CODE FOR MORE SEVEN RUE BOOKS

Chapter One

Valley

"Beautiful, baby. Wet your nipples a little more and show me how they glisten. Fuck...you are one incredible young thing, Dove."

His shaky voice came from my laptop while he rubbed his hard cock right in front of his webcam while I sat on my bed, naked, playing with my tits the way he liked me to.

I've been a cam girl for two years now, wanting to explore my own body but doing it while having men watch me from all over the country.

My screen name was Dove, not wanting anyone I knew to find out about my secret, and my age now said twenty instead of eighteen.

I might've been lying about my age and name, but my body was what intrigued those dirty old men the most.

Most of them were in their forties, some in their fifties, and a few already in their sixties.

I didn't care about their age as much as they cared about mine, and although it was wrong for me to tease them with my body, knowing I wasn't even old enough to drink alcohol yet, I didn't feel disgusted with them watching me strip and touch myself one bit.

You could say I had major daddy issues, although my father was right downstairs, living his best life with my stepmom and not knowing what was going on behind my closed door.

Not sure where those daddy issues came from, but I'd fight anyone who'd tell me it was wrong and disgusting.

Hell, they're men after all.

Who cares about how old they were?

They have dicks, and that's what my mind was set on for the majority of the time.

Also not sure where my love for sex came from, but I had my first kiss at fifteen, and without the same-aged boy having a clue about what we were doing, I decided to explore his body and see what those older girls in town always talked about.

I didn't have siblings to learn about these things, and God forbid I'd ever talk to my stepmother, Della, about it.

School didn't help much either, and in sex-ed, the teacher only showed us a documentary about safe sex while skipping over the parts where the people in the video could be seen naked.

So I took it upon myself to learn everything about the human body, orgasms, bodily fluids, and all the different kinks that people had.

I had a lot of them myself, not being turned off by any particular ones.

And the man who was stroking his cock while his face was filled with pure pleasure had a few kinks we explored together.

His name's Garett, and pissing on himself was one of those kinks, or rubbing his cum into his skin after I made him come by just playing with my tits or rubbing my clit, or fingering myself while he watched.

I had moments where I thought it was wrong to be okay with such things, but then...life wouldn't be fun.

How boring would it be to never push your own limits?

I've pushed mine, and was still pushing them at times.

I wasn't ashamed of receiving some pocket money from these men to put on a virtual show so they could feel good about not going out and meeting women in real life.

They were old, which often resulted in them not getting any dates anymore, so camgirls would do.

"Spread your legs wider, Dove. Come on, baby. Show me how wet that pussy is," he growled, rubbing his cock faster with his knuckles turning white and his other hand pulling at his balls.

I leaned back against my headboard, not afraid of showing my face as I was wearing a ski mask anyway.

It was a stupid choice, but the only one I had available the first time I sat in front of my webcam.

It worked out just fine, and since my blue eyes weren't too special when it came to the color of them, there wasn't really much identification possible.

My long, brown hair was hidden underneath the mask as well, so I felt comfortable enough to show off every part of my body without being afraid of getting caught by some random guy who happened to live in the same town as me.

I moved my fingers from my wet nipples down to my stomach, then I spread my folds with two fingers on my left hand while pushing two from my right hand into my pussy.

"Like that, daddy?" I purred, licking my lips and moving my fingers in and out of my tight hole.

"Just like that, baby. Daddy's about to come. I wish you were here to swallow every single drop of my cum while I push my dick deep into your throat."

I loved dirty talking men.

I didn't care what age they were in that case, but if they had the ability to make me wet by just talking...*dear God.*

"How about you swallow it instead while I taste my pussy?" I suggested, knowing he'd be up for that.

It wasn't the first time I made him taste his own cum, but the dirty man he was, he seemed to have enjoyed it.

I loved having this power over men, and I didn't judge them if they were into different things that most men would find revolting.

If women can swallow cum or taste their own juices, why couldn't men?

"Show me those wet fingers, Dove," he demanded, and I pushed into my pussy once more before pulling them back out and holding them close to the camera for him to see.

"Fuuuck!"

He couldn't hold back any longer.

His white cum shot up into the air, landing right on his chest and stomach, and some even on his chin.

This was the time where he would fall into some type of trance, not able to speak while he did exactly what I suggested he'd do.

His hand kept rubbing his cock, making sure every last drop came out and with his other hand, he rubbed his cum into his skin before lifting his fingers to taste himself.

I smiled, doing the same with my wet fingers.

I watched him closely and started to pinch my nipples again, starting to feel ready for another man after him.

But there was no time.

I had to study for a stupid test, so getting him off was all I had time for today.

"Dove..." he breathed, trying to come back down from his high. "You earned another bonus tonight, baby. Promise me you'll be back tomorrow night. I can't spend one evening without seeing you."

My smile turned into a grin, knowing his bonuses were mostly just my actual price multiplied or even tripled.

This man spent most of his money on me, which I didn't complain about at all.

"You're the best, daddy. I promise I'll be back the day after tomorrow. I have a birthday to attend," I told him in my fake soft and sweet voice.

"Will there be men?" he asked, showing off his jealous side.

"Of course there will be men."

He knew I had other guys wanting to see me through my webcam as well. "You know I don't belong to you, daddy."

Daddy.

One word I had to get used to saying again, but not to my real dad.

That was something that made me slightly uncomfortable.

Funny, because I did far worse things than calling a strange man daddy.

But he wanted it this way, and his wish was my command. And his money was mine.

"I wish I could be there to show you just how hard I would fuck you, Dove. Have a good night. I'll see you in two days."

I smiled and waved at him, blew him one last kiss before turning off the camera and exiting the website I built shortly after realizing that those cam girl websites didn't get me anywhere.

Men who were serious about paying girls to make them come through a damn webcam paid monthly subscriptions.

I had at least eighty men who supported me, and not even half of them turned on their cameras when we set up a meeting through webcams.

They liked to watch me play with myself, others liked to show me how hard I made them, and a few just wanted to talk.

Not my favorite, but hey...it's their money.

Safe to say that next to being a college student I had a busy schedule, but I somehow managed to get everything done in time so Dad and Della wouldn't suspect anything.

I pushed my laptop aside and took the mask off before getting up and walking into my bathroom.

I needed a shower because as much as I loved making these men come, I needed to be clean and fresh to focus on school.

"Val, dinner's almost ready!" Della called out from downstairs.

I liked her.

Ever since Mom decided she didn't wanna be part of the family anymore, Dad decided that instead of being sad, he could look for a new woman who wouldn't leave.

Della was that woman, and I was happy for them.

Still, her way of living and her beliefs weren't exactly my cup of tea.

She was a strict Christian, and no way I could keep living in this house if she'd find out I didn't just call her husband daddy.

"Five minutes!" I called back, looking at myself in the mirror and brushing through my hair before putting it up into a high, messy bun.

I quickly stepped into the shower, and after only a few minutes, I was out again to dry my body and put on my pajamas.

I looked innocent.

Like a wallflower who'd rather hide in every possible situation.

Thing was, I *had* to act all innocent.

For Dad's sake.

And, well...also Della's.

Dad was once the mayor of this town, and God forbid his sweet daughter would ever turn into what her mother turned into.

Selfish, rude, and always up to no good.

Definitely had my mother's traits when it came to being naughty, but my family or the public didn't have to know that.

But I didn't want to do what my father did either.

Politics were never my thing, and I was okay with ordering men around, but not a whole town.

Perks of being his daughter were the big house and garden that came with it, but being seen as someone who could potentially run this town someday wasn't what I aimed for.

Not sure what I wanted to become after college, but for now, I was studying biology.

Because, well...I liked human bodies, and everything that came with them.

"Valley!" I heard my dad's voice call out, and I snapped out of my trance quickly.

"I'm coming!" I called out, walking out of the bathroom to get my phone from my nightstand and then heading downstairs and into the dining room.

"Smells good in here. Indian?" I asked, knowing Della liked to recreate recipes from all over the world.

"Malaysian, to be exact," Dad said as he poured himself a glass of red wine.

"I finally used all those spices I got for my birthday, and I think it turned out pretty good," Della said enthusiastically.

"It definitely looks good," I told her, then sat down on the other side of her while Dad sat at the head of the table.

"Thank you. Try it with this bread."

"Did you make this yourself as well?"

"Oh, no. I bought the bread. You know I'm not good at baking," she said with a soft laugh.

I smiled and filled my plate with a little bit of everything.

All that dirty talk made me hungry.

"Have you decided on the food for tomorrow, Dad?"

He nodded and after taking a bite of his bread with rice and some of the chicken on it, he looked at me and said, "Finger food. Seems appropriate for a 55th birthday party."

Agreed.

"Sounds good to me. And who have you all invited?"

I didn't like most of his political friends. They liked to rub their amazing lives into your face, even though Dad's was just as great.

I also disliked their daughters and sons. Stuck up private schoolers who talked too much about how they'd someday run for president.

Would be funny to see what they'd say if I told them what I did in my free time after classes.

"Some of my friends from my early workplaces and your cousins will be here too. It's been a while since you've seen them."

True, but that didn't mean it was necessary.

But then, it was Dad's birthday after all, and I couldn't just hide in my room and stream my naked body to a guy who pays me to see me finger myself.

"Oh, and your friend, Riggs will be here too!" Della announced happily.

"Riggs? Really?"

Why, that was a person I was excited to see.

Riggs was only a year older than Dad, but at fifty-six, he sure knew what to do to keep in shape.

"Oh, yes. He moved back into town last week. I forgot to tell you, Val."

Riggs was a close family friend, and he even tried to talk some sense into my mother before she took off and ran away.

He was a good man, though he always seemed so lonely.

Don't even think about it, the angel on my shoulder said, whereas the devil just grinned.

I puckered my lips and tried to hold back a smile. "Does he still live in the same house as before?" I asked.

"Think so. Anyway," Dad said, taking another flatbread. "I want you to clean your room tomorrow after school so our guests won't have anything to talk about behind our backs."

"My room's clean," I assured him.

Well, as clean as it could get. Just push aside all the dirty things that happen when I lock myself in it.

Chapter Two

Valley

"So no party at the country club tonight?" my best friend, Kennedy, asked as we walked down the hallway of the main building to get to the bathrooms.

"Can't. It's Dad's birthday and he wants me to be there."

I looked at my phone and smirked, reading Garett's message and remembering last night.

He really enjoyed his own cum, and now he was telling me how excited he was to do it all over again tomorrow night.

"Sounds boring," Kennedy said as we walked into the bathroom.

I looked around, then shrugged. "Not as boring as the parties at the country club. Those guys put me to sleep trying to have a conversation. Not to mention how lazy they get once you let them take you to bed."

I pushed open each stall to ensure no one else was in the room, and with Kennedy standing in front of the door to block it, I started to unbutton the first three buttons of my shirt.

This school had uniforms, and although it wasn't a private college, I still enjoyed the skirts and tights we had to wear.

Of course I'd always find ways to style it in a way I was able to show some skin, teasing not only my fellow students, but all the teachers roaming the halls.

They loved to stare, and since none of them were interested in stopping me from teasing, no one ever complained.

Lucky me.

"Those guys have dads, you know?" Kennedy pointed out, watching me as I pushed the strap of my bra down my shoulder, then holding my phone in front of me to take a picture of my tits busting out of my too tiny bra.

Kennedy knew everything about me being a cam girl, and having sex with older men whenever I had the opportunity to.

"Those dads are boring and most of them are married," I replied, taking a few pictures with my head cropped out.

I should've brought my ski mask, I thought.

"Since when did a ring stop you from fucking a guy your dad's age?" she asked with a grin.

"I might have a daddy kink, but I'm not a homewrecker."

"Gotcha," she mumbled, letting her head fall back against the door. "Can I come to your dad's birthday party then?"

I shrugged. "Sure, just know I won't be available to talk much. Dad wants me to network. He still thinks he can change my mind and make me like politics."

"How annoying," she said, brushing her long, blonde hair back and sighing.

"Who are those pictures for?" she then asked, nodding toward my phone as I was making sure no more than my tits could be seen in the pictures.

"His name is Garett," I told her, pulling my bra strap back up and covering myself again. "We had a fun time last night, and he wants to see me again tomorrow."

"I wish I could do what you're doing. Must be fun earning money by making yourself come," she said in a whiny tone.

"I told you it's not hard. Just get yourself a cam, set up a website, and I'll tell my men about you. I'm sure they would love you."

"I'm not nearly as hot as you are, Val. And I could never tease a man the way you do. You're a literal goddess. A dirty one, but in a good way."

I laughed, sending Garett the pictures and adding a few heart emojis.

They didn't have my actual number. I used my old phone to text with some of the guys, which made it easy to hide my identity.

"Next time I meet with a man, I'll let you be in the picture and we could have some fun to show them a good time."

"Lesbian stuff?" she asked with a frown. Although she wasn't judgmental toward me and everything I did, she was a little bit of a prude. "Have you done things like that before?"

"I hooked up with a girl when I was on vacation in South Africa last year, and I also made Maya come that night we were at the bonfire. Didn't I tell you about that?" I asked.

I was fairly open with her, but I guess I forgot to tell her about the girls I had fun with.

I was an open book when it came to sexuality, although I did prefer men.

Older, silver foxes who had experience and weren't afraid to be rough.

Through the cam or in real life.

God, it's been a while since I had sex with a man.

"Now I know," she said, puckering her lips and then smiling. "I think I'll pass for now. You're far too wild for me."

I chuckled and pushed my phone back into my jacket's pocket, then I nodded toward her to let her know we could leave the bathroom.

"I take that as a compliment. As long as you stay my best friend, I don't care if you let me suck on your clit or not."

"Is that the way you're supposed to talk in this school, Ms. Bentley?"

I stopped to turn around and look at Mr. Trapani.

Most definitely the hottest Italian teacher we had at this school.

Well, he was the only Italian teacher here, still...he had great potential.

A few more years, and a few more white hairs, and I'd put him on my list of men I'd want to fuck.

After graduating from college, of course.

I tilted my head and smiled at him sweetly, then I wrapped an arm around Kennedy's shoulders and leaned against her as she was almost a head shorter than me.

I wasn't the tallest girl at this school, standing at only five-foot-three, but I liked to think I was the perfect height.

"I'm sorry, Mr. T. I didn't mean to offend you," I told him, knowing that would only piss him off even more.

"Offend me? I'm not offended. I just think it's inappropriate for a girl your age to talk like that. Especially not in this school."

He was being dramatic.

Either that, or he just needed an excuse to talk to me.

His eyes had already moved to my tits five times in this short interaction we were having, and I had to admit...I liked the way he tried his hardest not to make it so obvious.

I pushed my chest out more, making my shirt open up a bit more to reveal my tits which were pushed up thanks to the tightness of my bra.

Would he have wanted me to talk about dicks instead? Because I'd gladly talk to him about those fascinating things.

"It won't happen again, Mr. T. Mi scuso," I said in Italian, showing off my language skills that I learned from him.

That made him grin, not able to hold it back.

With a shake of his head, he let out a soft chuckle. "All right, you two. Go to class."

One last look at my tits, a lick of his lips, then he disappeared.

"How have you not been kicked out of this school yet?" Kennedy asked, laughing.

"Simple. Dad's money."

***

"And I want you to go talk to people as well. No standing around and waiting for someone to come talk to you. And if you need to get out of a conversation, call out to me," Dad said as I made sure his tie wasn't crooked and the knot nice and tight.

"What if there's no one I want to talk to?" I asked, brushing along his chest to smooth out his white, button up shirt before helping him get his suit jacket on.

"There's no such thing, Valley. You'll find someone to talk to, and you will allow them to talk to you," he demanded.

He didn't take no for an answer, and the best thing for me to do was just do what I was told.

Even at his birthday he had to be this bossy.

A few glasses of wine and champagne would surely make him relax a little bit.

"How does it feel being fifty-five, Dad?" I asked with a smile as we looked into the big mirror in his closet.

"Not much different. I feel surprisingly healthy. Good thing I started working out a few weeks ago. All this food Della cooks can't be good if you want to stay in shape," he said.

I smiled, leaning against him and wrapping my arms around his arm. "I'm still in great shape," I pointed out, mostly to get a rise out of him.

I ate a lot, yet, my body didn't feel like gaining weight.

It didn't bother me much, as I had the necessary curves that made me look like an hourglass, but Dad always complained about me being too skinny.

He let his eyes wander over my body which was covered by a tight, short dress, and before he said something, I could tell he was trying to hide a frown and negative comment.

"You're beautiful as always, Val." He kissed the top of my head, then cleared his throat.

"We should head downstairs. The catering staff is here already, and the guests should arrive soon."

I nodded and smiled at him before pushing myself up onto my tiptoes to kiss his cheek. "Let's go."

With my arm hooked with Dad's, we walked out of his bedroom and down the stairs to find a few guests already standing in the foyer with a drink in their hands.

"Ah, there he is. The birthday boy!"

I smiled as one of his best and oldest friends, Lennard, announced Dad's arrival, raising his glass.

"Good to see you again," Dad said, greeting everyone and then looking back at me.

"Valley, come say hello."

Lennard and all the other guests weren't strangers to me, yet there was some type of distance between them and me which I wasn't sure why it even existed.

I grew up with all these people around me, but none of them became more than Dad's business partners or friends, and only a few of them ever came over to have dinner with us.

I'd say they were acquaintances to me. Not too close, yet familiar enough to trust them.

"Hello, Lennard," I said, smiling at him and letting him shake my hand with a firm grip.

He wasn't as tall as Dad was, and although they were the same age, Dad looked younger.

Must've been his clean-shaven face.

"Valley. You're getting more beautiful each day. Shame your mother isn't around to see you grow into a wonderful young woman."

If he hadn't mentioned my mother, I probably would've taken that as a compliment and even as a flirtatious try to get closer to me.

Mentioning my mother was never a good idea, and Dad thought the same.

"No need to bring up my ex-wife," he spat, trying not to sound too annoyed with his friend.

"Why, it's true, isn't it? She's a wonderful young lady. Sure you don't want to help run this town?"

Help run it.

As if a woman wasn't able to run a damn town on her own.

That sexist comment made me want to run for mayor, but that motivation quickly washed away as more guests arrived, interrupting this lovely conversation with Lennard.

"Excuse me. I'll go check on Della and see if she needs my help in the kitchen," I told him and my father, and after shooting a glare at Lennard, I turned and walked to the kitchen where Della was checking on her appetizers.

She insisted on making some of her own as she wanted to impress Dad's friends with her culinary skills.

"Oh, Valley. Come try one of these Bruschetta's I made."

Those weren't hard to make.

Just put some diced cherry tomatoes drizzled with olive oil, balsamic vinegar and salt onto a small piece of bread of your choice, sprinkle some basil on top and you're done.

But I didn't want to upset her, so I took a bite and smiled at her as the different tastes mixed together in my mouth.

"Delicious," I told her, eating the rest and then washing my hands in the sink to avoid oil stains on my dress.

"Thank you, sweetie. You look wonderful tonight," she complimented, looking down at my dress and then rubbing my arm.

"You too. That's a really lovely dress, Della."

I loved her like I should've loved my biological mother, but I had never had a real connection with her the way I did with Della.

She was the kindest woman I had ever met, and Dad was lucky to have her by his side.

"Thank you, darling. Here, take this," she said, handing me a glass with what looked like champagne in it.

I frowned at her and smelled what was inside the glass, and as the bubbles tickled my nose, I grinned. "You'll let me drink?"

"You somehow have to make it through the night, don't you?" she asked, winking at me.

"Go have fun, sweetie. I'll be right with you guys. Just have to finish up these salmon parfaits."

I smiled at her and nodded, and once I walked out of the kitchen to go back to Dad, I stopped in my tracks to take in all the new guests that had arrived in a matter of minutes.

How on earth would I find my father in this crowd?

I sighed, standing right there between the dining and living room, wondering where to go while our house filled up with more people.

"Dear God," I muttered, wishing the party would already be over.

I took a few sips of the champagne, not liking it at first but then forcing myself to enjoy it and taking another sip.

Although I illegally showed my body to adult men when I was only sixteen, I never tried alcohol before, and after this one glass I was afraid to already be addicted to it.

It soothed me in a way, and my heartbeat calmed for a while.

Until *he* walked in, making my heart pick up speed immediately.

Chapter Three

Riggs

Too many people for my liking.

No, let me correct myself.

Too many stuck up and arrogant people for my liking.

This wasn't really my scene, all these politicians thinking they'd do great things someday.

Most of them were in it for the money anyway, coming from rich families and wanting to make their ancestors proud by bragging with the money they received after their funerals.

It was all a damn game to them, and sadly, I couldn't say anything different about Andrew.

Sure, he's been my close friend for years, and if it hadn't been for my own damn parents feeling the need to push themselves between all these rich people in the city, I would've never met him or his family.

Shame his ex-wife ran away and left him and his daughter all alone, but that woman was a literal devil.

Too damn crazy and wild, and no good for this neighborhood.

But lucky him, he found a woman who was loyal and not crazy for his money, but for him.

Della was a wonderful woman, and I knew she was loved by Andrew and Valley.

Valley.

Seen her grow up right in front of my eyes and spent a few holidays watching her open presents with her big, blue eyes.

The same eyes that were watching me closely in this very moment.

I felt them on me as I walked through the crowd in the foyer, but I didn't look at her as her eyes could be used as a damn weapon.

She was only eighteen, but behind all that sweetness and obedience, there was a little devil hiding.

I've seen her around town a few times with her friends, showing off her perfect curves and shooting those sensual looks to every man that walked past her.

She knew exactly what she was doing, and although it didn't seem like much, she had the power to make a grown ass man fall to his knees and surrender with just her eyes.

There was so much more to her, and I'd shoot a damn bullet through my head if I'd ever let her show me just how powerful she could be.

I tried my hardest not to look her way, but that tight, pine green dress hugging her body made it hard to keep my eyes off her.

I had enough control to push the thought of her aside and move closer to her father who was standing next to the stairs, talking to a few men I've seen before.

"He made it!" Andrew called out, lifting his glass and grinning at me before he pulled me into a hug.

"Happy birthday, brother," I said, patting his back and then stepping away to nod at the other men.

"Gentlemen, you remember Riggs? He's been out of town a lot in the past year, but he finally decided to stop working his ass off and enjoy his retirement."

I sure earned it.

I've been an Air Force pilot most of my life, and six years ago, I decided to step down and continue as an aircraft repairer, letting me travel all over the country.

It wasn't as fun as flying those things, but I didn't wanna stay home and wait for the day I die to come.

I liked the traveling part anyway, but now that I retired, I was ready to just relax and enjoy the rest of my life.

"Good to see you," I told them, pushing my hands into the pockets of my pants.

"Glad you could make it. Della will be happy to see you, and Valley—"

"I'm excited to see them as well," I interrupted him, not wanting to hear him talk about his daughter while she was still watching me closely.

Didn't she know it wasn't very kind to stare?

Then again...she did this to every man. Messing with their heads for her enjoyment.

My grumpiness quickly made the three men step aside to continue their conversation, and I was left with Andrew who was eyeing me closely.

"You doing okay, brother? You don't look too happy to be here and celebrate me getting a year older," he said with a chuckle.

"I'm fine. Had a long day unpacking and getting my shit together," I told him. "How are things going?"

"Not too bad. Renovated my office so I can work from home instead of heading into work every day. Can't stand those interns at the firm, and I need a quiet place to work and answer calls."

"Still wondering how you went from being the damn mayor of this town to owning a law firm," I said, letting out a low chuckle.

"You're forgetting that I studied law. I invested in that firm, and I'm not ready to let anyone else run it. Not until I find the right man to handle it all."

"Or woman. Let's not forget how smart and powerful women can be," Della pointed out as she walked up to us with a big smile on her face. "Riggs, I'm so happy you're finally back. It's time you took a few steps back from working so hard."

I placed my hand on her waist and leaned in to kiss her cheeks to greet her. "Good to see you, Della. You look lovely," I told her.

"Thank you. Would you like something to drink?"

"Whiskey neat," I replied, but instead of letting her go get me the drink, I stopped one of the catering staff and told him to bring it to me.

"Right away, sir," the guy said, and as he walked away, I looked straight into those passionate and lustful blue eyes.

She was standing by the archway leading into the dining room with an empty glass in her hand, her hair flowing down over one shoulder and almost reaching her hips.

Before I tore my gaze off her, I couldn't help but smirk at the way she kept teasing me with those eyes.

Safe to say she was up for playing games, but there were thirty-eight years between us, and there was no way she could handle the way I played.

"Ah, there she is. Val!" Andrew called out, waving his hand to finally make her look away from me.

I watched as she tensed up, then she set her glass down on one of the round tables before she started to walk over to us in those incredible black heels.

"It's been a while since you two saw each other, hm? You remember Riggs, don't you?" he asked his daughter.

Of course she does.

It's only been about a year.

My jaw clenched as her lips curled up into a sweet but devilish smile, and I fisted my hands in my pockets before pulling them out to greet her the same way I greeted her stepmother.

"Of course I remember him," she said in a playful voice, stepping closer and placing her hand on my shoulder while I kissed her cheeks gently.

I had placed one hand on her lower back, close to the curve of her ass, pulling her closer to me.

Her tight body pressed against mine as we hugged, and I couldn't help but move my fingertips toward her round ass, ready to squeeze it but deciding against it as we weren't alone in this house.

Besides...I could tease just as much as she teased me.

I stepped back and pushed my hands back into my pockets to keep them from doing something I'd later regret, and after taking a good look at her body, I looked back into her eyes.

"You doing okay, Valley?" I asked.

"Everything's perfect. Dad told me you retired," she said, and I gave her a quick nod as the catering guy came back with my whiskey.

"I did. Not sure if it was the right decision at fifty-six," I told her, mentioning my age just to make sure she knew I was more than triple her age.

But she was very well aware of that, smiling at me as I said those two numbers. "You worked hard all your life. You deserve a break," she told me, now smiling without any bad intentions behind it.

"Guess I do. Think it's time for your father to do the same. Don't want him to suffer from a heart attack if he keeps working hard like that."

Andrew and Della laughed as I kept my eyes on Valley.

I couldn't tear my eyes off her, no matter how hard I tried.

There was something intriguing and playful lingering in her gaze, and although I thought at first that she was only teasing to get a rise out of me, she was doing it because she wanted something.

Wanted me.

Shit.

A young girl like her shouldn't go after men my age, but who the fuck was I to stop her?

I took a sip of my whiskey while my eyes stayed on hers, but when someone called out her name, we both turned our heads to look at her friend walking toward us.

"Hello, Mr. and Mrs. Bentley," the girl said, smiling at them and losing it quickly as she stared up at me.

"Holy mother..." she whispered, quickly looking away and turning her attention to Valley.

"Hello, Kennedy. Didn't know Valley invited you," Andrew said.

"I forgot to tell you," Val said, smiling at her father apologetically. "You don't mind her being here, right?"

"Of course not. How are your parents, Kennedy?" Andrew asked.

"Oh, they're great. Happy birthday, by the way. Fifty-five looks good on you, Mr. Bentley," Kennedy said.

Unlike Valley, Kennedy was able to make that compliment without a flirtatious undertone.

"Thank you," he replied, making me wonder if he thought the same way about girls his daughter's age as I did.

I wasn't a creep, but I liked my women young.

Maybe in their early thirties, or even late twenties, but something about Valley and how she teased the shit outta me intrigued me.

I wanted more.

Wanted to taste the forbidden, but I couldn't.

"Would you girls like to help me in the kitchen really quick? I have a little surprise for the birthday boy," Della said, winking at Andrew.

"Of course," Valley said, reaching for her friend's hand and shooting me one last look and letting her eyes wander down my body.

Yeah, she definitely wasn't just flirting for fun.

She wanted so much more.

"Nice seeing you again, Riggs," she then said, making my dick twitch as if I was a fucking teenage boy not able to control my damn body.

I gave her a quick nod, then took another sip of my whiskey before turning back around to talk to Andrew.

As the women walked away, Valley put on quite a show with those long, smooth legs and round ass bouncing and her hips moving gracefully.

She checked if I was watching her, and when she noticed I was, she smirked before turning back around and making me look like a total fool.

Let's play then.

But by my rules.

Chapter Four

Valley

Riggs was one hell of a man.

I didn't care about his age, but him being a family friend might've been a slight issue.

He definitely noticed me teasing him, and although he liked to watch me, he didn't seem too pleased with my behavior.

Grumpy old man, I thought. *Just what I like.*

I couldn't help a grin as I left my bathroom to head back downstairs where Kennedy was waiting on me, but I took a second to take a faceless mirror selfie and send it to five of the men who I would be seeing later this week via web cam.

A little something to get you excited for our night alone soon, I wrote in the text underneath the picture, and once I sent the messages, I left my phone on my bed to head downstairs again.

Kennedy was standing next to the group of teens consisting mostly of my cousins, and when I reached them, I smiled at everyone before inviting them to go outside and hang out by the pool.

The weather was nice, and although summer was already over, it was warm outside.

"Hey, Valley?" Milo, my fifteen-year-old cousin stopped next to me as we stepped outside, and I turned to look at him.

"What's up, Milo? Heard you're attending private school now as well," I said, not really caring about that as they lived about two hours away from here.

"I do. Is it true you slept with one of your teachers?" he asked without a filter in front of his mouth.

Guess we really were related.

"Who told you that?" I asked, tilting my head to the side with an amused smile.

"Everyone's saying it, but I heard it from Joe."

Joe was seventeen and attended the private school here in town.

The same one I would've attended if I didn't have to beg Dad to not make me go there.

I turned to look for Joe, and when I found him standing there with his brother and our other cousin, I laughed and shook my head.

"Which teacher, Joe?"

He looked at me with some type of unsureness in his eyes, but then he puffed up his chest to seem more confident. "Mr. Trapani. I've heard it from Penn."

"So, is it true?" Milo asked, grinning like an idiot.

"God, I wish. Mr. T is hot," I said to confuse but also shock them.

I didn't have sex with Mr. T, although I wouldn't shy away from it if he weren't my teacher.

"She didn't sleep with him," Kennedy assured them, and I rolled my eyes at her for ruining all the fun.

"Why not?" Joe asked.

I ignored his question and sat down on the lounger close to the pool with Kennedy next to me and my other cousin, Beatrix following us.

She was Milo's older sister, and since she was my age, I didn't feel like I had to check what I said before talking like with the boys.

"Joe texted about it in our group chat. Didn't you read it?" Trix asked.

"No, I have that chat on mute and never open it," I explained, leaning back and crossing my legs to make sure none of those little rascals would get the stupid idea of taking a peek underneath my dress.

I wasn't wearing any underwear.

It would only look weird underneath a tight dress like this one, so I decided to skip that step when I got dressed.

"Why don't you have an Instagram, by the way? I tried to look you up, but your old account has been deleted," she said, puckering her lips.

Trix was a sweet girl, but a little too naïve for my liking.

She and Kennedy would be great friends, but they lived too far away to start an actual friendship.

"I don't use Instagram anymore."

"Why not?"

Because I use other socials to interact with people.

Men much older than me, to be exact.

"I don't like the app. It's boring, and I don't need to see pictures of people I see daily in school."

Trix nodded, smiling and then looking at Kennedy. "Do you have Instagram?"

I quickly ignored their conversation when Riggs stepped outside with his phone pressed to his ear and a cigarette ready between his fingers.

He had a deep frown between his brows, and his low voice made my chest vibrate without me being close to him.

I watched him as he moved toward the pool house, and when he stopped, listening to whoever he was talking to, he used that opportunity to light his cigarette.

Riggs was a handsome man.

White hair peeked through his natural black hair, and the highlights that came along with age made his gray eyes stand out even more.

He always looked grumpy, always frowning and silently cursing the world around him, but with all the new wrinkles he got in the past year, he didn't look like a fifty-six-year-old.

His thick beard was slowly turning white as well, hiding most of his wrinkles around his mouth and nose.

Yeah, Riggs was a handsome guy, and he definitely knew how to dress.

His black pants fit nicely on his narrow hips, and the gray, V-neck sweater covering the white dress shirt underneath hugged his chest perfectly.

His shoulders were wide and his arms thick, making me remember how they felt when he hugged me.

I felt the muscles underneath his clothes, and for his age, he seemed to have quite a few of them to show off.

Riggs had tattoos.

I knew because years back, when I was little, he used to come over to hang out with Dad and other guys right here in our garden, having a BBQ and drinking beers shirtless.

I wondered if I'd ever see him without a shirt on again.

"Val?"

I snapped out of my trance and looked at Kennedy who was smirking at me. "What?"

"Trix asked if you'd like to head back inside and get some food. We're both hungry, and that cake Della ordered looks delicious."

I looked back at Riggs who was still on the phone, but as he took another drag of his cigarette, he hung up the phone and let out a harsh laugh.

"You two go ahead. I wanna go talk to Riggs," I said.

I was hiding my attraction toward him, but Kennedy knew exactly what was going on in my mind.

I got up from the lounger and stopped as she grabbed my wrist. "At your dad's birthday party?" she asked with a raised brow.

"I'm just gonna talk to him," I said with a laugh, freeing my arm and then walking around the large pool to get to Riggs.

"Oh, boy," I heard Kennedy whisper, but there was nothing holding me back from making sure good ol' Riggs was okay.

He's Dad's friend. Why wouldn't I check in on him?

"Important call?" I asked as I stopped a few feet away from him, holding up my hand to shield my eyes to stop squinting because of the sun.

He puckered his lips under that thick beard of his, and with a quick shrug he answered, "Not really."

He studied me for a while before putting out the cigarette and throwing it into the strategically placed cigarette bin next to the pool house's entrance.

Dad spent most of his time in there during the summer, and when his friends were over, they liked to come out here and smoke before continuing with whatever they did in that pool house.

"That's a nice dress," he said, looking down at it and stopping at my shoes before he lifted his gaze again.

"Thank you. Dad says this color looks good on me," I told him.

"It does. But if you were my daughter, I wouldn't let you walk around like this. Not with all these men at this party."

"Good thing you aren't my father," I said, not able to hold back a smirk. "Would be a shame."

I moved my eyes from his down to his chest, then over his stomach and finally stopping at his crotch.

I wasn't one to brag, but the bulge wasn't there just seconds before.

Riggs muttered something under his breath I couldn't quite understand, but from the crease between his brows it was clear he was trying to keep his cool.

I liked him like this, on the verge of cracking, but Riggs wasn't like Garett. Or Fred. Or any other man I showed my young body to.

Another difference was...Riggs was here. Standing right in front of me.

I could touch him again. Get closer and let him feel my body with his big, rough hands.

But shortly after having those thoughts I wondered if he'd be brave enough to do it.

I knew he wanted to, but there was hesitation in his eyes.

His next words surprised me though.

"What are you up to?" he asked, raising a brow and keeping his eyes fixed on mine.

His stern look was dark, and when I tilted my head to look at him as innocently as possible, he spoke again.

"Don't play games with me, Valley."

I frowned and pouted. "What do you mean?"

He'd already broken through the wall I built up to try and hide my real self, and he didn't seem too happy with me teasing him like this.

"I mean for you to stop fucking around. It's not working, and whatever your goal is, you won't reach it. You're eighteen."

As if my age was statement enough for me to stop messing with him.

"What is it that you think I want to achieve?" I asked, sounding calm but being very amused by his sudden change of personality.

I liked this side of him.

He was rough and annoyed, with a dash of anger.

But, fuck me...he was so incredibly handsome.

Maybe I should start giving those older men a little more attention through my web cam from now on.

One thing was for sure...Garett could clear his schedule for tonight because I'd one hundred percent move our meeting to today instead of tomorrow.

"Just drop it. You're acting inappropriate and it's your father's birthday. You should go back inside."

His bossy voice sent shivers down my spine and right to my pussy.

Hell, I had no shame in finding his behavior attractive, and I was seriously trying to figure out if I should've kept going or do what he told me.

Either way, this wouldn't be our last interaction.

I licked my lips and bit down on my bottom one with my eyes taking another good look at him.

"See it as a compliment, Riggs. Out of all these men, young and old, you're the one I would wanna fuck."

That might've been a little too much, but I wasn't one to hide my attraction. Especially not toward a man like Riggs.

I turned on my heels and walked back around the pool, not looking back to see if he was looking because I was positive he was.

When I passed my cousins, I smiled at them and winked, knowing how much they wished we weren't related.

They already suspected me being into older men, so they wouldn't have a chance anyway.

As I entered the house, a few guests had already left, and Dad was sitting on the couch with Della next to him and a few others on the other couches.

"Ah, there she is. Valley, come sit with us," Dad said, holding out his hand to me.

I walked over to him and sat down next to him and Della, and with my hand on his knee, I looked up at him with a smile. "Enjoying your party, Dad?"

"It's wonderful. Gregory wants to ask you a few questions about college. He's been thinking about transferring Beatrix, and he wants to know what the teachers are like."

I looked over at uncle Greg who was sitting on the big chair with Trix next to him on the armrest.

I smiled at her, seeing her unsureness as I was sure she wouldn't want to leave her friends behind.

"The teachers are great, but I'm sure they're nothing compared to Trix's teachers at the private college."

A relieved look flashed in her eyes, and she knew I was helping her stay right where she was comfortable.

"But I've heard your school has a lot more to offer. I want Beatrix to follow in my footsteps. She knows a lot about politics and is on the right track to become the first female mayor of our town."

At least he wasn't sexist like some of Dad's other friends.

But then, the town they lived in was smaller, far closer than ours.

"Really, uncle Greg. My school isn't nearly as good as hers. She should stay where she feels most comfortable, and as much as I would love to go to school with my cousin, I think it's safe to say that she needs her friends back home more."

Just as Greg started to talk, Riggs walked back inside and stopped behind one of the couches to listen in on our conversation.

But instead of focusing on Greg, I couldn't stop looking at Riggs.

He looked pissed, and that intrigued me so damn much.

But maybe it was really the wrong time and place to tease and flirt with him.

Chapter Five

Valley

To my luck, Dad didn't need me to sit there and talk for much longer after the conversation I had with Greg, and I headed upstairs with Trix and Kennedy to get away from the adults.

We had been hanging out on my bed for almost two hours now, often trying to push our other cousins out of my room so they wouldn't bother our girls-night.

A knock at the door made us all roll our eyes, but when we heard Greg's voice, Trix quickly got up and sighed.

"Thank you for talking him out of transferring me. You're the best," she said with a thankful smile.

"Anytime." I got up as well and hugged her tight, then she said goodbye to Kennedy and left the room.

"Bye, Uncle Greg," I called out, waving at him and then closing the door again and locking it this time.

"Wanna watch me make a man come?" I asked Kennedy, and her eyes immediately widened.

"I, uh..."

I laughed, shaking my head at her. "Relax, I was just messing with you. But I do have to take a few pictures in this dress before I take it off later tonight."

I grabbed my phone from the bedside table and read the messages from those five men I had sent the pictures to.

Two responded with heart emojis, Garett replied with a long paragraph telling me how excited he was to see me again, and the other two sent dick pics back.

They looked great, and I immediately felt my pussy ache at the sight of those thick, veiny cocks.

I licked my lips and wondered what Riggs' cock looked like.

Was it as thick and long as these two?

I quickly texted Garett back to tell him that I'd have time for him tonight, and his response came back fast.

"Want me to take the pictures?" Kennedy offered.

"You know what...sure!"

I gave her my phone and pulled out the ski mask from under the mattress, knowing that was a place my parents would never look.

They didn't come into my room much anyway, and if they did, it was to make sure the room was clean.

Kennedy got up from the bed while I pulled the mask over my face and my hair back to then lie down on the bed and pose as sexy as possible.

After a few photos with the dress on, I slowly started to undress, letting one tit peek out first, then the other.

For a few pictures I pushed my fingers into my mouth to wet them, and then circled them around my nipples to make them glisten the way I knew the men would love.

Kennedy was fully focused on taking the picture that it took her a while to realize I was starting to finger myself.

I had no shame in what I did to earn some extra money, and Kennedy didn't see me as anything other than her best friend.

Her dirty best friend.

"Mind if you come a little closer?" I asked her, but she shook her head with no hesitation and walked closer to the bed.

"And they like these kinds of pictures?" she asked while I continued to push my two fingers into my tight pussy.

God, it's been a while since I had more than just my fingers in there, and I made a mental note to pull out my dildo for tonight.

Garett will love it.

"They are addicted to these kinds of pictures. You should try," I offered, but she quickly shook her head.

When we were done with the photoshoot, she gave me back my phone and sighed. "I wish I could do the things you do. You're so confident."

I knew I was, and at times it wasn't much of a good trait.

But it did make me feel powerful.

"You'll see. One day you'll be able to open up your heart and mind and do what you like to do."

"But being a cam girl doesn't fit me like it fits you," she said, puckering her lips and frowning.

"Being a cam girl doesn't require a certain characteristic, Kennedy. There are shy cam girls too, you know?"

"Yeah, but...your body is perfect. Have you noticed how all those men downstairs have been staring at you all evening long? I look like a—"

I covered her mouth with my hand—the one I didn't use to finger myself a few minutes before.

"You have perfect curves and your skin is smoother than my freshly-shaved vagina. One day, when you're ready, I'll teach you everything you need to know. You're a strong, powerful, and beautiful woman. Don't tear yourself down."

Her eyes never left mine during my short speech, and when she started to nod, I took my hand away from her mouth.

"Now, choose the pictures you think I should send them while I put on my sleepwear."

I heard a few cars outside drive away, and when I looked out the bedroom window, there were only five cars left outside.

One was mine, the one next to it belonged to Kennedy, two were Dad's, and the one next those was Riggs's.

So he's still here...

I put on my black satin pants and button up shirt which I liked to lounge in before taking it off again for sleep, then I took off my makeup and walked back into the bedroom.

"I think these ones are amazing," she told me, handing me back my phone.

I swiped through the ones she kept and I quickly sent them to some of the men.

"Wanna hang out a little longer? You could sleep here and we'll have a nice breakfast tomorrow morning," I suggested.

"I'd love to, but Dad will kill me if I'm not back before midnight. Rain check?"

I nodded, setting my phone down. "That's fine. So you're leaving right now?"

"Yeah, I better. But I'll see you on Monday, okay?"

I walked her to the front door, passing my parents and Riggs in the dining room.

"Goodnight, everyone," Kennedy said with a wave of her hand, and once they all said goodbye back, I hugged her and opened the door for her.

"See you Monday."

"Come join us, Valley. We're looking at some of my old photographs," Dad said as I walked back through the foyer.

I stopped at the dining table and looked at the photo albums spread out on the table with pictures of Dad when he was little, a teenager, and a young adult.

There were even a few from his and Della's wedding.

I smiled and took a seat next to Riggs who was sitting across from the other two.

"I love how vintage these pictures look," I said, taking one with Dad pictured on it when he was a toddler.

"They make me feel nostalgic. Cameras back then weren't as high quality as they are now," Dad said.

I knew that, but Dad had this thing of explaining things to me that I already knew about.

It somewhat bothered me, but I couldn't tell him to stop or he'd get upset.

"I think we still have the camera my parents owned. I put all those things in the attic years ago. We might be able to find it again and see if it works," he suggested.

While I looked at all the pictures, I felt Riggs tense next to me as I leaned in over the table to grab Della's wedding picture with her wedding dress on.

"This dress was amazing. Do you still have it?" I asked.

They got married eight years ago.

Riggs was there too, and I was only ten. The wedding itself was a lot of fun, but other than the ceremony and all the delicious food after, there wasn't much I remembered.

"I do, yes. Your father and I joked about you wearing it to your own wedding, but I didn't think you'd grow up to be taller than me."

Because my biological mother was short.

She was a petite woman, just like Della, but that didn't matter anyway.

"I'm not getting married," I said, placing the picture back down and receiving strange looks from my father.

"Where does that kind of statement suddenly come from?" he asked, his brows raised in confusion.

I shrugged. "I've never wanted to get married, Dad."

"Why not?"

Because the men I would fall for wouldn't be the ones you'd accept.

I shrugged again. "I don't need a ring and piece of paper to assure the man I love that I'll be faithful to him for the rest of my life," I said.

Riggs tensed again, and I had the sudden urge to touch him.

My hand moved to his lap and I wrapped my fingers along the inside of his thigh, squeezing gently.

My pussy ached again, and it seemed he was the one guy making me feel this way today.

Sure, I was excited for Garett later, but Riggs was right here.

Close enough to touch him.

So why wouldn't I?

A lump in my throat formed, making me unsure about what I was doing.

Was I scared of his reaction? No, way...

Riggs cleared his throat, but instead of pushing my hand away or pulling his leg aside, he spread his legs wider so I could reach even further down his inner thigh.

Muscular, and so damn thick.

He definitely still worked out daily, and for his age, that was quite impressive.

"She's eighteen, darling. And nowadays kids have other plans than to settle down and marry in their twenties," Della said, understanding what I was saying.

"I'm not saying she has to get married in her twenties, but it would be nice to have a son-in-law someday. Even grandkids."

And that was something I definitely would never have.

"You know how I feel about kids, Dad. I don't think I'll ever have any."

"Oh, nonsense. You're just not ready to have a family of your own yet, but soon enough you'll see that it's something you'll definitely want."

I didn't think so.

I knew I wouldn't, and no matter how much he wanted grandkids, there was no way I'd make that wish come true for him.

I tightened my grip on Riggs's inner thigh again, and after he moved his leg again, he placed his hand on mine and squeezed it hard, not caring if he was hurting me or not.

My breath hitched as he did it again, and after shooting a glance his way, he moved my hand further down toward his knee.

That's not where I wanted my hand to go.

I stopped him from pushing my hand further away, and when he realized I was fighting him, he shot a glare at me and growled quietly.

He fucking growled!

Luckily, Della was talking Dad into not pushing me to do what he wanted, but letting me decide what went on in my life.

Dear God, if they only knew...

I kept looking at Riggs while he gripped my hand tighter now, and seeing him this worked up I couldn't bite back a smile.

"You're awfully quiet tonight, Riggs," I told him, making Dad and Della look at me again.

"He's had a long day, sweetie. Why don't go make him a cup of tea?"

I nodded, pressing my lips into a tight line and then pulling my hand away from his thigh.

"What kind of tea would you like?" I asked him, trying not to sound like a tease.

"Surprise me," he mumbled, finally letting go of my hand.

Chapter Six

Riggs

Whatever game she was playing with me, I wasn't here to fuck around.

Not tonight.

Not after the many calls from my younger brother who's got himself into some major trouble.

He was stupid enough to mess with the law, and like always, I had to get him out of it again.

I'd let him suffer a while longer while I dealt with my own little problem.

She knew exactly what she was doing to me, and it was a pain in the ass getting up from the table without Andrew and Della noticing the bulge forming in my pants.

Valley had only touched my thigh, but as close as she got to my dick, it was impossible to make it stop twitching and growing in my damn pants.

I had noticed before that she hadn't been wearing any underwear underneath that tight dress, and if she did, they must've been made out of the thinnest damn fabric in the world.

I excused myself to go to the bathroom and tuck my damn dick away so it wouldn't be too obvious that Valley was turning me on with just her presence.

When I came back from the bathroom, I decided to walk through the kitchen and stop right behind Valley, as close to her as possible.

This whole house was shaped weirdly, so the dining room was in a large, rainbow-like shape.

Although I couldn't see or hear the others, I had to be careful.

But this girl was driving me insane, and she had to realize that it wasn't okay to tease an old man like this.

Not unless she wanted to be teased right back.

She tensed immediately, and I reached around her to cup her throat with my hand and tilt her head back against my shoulder.

"I told you not to play games with me," I growled, my lips close to her ear.

I felt her shiver underneath my touch, but instead of me making her feel uncomfortable, she fucking leaned back against me and closed her eyes while her lips slowly parted.

"But you seem to like the games I play," she breathed, her ass pressing against my crotch.

I tightened my grip on her throat and clenched my jaw. "And you dare to keep this up with your father sitting in the room next to us?"

She was reckless.

"Yes," she replied, as if it were the easiest question to answer.

My dick throbbed in my pants, and I cursed myself for even getting this close to her when I just could've gone back to the dining room.

I looked at her relaxed face, her eyes still closed as her tongue came out to lick her pale, pink lips.

"You are something else," I murmured under my breath, letting my lips trace her ear and my beard tickle her soft skin. "Tell me, Valley. How often do you go after guys your dad's age?"

I could already imagine what her answer would be, but I waited for her to catch her breath as I loosened my grip to let her talk.

"Almost always," she whispered back with a slight smirk on her lips.

She didn't seem afraid one bit of getting caught.

Maybe she liked that just as much as she liked older men.

I tightened my grip on her throat again, making her hold her breath while I pressed her against the kitchen counter.

She was just about to put the teabags into the cups filled with hot water, but she placed them onto the counter to reach up to me with one hand, and put the other between her back and my stomach.

She was also not afraid to get what she wanted.

Her hand moved closer to my crotch, but before she could get to it, I pressed my body against her tighter to lock her arm in between us, making it hard for her to move.

"Is that what you really want, Val? You know if I let you touch me, there's no going back," I warned, but she saw it as an open invitation.

I was still pressing my thumb and fingers against her airway, making it hard for her to breathe and speak.

Her hand wiggled between my stomach and her back, waiting a few more seconds before I left her suddenly, making her take in a deep breath and turn her head to look at me with teary eyes.

"Stay away from me, Valley," I warned again, hoping she would take the hint.

As hot and beautiful as she was, I would wreck her in no time.

I might not be the youngest anymore, but my body would destroy her.

My warning seemed to have been enough for now, and I walked back from where I came from to adjust my dick once again before heading back into the dining room.

I knew exactly what I had done just seconds before, but my mind was still blurry and needed to clear itself before I could start conversing with Andrew and Della again.

That little girl almost brought me to my knees, but as powerful as she was, I wouldn't fall to her feet whenever she wanted me to.

If anything, it'd be her on her knees in front of me with my damn dick deep in her mouth.

"Your brother doing okay? Do I need to help or something?" Andrew asked.

"No, I'll handle it. He needs to stop fucking around with shit he has no business with. That's all."

My brother was always a troublemaker, and while I did everything to have a good, long career, he decided to mess with drugs.

He wasn't an addict or anything, he just liked the money he received from selling and importing it.

He's been to jail before, and I wouldn't mind them getting him back in there for another few years to get his head straight.

He was almost fifty. Time to fucking grow up.

"I think I'm going to lie down. I'm tired, and I should be up early to study tomorrow morning."

We all looked up at Valley who placed a tray with three cups on it on the table, and with a gentle smile, she leaned in to kiss Della's cheek, then Andrew's.

"I'll see you in the morning, sweetie. Have a good night," Della said, and Valley nodded as she looked at me.

At first, I thought I had made her speechless, which to be honest, would've been best for us both.

Instead, she straightened up her back and swallowed hard, looking straight into my eyes with determination.

"Now that you're back in town, I hope to see you again soon, Riggs."

That sounded like a challenge, and I couldn't help but grin at her facial expression.

"Good night, Valley," was my response, and with a quick frown she left to go upstairs.

Definitely made her rethink everything she thought she could do to tease me, but that obviously didn't go as planned.

Valley

Even with Garett's moans and groans coming from my headphones, it was Riggs I imagined sitting there on that black, leather couch, stroking his cock while his other hand played with his balls.

I was horny, and it was all thanks to Riggs.

The way he grabbed me in the kitchen, the way he made me gasp for air, and the way he talked to me in that dirty, deep growling voice made me want to strip bare in front of him and let him do whatever he wanted to me.

I didn't care how much it hurt, as long as it was him doing all those things to me.

"Now fuck your tight pussy with that thing, Dove. Show me how hard you like to be fucked." Garett's voice made me snap out of my thoughts and I pulled the large dildo out of my mouth to place it at my entrance.

I was leaned back against the headboard of my bed with my legs spread wide and my other hand pulling at my nipples the way he asked me to just minutes before.

Getting the dildo out was a good idea, and when I closed my eyes, I imagined Riggs's cock pushing inside of my tightness.

"Oh, fuck..." I breathed, trying to be as quiet as possible.

Riggs had left a few minutes ago, and my parents were still downstairs, cleaning up what the catering staff didn't have to.

Their bedroom was on the other side of the house, but they still had to walk up the same stairs to get to the top floor.

"I want you to watch me, Dove. Keep those eyes on me while you fuck yourself. God, baby...my dick is so damn hard."

I tried to imagine his voice to be as low and mysterious as Riggs's, but just thinking about him helped me move closer toward an orgasm.

I really needed a real cock inside of me soon.

"Deeper, baby. I want you to fuck yourself deeper and harder. Fuck...I can see all your juices coming out of that sweet pussy," he muttered, rubbing his cock faster and pulling at his balls by gripping them tighter.

"Oh, yes, Daddy," I moaned, throwing my head back into the pillow and biting down on my bottom lip to stop myself from being too loud.

I had to get myself under control before Della or Dad would hear me.

That's the last thing I wanted, but being heard by Riggs wouldn't be so bad.

To keep myself from moaning too loudly, I pushed three fingers of my left hand into my mouth and started to suck on them, imagining them being Riggs' hard, thick cock.

I wondered what he tasted like.

What his cum tasted like.

I wanted him to come on my face, tits, stomach, pussy. Anywhere he pleased.

Because just from our short but intense interaction we had in the kitchen I knew he was a dirty man.

Maybe even dirtier than Garett who liked to drink and swallow his own piss and cum.

I didn't kink shame, and to be honest, some of those kinks turned me on as well.

Maybe more when I watched instead of participating, but seeing others push their limits, like the first time I told Garett I'd enjoy watching him drink his own urine, did something to me.

I wondered if Riggs had boundaries.

He didn't seem like the type of guy who would shy away from anything when it came to sex, and maybe one day I'd find out about everything he liked.

My legs started to tense, and I pulled my fingers out of my mouth to place them on one of my nipples again, circling it while pushing the dildo deeper into my pussy.

"Keep going, baby. Daddy wants to see you come. Make me proud, baby. Show Daddy just how much you like to be fucked hard."

His groans got louder and I was happy to have made the decision to put my headphones in.

I felt the tingles in my toes start to slowly creep up my legs, skipping right over my pussy but forming a ball of tension in my lower stomach.

I needed more, so I moved my hand to my clit and started to rub it with my wet fingers.

"GAH!"

Garett was way closer than I was, but I wanted to take my time and hope for an intense, hard-hitting orgasm while he muttered things through gritted teeth.

My breath started to hitch, wishing Riggs's hand was around my throat again.

I tried my hardest not to moan or make any loud noises, so I forced my voice to disappear while I kept rubbing my clit and fucking my pussy with the almost too realistic dildo.

Luckily those things came in boxes without logos on them, or else I could've never ordered all these sex toys right to my doorstep.

My toes curled as the orgasm washed over me, and I had to cover my mouth with my hand to keep every little noise to myself.

"That's it, baby. Show Daddy just how much you wanted this," he said, making me come down from my high quicker than I wanted to.

It was his voice.

Normally, he sounded great, but ever since Riggs...I only wanted his voice to talk dirty to me.

Chapter Seven

Valley

First thing I did in the morning was put away the dildo that was still lying next to me on my bed.

Last night was amazing, and after receiving an insane number of compliments from Garett before I turned off the webcam, I couldn't stop thinking about Riggs.

His voice echoed in my mind, making me squeeze my thighs together to stop the aching between them.

I could still feel his rough touch around my neck, and I wished I knew when I'd see him again.

Hopefully soon.

I got out of bed and looked into the mirror with a heavy sigh, then I walked into the bathroom to wash my face and put my hair back into a low ponytail.

It was only eight, but if I wanted to have a successful day studying, I needed to be up early enough.

Della was probably already making breakfast, but I took my time to do my morning routine before walking out of my room to head downstairs.

"Val?" Dad called out from the other side of the hallway, and I walked past the top of the stairs to get to his office.

"Good morning, Dad," I said, smiling at him sitting in his chair, and I waited for him to give me permission to enter his office.

He didn't like people walking into his office without asking permission, but when he saw me, he quickly nodded and smiled back at me.

"Sleep well?" he asked.

I nodded as I walked over to him, wrapping my arms around his neck and kissing his head.

I've always been a daddy's girl, and I was lucky to have him and Della, of course. But it's always been him, no matter how stern and strict he was while raising me.

"We went to sleep a little late, but I have a few things to deal with today before I can relax."

"You deserve a little break, Dad. When's the last time you had a vacation?" I asked, looking at the screen where he had three emails open at the same time.

"It's been more than a year. Della's birthday is coming up in a few weeks, and I was thinking of taking her somewhere. Don't worry, I'm taking care of myself."

I nodded, puckering my lips and looking at him again. "Take her to the Maldives. She's been talking about it for months."

Dad chuckled and nodded. "Guess she's been hinting it, huh?"

I laughed. "Seems like it."

Them going on vacation meant I'd have the house to myself, which was of course a great thing considering all the things I could do without them around.

"Are you coming downstairs?" I asked, stepping away from him.

"I'll be right with you girls. Tell Della to not use that Mexican seasoning on the eggs again. Salt on mine is just fine."

I smiled and nodded, then headed downstairs and into the kitchen where the smell of bacon filled my nose.

"Morning," I said, looking toward the stove to see if she was already cooking the eggs.

"Good morning, sweetie. You're up early," she pointed out, sounding surprised.

"I have to study, and if I sleep in, I won't find the motivation to get up and actually do something."

"That's good. Would you like some eggs as well?" she asked, smiling at me.

"Yes, please. Dad told me to let you know he wants just salt on the eggs. No special seasoning."

"Oh...he doesn't like it, hm? At least I know what not to buy anymore. I have so many things in the pantry I don't know what to do with."

"You'll find a way to use them," I encouraged. "Hey, when did Riggs leave last night?" I asked, knowing exactly when he did.

I heard his car, but I needed a way to start talking about him.

"A little after you went to bed. It's been nice seeing him again, hm?"

"Yes, very nice," I replied, biting the inside of my cheek. "So he retired...and he still lives alone," I stated, just wanting to be sure.

"I think he had a girlfriend a few months ago, but she lives in New York and he doesn't go back there anymore."

A girlfriend?

Did he touch her the way he touched me? And was she young like me?

Jealousy wasn't something I felt often, but knowing he had other women in his life bothered me a little.

I wasn't the relationship type myself, but I didn't want him to spend time with other women.

From now on.

"He looks good for his age, doesn't he?" I asked, needing to keep talking about him.

Maybe it wasn't the best idea to do so with my stepmother, but she wouldn't see my compliment as anything more than that.

"He really does. He told us last night that he turned his old office into a gym, and that he likes to go for runs a few times a week. I tried to talk your father into joining Riggs, but there's no way he would go on early morning runs," Della said, laughing softly.

I smiled. "Dad's getting lazier every day. His body more than his head though."

"He has to realize his life won't be over if he retires. I think that's what he's most afraid of. Feeling bored and lost without a job."

I nodded, knowing what she was saying was right.

"Maybe he'll realize it soon."

I helped her set the table and then we waited for Dad to come downstairs and sit down with us to eat breakfast.

My mind was already set on studying, and afterward, I wanted to reward myself with some online shopping.

Maybe I'd call up Kennedy and see if she could come over, but I knew how strict her parents were, and since she's gone out to a party last night already, that was probably enough for the week.

***

I lost time while studying, and it suddenly was five in the afternoon.

At least I had gotten a few things done, read a few chapters for an assignment, and got as much information into my head for the test on Tuesday.

I was so focused that I even forgot to eat lunch, and only snacked on the chocolate covered crackers I had lying around on my desk.

After pushing everything aside and packing my backpack for Monday, I got up and walked out of my room to find Della standing in the guest bathroom, folding towels.

"Your Dad and I thought you fell asleep. Have you been studying until now?" she asked with a smile.

"Yeah, and I have a major headache now," I said, sighing.

"Dinner will be ready soon. I'm sure it's food you're lacking." She looked at my body and puckered her lips. "Maybe your father is right, sweetie. You're losing weight again."

Again.

That wasn't true at all.

"Have you seen my tits and ass?" I asked bluntly, raising a brow at her.

She stopped moving and frowned. "Yes, and they're beautiful. But your waist and stomach...you look malnourished."

"I do not," I muttered. I simply didn't have the type of body to gain weight easily.

But it wasn't like I was trying to anyway.

I loved my body, and I knew the effect it had on men and women.

To avoid another one of her comments, I turned to walk back into my room to get my phone and then head downstairs to see Dad sitting on the couch and talking to someone on the phone.

"That doesn't matter. If he really wants to turn his life around, he'll accept my offer."

I listened in as I sat down on the couch next to him, and he gave me a quick nod to acknowledge me.

"I'm not offering again. He can agree, or keep on ruining his life. And that's final."

I puckered my lips as I kept listening while looking at my phone and going through Kennedy's messages she wrote throughout the day.

As focused as I was, I totally forgot to check my phone after asking her if she wanted to come by tonight.

Surprisingly, she had texted me *yes* five times, hoping for me to respond.

I quickly typed a reply, telling her she could come over later tonight after I had dinner.

A sleepover was just what I needed.

A good movie, snacks, and maybe a few nudes from my men.

Now that I let Garett see me last night instead of this evening, I had time to spend with my best friend.

"All right. Let me know what he says. I'll see you tomorrow."

He hung up and looked at me as I moved my gaze up to his, and with a smile, I said, "Kennedy is coming over later. We're having a sleepover."

He nodded. "Done studying?"

"Yes."

"Good," he said, standing up and placing his phone onto the coffee table. "Riggs will come over for dinner tomorrow night. We have a few things to talk about."

That made me sit up straight.

"Oh, that's great. You must've missed him the past year, huh?"

"Yeah. He's been the only one I could talk to about anything other than business. Great guy. I'm glad he's back," he told me.

If he only knew what his best friend did to me last night...

"I'm excited to see him again."

More excited than I've been in a long time.

It seemed like all the men I usually had fun with weren't as exciting as they once were, and no matter how hard I'd have to work for it, I wanted to see Riggs naked.

Touch and feel every inch of him, and show him just how bad I could be.

He liked the way I teased him, despite his grumpy and annoyed behavior last night.

He enjoyed touching me just as much, and I wanted more.

So much more.

"Help Della in the kitchen, will you? I have a few more emails to send and then we can have dinner."

I nodded as he walked out, leaving me all alone in the big living room with my naughty thoughts about my dad's best friend.

I looked at his phone on the coffee table and thought about unlocking it to get to Riggs's number.

Sending him a picture of me in my underwear sounded intriguing, and as reckless as I was, I grabbed the phone and put the password in to get to Dad's contacts.

It wasn't okay looking through his contacts, but it wasn't like I read his emails or messages, right?

When I found his name in the list, I quickly snapped a picture of his number with my phone as I couldn't use my actual phone to send him a naughty picture.

Might even be fun to make him guess who sent him pictures like that, which made it all even more exciting.

I grinned, because although I was used to doing crazy things like this, something about it being Riggs made my heart pump faster.

***

"Don't you think that's a little too…"

"Slutty?" I asked, finishing Kennedy's sentence after I told her my plan to send Riggs a naughty picture from my second phone.

How much fun would it be to know he got the message, saw a half-naked picture of me, but had no clue who was sending it?

"I just wanna have a little bit of fun with him, Kennedy. He was…intense last night. I wanna get back at him. Tease him a little more."

Kennedy studied me as she leaned back on the bed. We had both put on our pajamas, ready to cuddle up under the covers and watch a movie.

"But what if he knows it's you? If he's been as rude as he was last night, I can't imagine what he'd do if he figures out that's you in the picture."

He wasn't rude.

Well, at least that's how I interpreted it.

I was turned on by his asshole-behavior, and I desperately needed more.

I looked down at my phone and shrugged, checking his number which I had taken a picture of earlier this evening.

Riggs number was saved into my contacts of my second phone, and with a smug grin, I opened his chat and tapped on the camera icon.

"He won't figure it out if I don't show my face and have my hair up in a bun. Besides, he's never seen my lingerie, so there's no way he'll figure it out."

Although I wanted that to be how this turned out, I had no doubt he'd know sooner or later, seeing as there was probably no other eighteen-year-old wanting to mess with him.

I held my phone in front of me in selfie-mode, positioned myself in a way the wall behind me was empty, and snapped a few pictures with my other hand covering my tits or pulling down my bra strap just a little.

"You're wild," Kennedy muttered with a soft laugh.

"You should try it sometime. It's empowering," I told her.

"Empowering? In what way?"

I shrugged, sitting down next to her and getting under the covers before looking through the pictures I just took.

"I'm in control with what happens with this picture. My face isn't showing, and this bra isn't from a certain brand. You have the same one, if I'm not mistaken. I wasn't asked for such pictures by Riggs, but I know when he sees them, he will definitely keep his eyes on them for a little while before he starts to wonder who this mysterious girl is. And that, my friend, is what excites me."

It sounded stupid and not logical at all to her, but these little games I liked to play made me feel good.

It was fun, and to be fully honest, I wanted him to find out I sent him those pics to see how he'd act tomorrow night.

"So you're sending the pictures?" she asked.

"Yep. Right now," I replied with a smile, pressing *send* to get the pictures I was sure he'd like onto his phone.

"I hope he won't get angry. The way he looked last night frightened me. He was so...tall and scary. I've never seen a fifty-six-year-old like him."

Me neither, which was why Riggs was on my radar.

Chapter Eight

Valley

It took Riggs almost fourteen hours to see the pictures I sent him, and as expected, he didn't send anything back, nor did he block my number.

Guess he wouldn't mind me sending him a few more?

I grinned like a fool as I sat in front of the mirror in my bedroom the next day, curling my hair while Kennedy packed her clothes into her backpack.

"Sure you can't stay any longer?" I asked.

"Dad called me fifteen times already, and Mom has messaged me since eight this morning. If I'm not home in twenty minutes, I most likely won't be allowed to have a sleepover in the next twenty years."

I shook my head at her and sighed. "You're eighteen. When will they give you some privacy and space?"

I didn't dislike her parents, but I was glad they weren't mine.

Kennedy rolled her eyes and shrugged. "Probably the second I'm married. They wanna set me up with some guy. A friend's son who's just as rich and spoiled."

"They are too damn controlling," I mumbled, letting another long, beautiful curl fall over my chest.

"And now you should see why I could never become a cam girl. I'll see you Monday. I wanna hear all about tonight with Riggs," she said.

I smiled at her and nodded, then I turned back to look at myself in the mirror.

"See you Monday."

After Kennedy left, I finished curling my hair and put the curling iron away to then get dressed.

Having Riggs over for dinner was a great opportunity to put on something nice.

Maybe another dress, or a short skirt with a tight shirt.

I walked into my closet to look through my clothes, finding a skirt I used to wear a lot when I was sixteen.

It almost looked like my school uniform's skirt, but it was much shorter, barely covering my ass.

I grew a little over the past two years, but it still fit me and it was the perfect item to wear tonight.

I picked out a tight, white shirt with long sleeves to go with the skirt, and after quickly putting my outfit on, I tried to decide whether or not long socks would be needed.

It was warm enough in this house and I had shaved in the shower this morning, so maybe showing off some skin wasn't too bad.

I saw the way Riggs watched me last night, and it seemed like he quite enjoyed looking at my legs.

"This will do," I whispered, looking at myself in the mirror and choosing a pair of my whitest sneakers to finish up the look.

I didn't have to wear shoes inside, but sandals or Birkenstocks didn't really fit tonight.

"Val? Would you please come downstairs and help me with dinner?" I heard Della call out from the bottom of the stairs, and I quickly walked out of the bedroom to get to her.

"What's for dinner?" I asked as I walked into the kitchen where she was already cutting up some veggies.

"Mexican. And Italian. A little bit of everything," Della said.

"Interesting."

"We have so many things left in the fridge and I couldn't decide on one thing to cook. I've already put the pizza in the oven. Just help me season the chicken, please."

"Isn't it too early? Thought Riggs would come for dinner."

"It's almost five, sweetie, and I have a few more things to do before we can eat. He'll be here at six."

And the pizza really had to be in the oven for so long?

I turned to the oven to check, then noticed it wasn't even on or preheated.

As much as I wanted to, I wouldn't judge her cooking. It was her putting food on our table every day, so I couldn't allow myself to comment on the way she prepared our food.

"Isn't that skirt a little too short for you, Val? I thought you'd thrown it away years ago."

I had intended to, but then I discovered the world of cam girls and decided that I could put it to real good use.

Some of the men were into the whole schoolgirl thing, and since I still was one, they were still able to live their fantasies with the way I dressed for them at times.

"I thought I might be able to squeeze into it, so I kept it. Do I look bad?" I asked.

"Oh, no, you look beautiful. I just don't think your father will like the way you're dressed tonight."

Not only Dad.

I was excited to see Riggs's face when he saw me tonight.

I shrugged at her comment and continued to season the chicken with every spice she had put out for me to use, and since I was in control of them, I didn't put too much on the chicken, knowing those spices could quickly ruin a great dinner.

I felt good in what I was wearing, and I've always loved having tight clothes on.

The skirt was just a bonus, and although I was wearing underwear, the cool breeze between my thighs felt nice.

It got rid of all the hotness building down there, just waiting for Riggs to arrive and make me wetter than I already was.

Just the thought of him excited me, and I'd make sure to place my plate right next to his so I couldn't be sitting too far from him tonight.

***

"Just in time," Della said with a smile as the pizza was done.

I had already set the table for four and placed the bowls and plates with the food in the middle of it so everyone was able to reach it.

"Is Riggs here?" Dad asked as he walked down the stairs.

"He just arrived," I said, smiling at him. "You've been working all day again. It's Sunday, Dad."

"I had things to take care of. When you own a business, there's no time to take breaks. Just wait and see."

Still didn't think I would ever own a damn business.

Well, no business other than one for cam girls. That would be fun.

"Aren't you cold?" he asked as he noticed my exposed legs.

"No," I replied with a shrug, hoping he wouldn't say more.

To my luck, he only frowned for a few seconds before walking through the foyer to get to the front door right as Riggs rang the bell.

I brushed his judgemental glare off and followed him to see our guest come inside and hug him.

When Riggs noticed me, I couldn't help but grin at him before walking closer to greet him as well.

"Hi, Riggs," I said, trying not to sound too sweet.

He gave me a quick nod before looking away, and when he realized he couldn't just stay mute, he looked back at me and said, "Hello, Valley."

His deep voice sent shivers right down my spine and I bit my bottom lip to stop myself from grinning even wider.

"Oh, you're right on time, Riggs. Valley and I just finished cooking and we're ready to eat," Della announced from the dining room.

"Sounds wonderful, Della. It smells amazing," he said.

He was dressed almost same as last night, though a little less elegant. No dress shirt under his sweater, and his jeans looked comfortable enough to have a nice, laid-back dinner tonight.

I waited for Dad to pass me and then watched Riggs closely as he moved toward me with his eyes hooded and dark.

When he was close enough, he let his eyes move down my body, taking in every inch before pushing his fists into his pockets and blowing out air through his nose like a damn stallion.

As hot as he looked tonight, he didn't have that expected gleam in his eyes.

He really didn't know I sent him those pictures. Could that even be?

Not even a clue?

"No games tonight," he growled in a deep, warning voice, then he walked away to get to the dining room, leaving me standing by the entrance all alone.

Shame.

That's the only thing I wanted to do tonight.

But did he really think I would listen to him?

I let out a harsh laugh before turning around and heading to the dining room myself.

As planned, Riggs sat down right where I wanted him to, and when I sat next to him, he studied me for a moment before deciding it was okay for me to sit to his left.

"So, Riggs, did you have a nice Sunday?" Della asked while Dad poured wine into the glasses, leaving mine empty.

"Yeah, it was good. Had to handle a few things, but nothing too stressful."

"What things did you have to handle?" I asked.

He didn't answer at first, wondering if answering was worth it as he already knew I wasn't actually interested in what he did today, but what would happen tonight.

As if I would just sit there and listen to their conversations about whatever the hell they were interested in.

"Nothing special," he replied, his voice low. He moved his gaze to my parents who looked at him with more interest than expected, and Riggs let out a sigh and added more to his reply.

"I told you about my brother. He agreed to come back into town and stay with me until he gets his shit together."

That was a good enough answer for Dad to continue talking about Riggs's brother.

"And what did he say about my offer?"

"He's thinking about it. He's lazy. Often just sits arounds and smokes weed, waiting on whatever to happen."

"Have you ever smoked weed?" I asked, spicing up this conversation.

"Valley," Dad spat, giving me a look of disapproval.

"What? It's not like I asked him for his bank information," I said, holding up my hands to defend myself.

"You don't have to answer that," Della said apologetically.

And he didn't.

"He'll be back next week," he said instead.

I rolled my eyes and started to eat what I put onto my plate while the others continued to talk while eating their dinner as well.

I had imagined tonight to be a little more interesting and fun, and I hated how much control he had over me without ever saying another word.

Maybe I had to change my strategy.

I didn't even have the motivation to tease him under the table the way I did last night.

But it was useless either way, so I continued to enjoy my dinner, listening to their adult-talk, and hoping I would soon get to spend a few minutes alone with Riggs.

Chapter Nine

Valley

I was bored.

My parents and Riggs decided to continue their conversation in the living room after I helped Della clean up the dining table, and since I wasn't much into talking about Dad's business, I excused myself to go upstairs.

You could even say that I was upset that I didn't get to do the things I wanted to do tonight, and I hated the silent control Riggs had over me.

There were also my parents in the room with us, and although I liked to push the limits, I didn't feel like teasing Riggs.

Maybe one of my loyal men on my website want to see me in this cute outfit I'm wearing, I thought.

I walked into my bedroom and set up my laptop with the web cam clipped at the top.

I could've used my laptop's camera to video chat with them, but I liked to get close sometimes, holding the webcam up close to my nipples or pussy so they could see just how wet I was.

Just thinking about that excited me, and I smiled, pleased with myself.

I sent some of the men a message, telling them the first who's online could have some fun with me tonight, and the lucky winner was Frank.

A fifty-four-year-old British bus driver.

I liked his accent, and I was excited to see him again as he was extremely shy.

Maybe tonight I could get him to explore his body a little more, seeing as he only ever rubbed his cock while wanting to see me massage my tits.

Nothing more, so I figured it was time he'd come out of his shell.

His name appeared on my screen, but I quickly texted him that I needed another minute before I was ready.

I grabbed my ski mask from underneath my pillow and my vibrator I thought would be nice to play with while Frank played with himself.

Just as I wanted to sit down on my bed and accept Frank's call, Della called out from downstairs, making me sigh and head out of the bedroom.

"What is it?" I asked, seeing her at the bottom of the stairs.

"Would you like to come down for some dessert?" she asked.

"Uh, no, thank you. I'm pretty full from dinner," I replied.

She smiled and nodded, and once she walked away, I turned around to go back into my room.

That didn't go as planned though, as a large hand gripped the back of my head, fisting my hair tightly and pushing me against the wall next to my bedroom door.

I hadn't heard Riggs come upstairs and step close to me, but whatever he was doing seemed like an act of revenge.

Before I could look into his eyes without him forcing me to, he cupped my throat with his other hand and pushed my chin up, tilting my head back to meet his eyes.

"Does your daddy know you go through his phone?" he asked, his voice darker than ever, making me shiver.

So he knows that it was me in those pictures.

I couldn't help but grin, but it quickly vanished as he tightened his grip in my hair and around my neck, making me gasp for air.

God, he had no idea how much this was turning me on.

His body was pressed against mine with his knee between my legs and his thigh pressing against my wetness.

My skirt had ridden up, not covering much of my ass anymore, and this whole situation was getting steamier by just him staring back into my eyes.

"You thought I would just let it slip? Those damn pictures of you in that bra...God, Valley. Don't you know you should've listened to me when I told you to not mess with me?" he asked, letting out a deep chuckle which made his chest vibrate.

I didn't care what he was telling me to do or not to do.

This was exactly what I wanted, and although he must've been thinking he was teaching me a lesson, he was doing the exact opposite.

He was giving me exactly what I wanted.

His attention, and soon I'd have control over him the same way I had over all these other men.

Good thing was, he wasn't denying he liked the pictures.

I tried to talk, but he was still pushing down on my airway, making it not only hard to speak but also to breathe.

I started to like this, having to hold my breath while he pulled my hair tightly.

He noticed I was trying to say something, but he didn't let go at first.

Instead, he pushed his leg against my crotch, making me rub against his thigh.

Everything he was doing, thinking he was scaring me off, only made me want more.

Guess he wasn't as smart as he thought he was.

"I hate doing this, but just like you, I'm not afraid of getting caught. You're provoking me, and no matter your damn age, I won't let those fucking pictures slip."

If he hadn't loosened his grip on my throat, I would've definitely turned purple. But the kind man Riggs was, he let me take a deep breath.

I took the opportunity to talk back, and with a smug grin on my face I said, "How often did you look at those pictures before coming here tonight?"

I was forced to my knees in an instant, his hand still gripping my hair tightly and his crotch close to my face.

"Too many fucking times for my own good," he growled, his voice low so that my parents wouldn't hear him.

The upstairs hallway was built in a half-circle, having to turn the corner after walking up the stairs to get to each bedroom, and since we were quite a bit hidden, I was sure my parents had no clue about what was going on upstairs.

I looked up at him, my eyes wide and filled with lust.

He was really making this easy on me, and for a short second I wondered if it was still fun the way he played his game.

He said he played differently, yet it seemed I was beating him at his own game.

"Listen to me, Valley," he hissed, never taking his dark eyes off mine. "If this is really what you want, I'd advise you to stop messing around while your parents are around. Because if they find out you've been sending pictures to a man triple your age, there will be consequences."

I knew that, but the thing was...what I was doing wasn't much fun without the chance of getting caught.

Where was the fun in that?

His words didn't mean much to me, and since he was already right there, with his dick in front of my face, I used the opportunity to get a little taste.

I moved my hands up his legs while he watched me closely.

He wanted me just as much, or else he wouldn't even have bothered mentioning the pictures.

He could've ignored them.

Deleted them.

But he didn't.

"What if knowing my parents are around is what makes all of this so...thrilling?"

"Then you have no boundaries whatsoever," he spat, tightening his fist in my hair once more as my hands reached his ass.

He pulled my head back against the wall as his lips parted and his tongue came out to lick his bottom lip slowly, making my pussy ache while I started to rub against his shoe between my thighs.

I always found ways to please myself without the other person intending on letting me, but Riggs didn't seem to mind at all.

But just as the friction against my clit grew hotter, Riggs moved forward and pressed the bulge in his pants against my mouth while gritting his teeth.

See? Easy.

He was getting himself into more trouble.

"You're so fucking naughty, but you damn well know it," he muttered, moving my head to rub my face against the rough fabric of his pants.

My mouth was wide open, feeling the thickness in his pants getting harder as I pressed him even more against me by pulling his hips toward me.

"This really what you want, Val?" he asked, both hands now cupping the back of my head to keep my face pressed against him.

I nodded, looking up at him and curling my fingers into his ass to show him his physical threats were exactly what I wanted.

What I *needed*.

"Not sure you can handle me, darling. I will break you."

I took his warning as a challenge, moving my hands to his bulge and squeezing his balls to make him let me lean back.

Once he did, I cupped his cock and started rubbing it over his pants, and the heavy throbbing I could feel made me smile victoriously.

"Break me then," I challenged back, feeling his length getting harder underneath my touch.

He held his breath as I continued to stroke his cock and squeeze his balls, but as much as I wanted him to let me suck his shaft and then let him fuck me right here in the hallway, I had to let him go.

I had teased him enough, and I knew there was no way he wouldn't come back for more someday, so this was my opportunity to take control over him again.

I pushed him back and got up with his hands still in my hair, and after pulling them away from me, I stood on my tiptoes and stepped close enough to whisper in his ear.

"You have my number."

His body tensed for a second before he realized what was happening, and to show me that he wasn't giving up control so easily, he gripped my ass tightly, almost making it hurt before I turned to walk into my bedroom and lock myself in.

It took me a moment to catch my breath, seeing as he made it hard for me to breathe with his hand around my throat.

I heard him adjust his pants outside of my bedroom before he headed back downstairs to act as if nothing ever happened.

Tonight was more successful than I had thought after the disappointment at dinner, and with my heart racing in my chest, I hurried to my bed to start the web chat with Frank.

With Riggs still on my mind, I definitely wanted to use the vibrator more than once tonight.

Riggs

Reckless.

So fucking reckless with no filter in front of her mouth and no goddamn hesitation in her system.

Valley knew exactly what she wanted, and she knew she could get all of it from me.

The fact that I even played those games with her amazed me, as she was the last girl I would ever wanna mess with.

Ever since she was little there wasn't much about her that screamed she'd someday turn out the way she was now, but then again, as close as I was with her parents, I never had much to do with her.

Andrew kept his daughter locked away while he was in office for the most part, and at every event he attended or hosted, Valley was quietly standing in the background, observing people and not saying much.

Valley and I also never talked much.

The only time I remembered was over a year ago when I invited some of my closest friends over before I left for work, and not even then did she have the tendency of being mature enough to know how to turn a grown-ass man on.

Something must've changed in a short period of time, or she was just good at hiding her true self.

She was still good at that, as her parents had no clue about how dirty their daughter really was.

I've not come across girls her age being this mature, and although I knew there were enough teenage girls knowing exactly what they liked and needed, I never thought I'd come across one that would want me.

Sure, there were women younger than me trying to take me to bed whenever I sat alone in a bar just minding my own business, but none of them ever intrigued me as much as Valley did.

She was old enough to make her own decisions.

Valley was confident and had her own mindset, one that was strong enough to know her limits.

Though, the way I played was new to her. I saw it in her eyes when I grabbed a fistful of her hair and pushed her against the wall.

There was a quick sign of unsureness before she read me like a damn book and continued with her usual, unfazed-by-men, behavior.

I wouldn't make life easy for her from now on.

She had pushed enough buttons to get my attention, but I was positive that it wouldn't take too long for her to realize that no matter how much in control she was right now, I wouldn't let her go on like this.

She wanted me to fuck her?

Sure.

But I fucked hard, and I wouldn't hold back when it came to her.

"Ah, there you are," Della said with a smile as I arrived back in the dining room. "Would you like a cup of coffee with your dessert?" she asked.

"No, thank you, Della. I'm headed home after this. Dinner was great," I told her, taking a bite of the apple pie she didn't make herself.

Della was a great cook, but baking wasn't her strength.

"You're welcome to come by whenever you want, and I'd love for your brother to come have dinner with us sometime soon."

She didn't need to invite my brother just to show how kind she was, but if that's what she wanted, and if that meant I'd see Valley in a short skirt and tight shirt again, I definitely wouldn't say no to another dinner at the Bentley's.

Chapter Ten

Valley

"Miss Bentley, would you please come to my office?"

I turned to look at Mr. Thompson, the headmaster of this school. "Did I do something wrong?" I asked innocently, knowing the answer to that already.

I never did anything to be called into the headmaster's office, so this was new and surprising to me.

"Please, just come into my office," he repeated, holding out his hand to gesture the way to it.

I looked at Kennedy who was watching me with a questioning look, and when she raised her brows even higher, I let out a laugh.

"I did nothing wrong. He probably just wants to complain about my uniform," I said, knowing I had pulled my skirt up a little too high this morning, feeling even more confident than ever.

"Well, whatever it is...please don't provoke him. I don't want you to be kicked out of here."

I rolled my eyes at her words and shook my head. "I won't get kicked out. Remember all the money my Dad put into my education. Besides, I'm at the top of my class, if not the whole grade."

"You're right. I forgot that hiding behind all that dirtiness is a very smart brain," she said with a grin.

It was true, but just because I had enough knowledge and capability to finish college two years earlier, didn't mean I always put those things to good use in my free time.

I had a great night with Frank, imagining it was Riggs stroking his cock while I told him to use his other hand to massage his balls and even play a little with his asshole.

Frank was surprisingly brave last night, and he told me he really enjoyed how I pushed his limits and showed him that coming while one of his fingers was in his butt felt incredible.

It was time for him to explore a little more, and I was proud to be the one to show him all these new things.

I picked up my backpack from the floor and left Kennedy by our lockers while I followed Mr. Thompson into his office.

"Is it important?" I asked, but before he answered my question, Mr. Trapani was sitting in one of the chairs, leaned back and with his fingers brushing along his stubble covered jaw.

"Let's say it's important we find a solution for what I'm about to tell you."

Mr. Thompson sat down in his big chair and let out a heavy sigh, then he looked at Mr. T before clicking his pen a few times, unsure of how to start this conversation as he eyed my clothes.

Wait...this really is about my uniform.

"Am I dressed inappropriately?" I asked, sounding somewhat challenging and raising a brow at Mr. Trapani.

"Let's say we've had some complaints," Mr. Thompson said, his eyes back on my face again.

"From whom?"

"Some of the seniors."

Right.

They probably complained just to mess with me.

"Is this the first time they complained?" I asked, raising a brow and looking at Mr. Trapani again who was watching me closely.

Too bad he'd never let me stay in his classroom after school because the way he looked at me sure screamed for sexual attention from one of his students.

"Yes. First time, and hopefully also the last."

"And there were no complaints from the teachers?" I asked.

"No," Mr. Thompson replied, letting his eyes move to my uniform again.

"So I'm not really pushed to change the way I wear this beautiful school's uniform, am I?"

Mr. Trapani chuckled, sitting up straight and shaking his head at Mr. Thompson. "I told you this meeting wasn't necessary."

It really wasn't if they wouldn't tell me to button up my shirt or pull down my skirt to cover more of my legs.

"Can I leave, then?"

Mr. Thompson nodded, then he also shook his head as he realized this was really a waste of time.

"Just...stop giving those guys false hope. It's all they talk about in my classes, and I don't have time to hear them talk about you and the way you dress," Mr. Trapani said.

I knew boys at this school had nothing better to do than talk about me behind my back, feeling hurt because they damn well knew I would never hop into bed with them.

"I'm not even talking to them. They're immature. It's not my problem if they get a boner whenever they see me around campus."

"Ms. Bentley," the headmaster warned. "No reason to use such words. I'm sure your father wouldn't like the way you talk."

I smiled at him and shrugged. "My dad isn't here, and just because I talk like this in school, doesn't mean I use vulgar language at home as well," I told him.

When I got up from the chair to turn and walk back to the door, Mr. Trapani cleared his throat and muttered something in Italian under his breath, making me turn back around and look at him.

He called bullshit on my statement with just his gaze, and with a shrug, I left the office to head back to Kennedy.

"What did he say?" she asked as I reached her.

"What did *they* say. Mr. T. was in there too, saying his seniors talk about me all the time."

"And you must enjoy all the talk about your insanely hot body," a guy said, and when I turned around, four seniors I've had a few interactions with before stood there.

I crossed my arms over my chest and tilted my head to the side. "The attention's nice, yeah. Don't mind if you keep talking about me," I teased, making three of them widen their eyes.

The one talking was Cedric. Notorious bad and fuck boy of this college.

There were too many girls he had fucked over, Kennedy included.

That's why I didn't like him much. But then...Kennedy was very naïve, and even after telling her not to fall for his stupid games, she did just that.

"They still let you walk around like this? Even after we complained?"

"Maybe next time you should be more serious about your complaint. They didn't take it seriously, Ced."

He raised a brow, letting his eyes wander all over my body before stepping closer and leaning in to talk quieter just for me to hear.

"When will you finally drop that attitude and let a real man fuck you?"

I snorted, not able to help myself.

"You wish you could fuck like a real man. Stop bothering me and every other girl in this school and grow up."

"I am grown up. Didn't you hear from all those girls how good I made them feel? Don't you want that too? Those old men have nothing to offer anyway."

I wasn't going to talk about how much better it was having sex with an older guy, but I couldn't let his comment about the girls slip.

"Those are one-fifth of the girls you fucked who said those things, but the rest are disappointed by what they had to endure while sleeping with you. Get your facts straight, Cedric, and maybe one day, which I highly doubt, you might have a shot with me."

There it was again...me giving him false hope.

After what I said, Cedric's eyes filled with excitement and challenge, thinking he could really fuck me some day.

"So this isn't over," he said with a grin, but I just rolled my eyes and turned away to walk to class with Kennedy.

"He didn't even look at me," she whispered.

"Woah, no! You will not be offended by him, Ken! He screwed you over and used you.

Forget about him already. God, I really should set you up with a guy who doesn't play games."

She raised a brow at me. "But you play games with men all the time."

"I'm also not a relationship kind of girl," I told her with a sigh. "Come on. We'll go shopping after school and I will find you someone who knows how to treat a woman right."

"And where do you wanna find such a guy?" she asked.

"I don't know. Maybe we'll come across someone who seems nice."

She wasn't the type of girl who liked to be alone, and she had dated one guy in the past.

Her father was quick to shut their relationship down when he found out he didn't have rich parents, and was basically worthless in his eyes.

"What about you? I haven't seen you with a guy in real life in a while. You know, not one you hang out with on your laptop screen," she said, keeping her voice quiet as we entered the classroom.

"I do have someone now," I replied. "It's just a matter of time until I see him again."

***

"You went shopping without me?" Della asked with a pout as I entered the house.

I looked up at her and smiled apologetically. "It was a spontaneous decision. But I'd love to go shopping with you sometime soon," I told her.

We bonded over a lot of things, but spending money on clothes was what we liked doing the most.

"I wanna see everything you bought after dinner. Be down in an hour, okay, sweetie?"

I nodded and then hurried upstairs to put away my backpack with the homework I'd have to do later tonight, and then I pulled out every item I got to cut off the tags.

Shame most of these clothes would never be seen by anyone except the men through a webcam.

I got mostly lingerie, a few skirts and dresses, and two sweaters which I thought looked comfortable for when I decided to cover up for once.

I lifted the red bra with matching panties to admire its beauty, knowing my men would love it.

They weren't picky. Well, all but one.

Daryl always wanted me to wear nothing but a white, see-through shirt. No underwear, no toys, nothing.

He was forty-nine and had this recurring dream of a woman sitting in front of him on a bed, her nipples showing through a white shirt and her legs spread wide to expose her pussy.

He couldn't quite understand why that turned him on so much, but because I wasn't the one deciding what they wanted to see or do for their money, I always watched him rub his cock until he came without me doing much but sit there.

Some men were strange, but then...I did have a few things I liked to do before reaching an orgasm which most people would find weird.

But that was a whole other story.

The fact that only they would see me in this lingerie upset me, so I reached for my second phone and opened Riggs's chat, thinking about sending him a few pictures of me in it.

I had a little bit of time before dinner, so I set the phone back down and quickly changed into my new set of underwear, then I adjusted my hair and sat in front of the large mirror in my closet to take a few naughty pics.

He'd love them, and teasing him might just make him react the way he did last night.

The excitement rose inside of me, and after taking about twenty pictures in different positions, I looked through them and deleted the ones I didn't like.

I left my face out of them for the most part, mainly wanting him to focus on my body.

Once I chose three that I thought were good enough to send Riggs, I added them to his chat and sent them without hesitating or rethinking it.

A smirk appeared on my lips, knowing Riggs would definitely get mad at me for sending him those pics.

But just as much as he'd hate them, he would definitely enjoy looking at them.

***

I decided to take a quick shower before heading downstairs to help Della set the table, and since I left my phone upstairs, I had no way of knowing if Riggs had seen my pictures already.

I wanted him to text me back.

Maybe send a little tease my way, but the old, grumpy, short-tempered guy he was, the only thing I would probably get from him in return is the confirmation that he saw the pictures thanks to a little blue tick underneath them in our chat.

"Where's Dad?" I asked, wondering why she only put two plates onto the table.

"Oh, he's at the country club tonight. Didn't he tell you?"

"No. What's he doing there? Is there an event?"

Della shook her head. "He's just meeting with a few of his friends. He took Riggs with him so he wouldn't sit around in his house all alone. He's changed in the past year."

I wouldn't know, as we never really interacted much before, but there was one thing I was sure about.

He got my pictures, and the thought of him sitting right next to my father made the whole situation more fun.

Chapter Eleven

Valley

He blocked me.

After I sent him those insanely hot pictures of myself almost a week ago, he fucking blocked me.

Not only that, I've not seen him ever since he came over for dinner.

I was angry at him.

Why would he block me after what he did to me that night?

I basically had his dick pressed against my face and my hands on it as well, showing him how much I wanted him, and he had the audacity to block me?

If it was me pulling the same shit he pulled, he'd stand at my front door in no time, getting back at me with his short-tempered behavior.

But since it was him who blocked me, and I couldn't just show up at his house in case he was actually mad at me, I spent the whole week pleasing other men, even made them hurt themselves for pleasure, just to get back at Riggs.

Of course it was stupid, seeing as he had no idea what I did in my free time with all those men, but it felt good imagining him being the guy dripping wax on his chest or making him tie up his balls and dick until it turned blue.

Hell, even poor Frank had to torture himself for me last night, doing something he has never done before just because I imagined it being Riggs.

I made Frank push the end of a round brush into his ass, testing his limits but quickly finding out that after all the pain he endured, he actually enjoyed it.

Now, if only I could get Riggs to do what I told him to.

In just a small gesture, by blocking me, he took control over me again.

I felt defeated at first, thinking that was it for us.

He's had enough and didn't wanna mess around with me anymore.

But if it weren't for him inviting my family to have dinner at his place since his brother was back, I couldn't stay angry for too long.

I would see him tonight, if he liked it or not, and he could count on me looking like a goddess tonight.

No way I would hold back from now on.

He upset me enough to get me to hate him, and this little game we were playing would soon be won by me.

I walked out of my closet wearing one of the new skirts I bought on Monday, with no underwear on.

A bra was unnecessary as well, as I was lucky enough that my tits held themselves up if the shirt I wore was tight enough.

Dad and Della would definitely tell me to change into something more appropriate for dinner, but this outfit felt good, and it would definitely make Riggs rethink blocking me.

My phone was upright and against my pillow on the bed, with Kennedy on the screen doing homework and waiting for me to show her tonight's outfit.

"What do you think?" I asked, looking at myself in the tiny rectangle in the corner of the screen, then watching her reaction as she looked up from her book.

She frowned at first, then tilted her head and pulled the corners of her mouth down. "Even though that skirt is fairly short...you don't look slutty at all."

I looked down at myself, thinking slutty wasn't what I was going for anyway.

"You look like you're going to a business meeting, but will end up at a bar with every rich guy in this town," she added.

Good.

"And I love that sweater. Turtlenecks look great on you."

I smiled and adjusted my skirt on my waist. "Thanks. What about my shoes?" I asked, lifting my right foot to show her another pair of white sneakers with a little bit of a platform underneath.

"I like the whole school girl look. I'm sure Riggs will too."

I sighed, suddenly feeling unsure about everything.

"Is that confidence lacking?" Kennedy asked with a raised brow and smug grin on her face. "Come on, Valley. He's blocked you already, and that should actually be a good sign. What's the worst thing that could happen?"

"Him strangling me but not in an act of breath play," I muttered.

"You really think he's that mad at you?"

I shrugged. "I don't know him *that* well to know what he's thinking. I just know how rough he can be. He didn't hold back that night, but I do think he was taken aback a little by my own behavior."

"Well, he won't kill you, that I know. At least not with your parents around," she joked.

I rolled my eyes and sat down on the bed, then grabbed the phone to hold it up in front of my face.

"I gotta go. I'll let you know how it all went."

"Okay, enjoy your night," she said, smiling.

We said goodbye and hung up, then I quickly put on a little bit of mascara and blush to complete my school girl look, as Kennedy called it.

I looked good, there's no denying it.

But I was starting to feel a little nervous which wasn't usual for me.

I took a few deep breaths before heading downstairs where Dad was already sitting on the couch, dressed and ready to leave.

"You look handsome tonight," I told him, sitting down on the recliner next to the couch.

He looked up from his iPad, eyeing me carefully before looking back at the screen. "Aren't you gonna be cold in that skirt?" he asked, noticing my once again exposed legs.

"We're inside anyway, right?" I pointed out.

He shrugged, tapping the screen a few times before setting the iPad down next to him. "His brother will be there. Please, don't make any remarks about him."

I raised a brow at him. "Huh?"

"Just don't...say anything offensive or anything. You've said a few things in Riggs's presence that I didn't find very fitting at the dinner table."

I lifted my hand to my lips and gestured to lock my mouth and then throw away the key.

I could stay quiet for once. Maybe tease Riggs with just my eyes, and my outfit was enough to get his attention anyway.

"I'm ready. Sorry I took so long but this dress just didn't wanna fit right," Della said, sighing and tugging at her dark-red dress.

"You look beautiful," I told her with a smile.

"Oh, thank you, sweetie. Are we ready to go?"

"Yes. Let me get the champagne bottle," Dad said, getting up from the couch and walking back into the kitchen while Della and I headed to the front door.

"Aren't you going to be c—"

"No, I won't," I replied without her having to finish that sentence.

If there was one more human asking me if I was cold, I would lose it.

"Is that a new skirt?" she asked, changing the subject but still sounding a little judgmental.

"Yes. It's pretty, hm?"

"Very."

We got into the car once Dad was back with the champagne bottle, and after handing it to me, we drove off to get to Riggs's house.

I could still contain my excitement, whereas my nervousness was rising like never before.

It wasn't the way I was dressed that made me feel this way, but more so his reaction, and seeing me after blocking me.

Sure, I was upset about that, but if he thought that would make me stop, he was wrong.

I would only play harder, dirtier.

Ready or not, Riggs...here I fucking come.

***

We arrived after a few minutes at Riggs's house which was located a short drive away from the town's center on a small hill.

This part of town was a little quieter, with many families living close by but all of them were surrounded by big trees, separating them and ensuring some privacy.

I liked where Riggs lived, but this was one of the few reasons for me to come here.

I could easily come by unannounced, surprising him with nothing but lingerie underneath a long coat, but after what he did, blocking me, he surely wouldn't want that to happen.

My heart started to beat faster as I got out of the car with my parents to get to his large front door.

All the lights were on, and it was easy to see what was inside his home, but only if you stood right in front of it.

I knew he had a great view on the other side of the house, where there was a steep cliff right underneath it.

I only remembered the inside of his house because we've been here once before for some kind of party.

Not sure if it was one of his birthdays, but I was still little, and even back then I didn't really cross his path much.

Riggs was always in the background, but Dad talked a lot about him and often spent time with him, but other than that, Riggs wasn't really a big part of my life.

Until now.

I left my phone in the car because I hated carrying it around all the time, and since we'd have dinner anyway, there was no need for me to use it tonight.

I also never brought a clutch or purse with me, not really liking either.

"Behave," Dad murmured as Della pushed the doorbell, and I looked at him with a frown, questioning his request.

"I always behave," I replied as the door swung open.

"Andrew, good to see you again," Riggs said in his typical low voice, though it didn't have that growly undertone it always had when he talked to me.

Guess that way of talking was reserved for me.

"Thanks for inviting us. I got you something," Dad said, pointing at the champagne bottle Della was holding.

"Thanks, that's my favorite," Riggs replied with a nod. "Good to see you again too, Della. You look beautiful," he told her, kissing her cheeks the way he did that first night we encountered him after more than a year.

"Please, come inside. I have prepared a few appetizers. Dinner's in the oven and will be ready soon," he explained, and when my parents went inside, he looked at me and his gaze immediately darkened.

I felt like grinning at him out of spite, but the thought of him blocking me made me stop from doing just that.

"Valley," he muttered, probably hoping for me to just say hello and pass him to follow my parents into the living room.

"Hello, Riggs," I replied, stepping closer and wrapping my arms around his neck to hug him while pressing my petite body against him.

He immediately tensed, and when he realized I wouldn't let go unless he hugged me back, he put one arm around my back, not hesitating to place his hand on my ass.

"You're careless," he spat, tightening his grip and making me press my hips against his crotch tighter.

My parents were out of sight, and since he was unexpectedly daring, I thought I would play along.

"You liked them," I pointed out, referring to the pictures.

I moved one hand to the back of his head, feeling his wavy, black and gray hair between my fingers as I turned my head to press my lips against his neck.

"I blocked you for a damn reason," he growled, giving my ass one last, almost hurtful squeeze before pushing me away from him with both his hands on my shoulders.

"I told you not to fucking play with me, Valley. Wasn't that warning enough?"

I puckered my lips to keep from smiling, brushing my hands along my skirt to straighten it again.

"Didn't seem like a warning to me."

"Get inside," he barked through gritted teeth, not wanting to hear more of me.

I bit back a laugh and let out a heavy sigh, and when I passed him, I let my hand brush his thigh and got a nasty look back from him.

Gosh...someone's grumpy tonight.

I heard him follow me into the living room, but I had to stop in the archway as I saw the man who supposedly was Riggs's brother.

My parents were talking to him, introducing each other and already laughing about something.

Could it really be...?

No way.

He said he lived in Canada. That's nowhere near Nevada.

I stood there with my eyes glued on Riggs's brother, and as awkward as this could turn into, I was more amused by what was going on.

"Don't fucking mess with him as well," Riggs growled as he passed me.

"Too late," I mumbled under my breath, grinning at the sight of Garett next to my parents.

What a damn coincidence, I thought.

This night could only get better.

I stepped closer to them, and when Garett noticed me, he smiled as friendly as possible and reached out his hand.

"You must be Valley. I'm Marcus," he told me, making me raise a brow at what I supposed was his actual name.

"Nice to meet you, Marcus," I replied, shaking his hand and looking into his eyes.

He was taller than I had imagined, but then again...I only ever saw him on my computer screen. The other strange thing was that he and Riggs had no similarities whatsoever.

Sure, they were both very tall, but Riggs had a wide, well-built frame while Garett—uh, Marcus, didn't have a lot of muscles.

Riggs's face was also more structured, with a not very straight nose which must've been broken a few times in his life.

But Garett's, shit...ah, what the hell. He's Garett to me.

Garett's was much smaller, straighter, and a little turned up at the tip.

Now that he stood right in front of me, he wasn't as attractive anymore, but he was still the same man drinking his own piss in front of my eyes.

Good thing he didn't know what I looked like, or else he would've recognized me the second he laid eyes on me.

"Marcus just came here from New Mexico. You've always wanted to go there, didn't you?" Della asked me with a smile.

So he lied to me about being in Canada. Or he could've been lying about where he came from.

Either way, it didn't really matter as long as he didn't know I was the alleged twenty-year-old he paid to sit in front of her webcam without any clothes on.

"Would love to go to New Mexico sometime. What's it like?" I asked, taking a quick look at Riggs who was standing there with his glass in his hand and a raised brow on his grumpy face.

"It's beautiful. Worth a trip," he told me with a smile.

Yeah, this guy definitely wasn't who he pretended to be. Then again...I wasn't who I really was either.

Chapter Twelve

Riggs

Her attention was set on my damn brother.

After blocking her and hoping I wouldn't have to see her again wearing fucking lingerie, I made the fatal mistake to invite her family over for dinner because of Marcus's arrival.

Worst thing about it all? She wasn't wearing a fucking bra.

Her nipples practically pushed holes into the fabric of her tight sweater, and the sight of it made me wonder if she wasn't wearing anything underneath her skirt either.

Who was I kidding?

That girl had no boundaries, so why would she only get rid of her bra?

And the way she greeted me at the door...I wanted to spank her right there.

Push her against the wall and teach her another lesson. Not that she learned anything from the first one anyway.

As innocent and unfazed as she acted around my brother, I wasn't done with her yet.

Squeezing her ass and feeling her tits pressed against my chest wasn't enough, and the second I got her to myself tonight, even just for a few seconds, I would show her how much anger I had in me because of those pictures she sent without me asking for them.

She knew exactly what she did, knowing how hot she looked, but just because I might've rubbed my dick and came while looking at those pictures, doesn't mean I'd let it slip just like that.

She was playing with me, and although I told her I wasn't up for that kind of bullshit, I couldn't be an adult and step away.

All through dinner, Valley was talking to Marcus about this and that, mentioning how well she was doing in school and what her future plans were.

All while her parents asked me thousands of questions concerning either my past as an Air Force pilot, or my current situation about being retired.

They knew a lot about my life already, and to change things up a bit, I turned the questions around to make them talk a little more and let me keep quiet for once.

Valley was focused on Marcus, and they seemed to have found each other in such a short time span.

Not that it bothered me, but the way Valley was, I was hoping she wouldn't try and get too close to him.

"Anyone want some dessert?" I asked to interrupt Valley and Marcus's conversation about biology.

They both seemed to be very much into human bodies, which wasn't a surprise coming from a sexually driven kitten like Valley and an almost fifty-year-old single man.

"I would love something sweet after this delicious dinner. I didn't know you can cook so well, Riggs," Della said with a bright smile.

"It's something I've always loved to do," I simply responded, getting up from the table and walking back into the kitchen with the empty plates.

Only a few more hours and I could finally stop being this tense.

I had to try and keep my eyes off Valley while she pushed her tits right into my brother's face.

She was trying to tease him, but Marcus didn't react much to it surprisingly.

Maybe he knew not to go after an eighteen-year-old teenage girl whose parents were sitting right next to them.

He had at least some self-control, unlike me.

**

It was almost eleven, and the Bentley's were still in my house.

Kicking them out was wrong, but to my luck, Della told her husband that after she came back from the bathroom, she wanted to go home and sleep.

Good.

They could take Valley with them and lock her up in her damn room so she wouldn't get to show off her body to anyone anymore.

Why did she have to look so goddamn hot anyway?

"Let's say goodbye, Valley. Della will be back quickly," Andrew told his daughter, but when she looked up from the book she was studying, with Marcus sitting next to her, she frowned and pouted.

She wasn't ready to leave.

"Marcus and I are talking about something I'm learning in school right now. He knows a lot about living organisms, and he's pretty good at chemistry too. You know that's the only class I have trouble with."

"You have an A minus in chemistry, Valley. I told you it's okay to have one imperfect grade."

Valley tilted her head to the side and shrugged. "But I wanna get even better at it. Maybe Marcus can teach me things I don't know yet. I'm not tired, and I'm sure one of these men can take me home later," she said, making my blood boil in an instant.

I fisted my hands and held my breath to wait for Andrew's response while I tried not to shoot angry glares at Valley.

"I guess letting you stay to study isn't such a bad thing. After all, there aren't many kids who willingly sit down and study anymore," he said with a chuckle.

Valley smiled brightly at her father. "Thank you, Dad!"

At this point, I wasn't even sure if she was just trying to mess with me, or if she's actually serious.

Either way, I wanted her out of my house, but kicking her out right in front of her father wasn't gonna work.

I didn't have an excuse either, as it was Marcus who'd have to keep up with her.

And this way I could make sure they wouldn't do something stupid. Like make out. Or fuck.

That's what I wanted to do with her.

"Get her home by midnight, will you?" Andrew asked me.

I couldn't say no, so I nodded and shot Valley one quick glance before Della came back.

"Are you coming, Val?" she asked.

"She's staying a little while longer to study. Marcus knows a few things about biology and all that stuff."

"Oh, you do? Did you study it?" she asked surprised.

Marcus turned to look at Della and nodded. "Always liked that subject in school. If I would've had my life under control a little more when I was Valley's age, I might've become a teacher."

You're just a lazy fuck, I thought, taking my eyes off Valley's again.

"Oh, it's never too late, you know? I'll see you again soon, Marcus. It was nice to finally meet you."

"You too, Della. Good night," Marcus said, nodding at Andrew.

They were both playing a role tonight, and I wasn't sure if they knew that about each other.

I walked Andrew and Della to the front door and thanked them for coming, and after saying goodbye, I took a deep breath before heading back to the living room where Valley and Marcus were sitting close to each other with the book Marcus got from the guest bedroom he was staying in.

Not sure why he had that book with him, but he brought more things than needed from New Mexico.

Guess he planned on staying a little while longer than I had anticipated.

While they talked about things I didn't understand much about, I went into the kitchen and poured myself a glass of whiskey, needing something strong and pure.

Words I would describe Valley with if I didn't have this anger toward her.

She made me mad and she damn well knew it. But instead of sparing me from even more hatred, she continued to push my limits in any way possible.

I took long sips of my drink and poured some more into my glass to head back to the living room.

I sat down on the couch on the other side of the coffee table and watched them as they read through another page of the book, mumbling things and pointing at certain parts of a paragraph.

"What a couple of nerds," I muttered, not able to hold those words back.

Valley immediately looked up at me with a raised brow, and the serious look on her face wasn't much proof that she actually liked sitting there on a Friday night with a damn biology book in her lap.

She wasn't fooling me the way she was fooling Marcus.

"You're not a very friendly host tonight, Riggs. Is my presence bothering you that much?" she asked, sounding almost like a lost kid asking an employee at the store to help find their mother.

"No," I answered nonchalant, wishing I could drag her upstairs with my hand in her hair.

She knew exactly what she was doing, and I had to admit...she was good at it.

"Come on, man. This won't take too long. I'm tired anyway, and you can get her home in half an hour," Marcus said.

I looked at him for a while, then at Valley before leaning back and taking another sip of my whiskey.

"Continue."

***

Half an hour went by quick, and like he had promised, Marcus got up from the couch, said goodbye to Valley by shaking her hand politely before heading upstairs where the guest bedrooms were.

The top floor of my house wasn't lived in much since I had my bedroom down the hallway.

I told him he could get comfortable up there and use whatever rooms he needed to, but he'd also have to clean them himself.

I watched Valley get up from the couch, and as she brushed her hair back to tuck it behind her ears, I had to let my eyes wander over her body.

Her waist was so damn tight, making her tits and ass seem even bigger than they already were.

I liked women in all shapes or sizes, but Valley was different with her curves and long legs.

"Guess you're taking me home now," she said, lifting her brow in an almost challenging way.

"Guess I am."

I got up as well and set down my glass to then follow her out of the living room. But before she could reach the front door, I couldn't just let her go without showing her just how those pictures made me feel.

I reached around her to wrap my fingers around her throat tightly, pulling her back against me and my other hand flat on her stomach.

Tilting her head back, I moved closer to whisper in her ear. "Don't think I'm letting you leave without consequences after those fucking pictures you sent," I growled, my voice lower than ever and making my chest vibrate.

Her breath hitched immediately, but just like last time, her face was relaxed, looking pleased and excited.

Damn her.

"I'm trying to teach you a fucking lesson, but all you do is not take it seriously. Think I might have to go harder on you, huh?"

And the little daredevil she was, she nodded.

I let out a harsh laugh. "Fuck, darling. You're not afraid of what's gonna happen, are you?"

My fingers squeezed her airway tight, and I saw the slight panic on her face as she couldn't breathe anymore.

But even that made her body relax more and more, making me think there was nothing she wasn't ready for.

Without saying another word, I started to walk down the hall to my bedroom which was luckily hidden around the corner and therefore soundproof from the rest of the house.

She came willingly, her steps confident.

When we entered my room, I loosened the grip around her throat to make sure I wouldn't actually choke her, but the second I did, she turned around to face me with a devilish grin on her face.

"Are you going to punish me now?" she asked in an angelic voice, contradicting her facial expression.

I felt my dick in my pants harden, wanting to come out and let her play with it for the rest of the night.

But as much as I wanted that, I couldn't let her take control over me this time.

It was my turn, and afterward, I wanted to keep that control over her.

"On your knees," I ordered, and with no hesitation, she dropped to her knees and licked her lips slowly.

"Will you let me play with your cock, Daddy?"

"Don't fucking call me that without my permission," I spat, reaching down to cup her jaw tightly. "Keep your damn mouth shut."

She did, and the excitement in her eyes grew bigger.

I wasn't much into the whole daddy-kink, but the way she said that word made my dick jolt.

"Open," I ordered, my thumb on her bottom lip. "I said open!"

She was starting to learn not to mess with me while she was on her knees, and when she parted her lips, I pushed my thumb inside of her mouth to wet it before taking it back out and inserting three fingers to rub against her tongue.

"Stick that tongue out, baby."

Baby.

Never had I called a girl that, but it fit her.

I rubbed my fingers against her tongue to collect enough spit, and while I did, I unbuttoned my pants with my other hand.

"Let's see how much you can really take. Think you can handle me? Ever been with an old man like me?"

She shook her head, but something told me she had already experienced something with a much older man before.

Maybe she didn't let someone my age fuck her yet, but I was sure she teased them just as much as she teased me.

And thinking of her as a virgin was so wrong, although I would've loved to be the one to break through that wall inside of her hot pussy.

Once my dick was out, I started to rub on it with her face right there in front of it, and with the three wet fingers, I pulled them out and rubbed her own spit all over her beautiful face.

She enjoyed it, closing her eyes for a second before looking back into mine with lustful eyes.

"Lean back against the bed," I ordered, and the second the back of her head hit the bed, I pushed my dick inside her mouth without warning.

She gagged as the tip of my length hit the back of her throat, and I kept it deep inside of her mouth for a few more seconds until she started to move her head.

"Not so damn confident anymore, huh? Shit, baby. You bit off far more than you can chew," I said with a grin.

Her face started to turn red, but instead of letting her breathe, I pushed further into her mouth, fisting her hair on the top of her head and cupping her jaw again to keep her in place.

Safe to say she wasn't expecting this from me, and the more she struggled, the longer I would keep my dick in deep in her throat.

Chapter Thirteen

Valley

All those things I wished those men would do to me were coming through thanks to Riggs who was being more than just rough with me.

He was torturing me in the best way possible, keeping his cock deep in my mouth without letting me breathe or push against him.

That was something that turned me on a whole damn lot, so while he kept me from breathing, I reached underneath my skirt to rub my pussy to intensify what I was feeling.

My eyes were on his, wide and teary as I tried my best not to lose consciousness.

I've always been good at holding my breath for a long time under water, but up until this moment I was never lucky enough to show my talent with a wide and long cock in my mouth.

It was thrilling knowing he was doing this to get back at me for sending him those pictures, and the more he growled things under his breath while pushing into my mouth deeper, the more this whole situation excited me.

"You're not giving up yet?" he challenged, and I shook my head as much as possible as he was still holding me in place and pressed against the bed.

"Gotta get some air into those pretty lungs sooner or later," he smirked, moving his hips once more as spit started to drool from my mouth.

A loud groan left his chest as he finally pulled back, strings of my saliva stretching from my mouth to his cock and dripping down onto my lap while I continued to rub my clit.

I took a deep breath now that I had the chance to, but after a quick slap to my cheek, he tilted my head back against the bed and pushed his rigid cock back into my mouth.

"Fuck, baby. You look fucking beautiful with my dick in your pretty mouth. Think you'd look even better with it deep inside your tight pussy," he growled, now slowly thrusting in and out of my mouth.

I kept my eyes on his, my mouth wrapped around his shaft and my tongue twirling around his tip every time he pulled back.

Precum had already dropped onto my tongue, letting me taste him while he held control over me.

"Take that hand off your pussy, Valley," he ordered as he noticed how I moved my hips against my hand, but I was already feeling the orgasm building up inside of me, and I didn't wanna stop.

"I said, take your fucking hand off your pussy!"

But before I could listen to him and do what he said, Riggs pulled his cock out of my mouth, grabbed me by the hair with both fists and pulled me up onto my feet to then turn me around and push me onto the bed with my legs dangling from the side of it.

A loud smack, then a burning sensation spread across my ass as he pushed my head against the mattress.

"Told you we're playing by my damn rules, and if you don't listen, I will punish you," he warned with his deep voice.

I bit my bottom lip and moved my hands to my side to lift up the skirt a little more, to show him just how wet this short but very intense interaction made me.

With my legs spread, I could hear him mutter something under his breath as he definitely was looking straight at my exposed pussy.

"Will you play with my pussy then?" I asked, my voice hoarse but filled with confidence and excitement.

His hand in my hair tightened, and since I couldn't see what he was doing behind me, I waited patiently for him to react to what I said.

The suspense was killing me, and my clit throbbed, needing attention.

Then, another loud smack, burning on my right ass cheek again.

I moaned, not able to hold back the way that made me feel, and as I slowly recovered from it, he spanked me one last time before he let go of my hair, gripping my wrists in one hand behind my back and spreading my legs wider apart with his other.

He wasn't saying a word of what his intentions were, but when I felt his beard tickle my skin, I knew exactly what was coming.

Spit flowed down between my folds, and shortly after, his tongue licked all the way from my clit up to my asshole.

My body shivered, wanting him to taste more of me.

I wiggled my ass to show him that I wanted him to do that again, but the tease that he was, he got up again and placed his large hand on my ass to squeeze it tight.

"I'm not gonna fuck you tonight. You don't deserve it. But you will make me come. Turn around."

He let go of my wrists and I slowly turned to sit up straight in front of him, with his rock-hard cock right in my face.

I lifted my hands to wrap my fingers around his shaft, but he slapped them away with a deep, angry frown between his brows.

"Did I tell you to fucking touch my dick?" he asked.

"No, Daddy."

It slipped, but the way he acted just made me wanna call him that.

It was a mistake though, as he slapped my cheek again, this time slightly harder and quickly cupping my jaw to avoid losing eye contact.

"Did I give you permission?" he asked, his voice dark and provoking.

I shook my head and couldn't stop from grinning. "No."

"Then why do you continue to push my limits and do the things I told you not to?"

"Because I know how much you hate the way I tease you. You want me," I purred, and my answer resulted in him pushing his fingers back into my mouth, pushing my tongue down and getting as far down my throat with his fingers as possible.

"I'm taking what I want when I want it. Don't need your naughty mouth to ask for it. I know you want my dick deep inside of you, but you don't deserve it that easily."

His fingers pushed further into my mouth, making me gag and close my eyes for a moment before he pulled them out again.

They were wet, and he put that to good use when he reached down between my legs and rubbed my saliva all over my pussy, wetting it even more.

"Shit, baby. This how I make you feel? You taste like a little slut. Too damn sweet for your own good," he growled, and without a warning, he pushed two of his large fingers into my pussy.

"You want me to fuck this tight hole, don't you? Too damn bad I'm not doing what you want. I told you I would wreck you, Val, but I'm holding back on that. You're not ready for me, darling."

I moaned as he fingered my pussy faster, pushing them into me harder and with more force until I had to tilt back my head and close my eyes to enjoy it.

His other hand gripped my hair again, making me look at him and see how his eyes turned darker.

He wasn't playing games anymore.

He was dead serious about this, but instead of being intimidated, I wanted more. So much more.

"Keep clenching that pussy around my fingers. Is that what you'll do when my dick's inside of you? Tease me like a little slut," he growled.

Him calling me a slut only intensified the way I felt, and so I nodded. "Fuck me," I begged, moving my hips against his hand while he continued to finger me.

"Keep that mouth shut," he spat back, and just as I had expected, he pulled his fingers out to cut off the orgasm building inside of me.

Asshole.

He lifted his hand, with his fingers covered in my own juices, then he held them up to my mouth but didn't say anything.

Instead, he looked at me with a challenging frown and I immediately did exactly what he wanted me to.

I wrapped my lips around his fingers, keeping my eyes on his while I licked every single drop off his fingers.

"Fuck..." he muttered, suddenly loosening the grip in my hair to fully enjoy watching me lick his fingers clean.

"You like that, huh? Dirty young thing..." he murmured, using his left hand to stroke his cock.

Once I was done tasting myself from his fingers, which wasn't new to me at all, he stepped closer to let me wrap my lips around his shaft.

"Show me what you can do with that mouth, baby," he ordered, and since he had calmed down a little bit, I used that moment to put my hands on the base of his cock and start blowing him.

He watched me closely, a frown appearing every now and then and his hands cupping each side of my head while I moved it back and forth.

His cock really was like none other, thick and long, and all veiny along the sides.

Despite his age, every part of his body resembled one of a mid-thirty-year-old instead of an almost sixty-year-old.

It was definitely worth all the work outs.

"Fuck," he groaned, tightening his grip in my hair slightly, but not showing me his harsh side again yet.

He wanted to see what I could do with my mouth, but after a little while of just giving him a blowjob, I wanted to spice it up a little.

I moved my right hand from the base of his cock to his balls, squeezing them as his shaft jolted.

There was no man who didn't like their balls played with, at least none of the ones I had the pleasure to interact with virtually but also in real life.

Riggs was slowly letting me take control again, but just as I moved my fingers to his anus, teasing and touching, he yanked my head back by my hair.

His cock fell out of my mouth, and the anger in his eyes was back again.

"Focus on my damn dick, Val," he hissed, making me think I had found a place on his body to use to make him angry.

He liked me rubbing along the rim of his asshole with my fingertip, he just didn't wanna admit it.

"There's so much shit you still have to learn, darling," he spat, letting out a harsh laugh.

"Make me come," he then ordered. "And keep those damn hands on my dick."

Definitely wouldn't say no to that, but I hoped one day we could do more than this.

My lips were wrapped around his cock again, but instead of letting me take over, he held my head in place and started to thrust into my mouth fast, hitting the back of my throat each time.

"Eyes on me," he ordered, and I looked up while I let him fuck my mouth hard, gagging when he unexpectedly thrusted in too deep.

More saliva dripped down into my lap, and since he didn't want me to touch myself, I started to rub my clit against his thigh.

"You don't listen, do you? You never fucking listen," he growled, thrusting harder than before.

I felt his body tense, and just like he stated, I didn't listen to him and moved my fingers to my pussy to wet them, then I placed them back on his asshole and pushed one finger inside his tight hole while he slowly moved closer to his high.

"GAAAH!" His body tensed up even more, but as he started to lose control over his own body, pushing his cock even deeper into my mouth, I started to move my finger to stimulate him even more.

I tasted his cum as the orgasm hit him, and to make things hard on me, he kept my head right there while I had no other option than to swallow his cum.

"Fuuuck!" His loud groans were hopefully not heard upstairs where Garett was staying, but even if...I wouldn't have minded Garett watching or even getting in on the fun, knowing he had many kinks I wanted to try out in real life one day.

Maybe Riggs would let me, but the way he acted tonight, so rough and bossy, I didn't think he'd ever let me watch him rub his own cum on his skin or even taste it.

I kept my eyes open while he slowly came down from what seemed like an intense and incredible high, and once he pulled his cock out of my mouth, I grinned at him and wrapped both hands around his shaft again.

"Don't tell me you can't go for round two," I teased, getting a low chuckle out of him.

"I gotta take you home," he murmured, pushing my hands off him and pulling up his boxer briefs and pants.

"This wasn't the last time I sucked your cock," I stated, wanting him to know that this wasn't over for me yet.

He buttoned his pants and eyed me carefully, then he reached out and brushed away a drop of his cum mixed with my saliva from the corner of my mouth and lifted it up to his lips to taste it.

That.

I wanted to see more of that.

"No, it wasn't," he replied, his voice stern as always.

That was good enough for me, and once I got up and straightened my skirt, I stepped closer to him and placed my hands on his chest.

"And maybe next time you can make me come too," I whispered close to his lips.

His right hand came around my body to cup my ass, but he moved it further down, underneath my skirt to let his fingers move along my wetness.

My inner thighs were sticky and wet from all the juices coming out of me.

"Maybe I'm lucky enough and you will lick and suck on my clit right now," I said quietly and full of hope.

A smug grin appeared on his lips, and as he entered two fingers inside my pussy from behind, he shook his head.

"Told you you're not deserving of that tonight."

My lips parted at the almost gentle way he fingered me again, not recognizing him when he was this careful not to hurt me.

Not sure I liked that part of him, but he was teasing again, and I had to keep that in mind.

He wouldn't make me come, leaving it up to me and my vibrator tonight.

"Too bad," I whispered, keeping my eyes on his and clenching my pussy, wanting more from him.

But before the tension in my lower belly started forming, he pulled his fingers out.

"Let's go," he drawled, turning away from me and heading out of the bedroom.

I used this moment to take a look around his room. It was furnished like the rest of his house.

It almost looked like a cabin in the woods, but instead of seeing trees when looking out of the big windows, there was an incredible view looking out over the city.

Must've been nice waking up here every morning with a view like that.

I followed Riggs and saw him waiting on me by the front door, and once he opened it, we walked out of the house to get to his car.

"Weren't you afraid your brother could hear us?" I asked once we got into the car.

"Where's the fun without the possibility of getting caught?" he asked back, making me laugh.

Touché.

It was still weird that Garett was Riggs's brother, but I was glad he had no clue about who I was.

It was a strange coincidence, but even with all the dirty things Garett and I did via webcam, he seemed like a genuinely nice guy tonight.

There was also no sign of him being weird or a bad guy like I had first imagined him to be with Riggs and my father talking about him liking to sell drugs and all that.

The drive to my house was quiet, and when he parked the car in front of our driveway, I turned to look at him with a slight grin on my face.

"When will I see you again?" I asked.

He studied my face for a while, making it look like he was unsure about wanting to see me again and continuing what we started just minutes before.

"When I say we will," he replied, making me roll my eyes at his response.

I unbuckled my seatbelt and leaned over to him, placing my hand at the side of his neck and then kissing his lips softly.

I couldn't hold back, but he didn't seem to mind.

His tongue moved along my bottom lip and then into my mouth, twirling around mine while he kept his hands to himself.

The lights were on in the house, and I knew Dad was waiting on me to get inside, but I couldn't leave without getting one last taste of Riggs.

"Maybe this will leave you wanting more sooner," I whispered against his lips, pressing one last kiss to them before sitting back and opening the car door.

"Goodnight, Riggs," I said, shooting him an intense glare.

He cleared his throat, seemingly fazed by our kiss. "Night, Valley."

I was happy with myself, and once I closed the door, I walked up to the house and entered it without looking back at him, knowing he was watching me the whole time anyway.

"It's me!" I called out, walking straight into the living room where Dad was sitting on the couch.

"How was studying?" he asked.

"So much fun," I replied with a bright smile, thinking back to the taste of Riggs's cock in my mouth.

God, I wished I could've stayed longer, or that he would've done more than just finger me.

"Good. I didn't think of Marcus as such an intelligent man. After all those stories I've heard about him," Dad said.

"What did you hear about him?" I asked, sitting down on the arm rest of the recliner, looking over at him.

"That he's had a few interactions with underaged girls. Don't know if that's true, but he looked trustworthy enough for me. Besides, Riggs was there, so there was no way Marcus could've done something to you."

I puckered my lips and tried to think about something other than how perverted Garett actually was, but that didn't mean he was a bad guy.

Also, Riggs wasn't as innocent as Dad thought he was, as he almost choked me to the point of unconsciousness just half an hour before.

"Well, Marcus was really nice and I learned something new today. I'm going to bed now. Goodnight, Dad," I said, walking over to him and kissing his head before heading upstairs.

Sleep was just what I needed after an evening like that, but before I that, I definitely had to pull out my vibrator and imagine it would be Riggs's tongue licking my clit.

I crawled under my covers and pulled my little friend out from underneath my mattress to finish off what he had started.

Chapter Fourteen

Valley

I felt powerful and strong when I walked inside Cedric's mansion the next evening, wearing another short skirt.

I usually wouldn't have accepted an invitation to his party, but since Kennedy desperately wanted to go, I agreed and went to see what his parties were all about.

There was alcohol and snacks, which was another reason why I came here tonight, and I told Kennedy that I would leave later because I had two men waiting for me to cam with them.

Despite the fact that all these boys weren't what I would usually aim for, I couldn't stay away from the dancefloor outside in the large garden.

Great music was playing, and since I didn't wanna stand around and watch others have fun, I decided to have some fun on my own until it was time to go.

Kennedy was roaming the place to make some boys notice her, but that never worked out well unless she caught the attention of a fuckboy who would happily take her upstairs to one of the bedrooms.

I just hoped she wouldn't let them fuck her over again the way Cedric did, and other than warn her about them, there wasn't much for me to do.

I moved my body to the music with my eyes closed and my arms in the air, swinging my hips and letting myself go.

It was what I needed after last night, and since I couldn't contact Riggs after he blocked me, I hoped to get my mind off him to see if he's really what my body ached for.

Of course, I could've added his number into my actual phone, or just go over to his house, but for some reason, I wanted him to come after me for once.

I took enough steps toward him in the past weeks, and if he really wanted more of me, he surely wouldn't stay back and avoid me.

Two arms wrapped around me from behind while I kept dancing, and for a split second I was determined to get that guy off of me.

But before I could do so, a second pair of hands moved over my body.

When I opened my eyes, I looked straight into the ones of Cedric who had a cocky grin on his face.

"Thought you could use some company tonight, babe," he told me, pulling me closer against his body while the guy behind me pushed his crotch against me.

As much as I liked the idea of a threesome, those two were not my first choice.

"I don't need your company, Ced."

I tried to push them both away, but they only held me tighter, laughing like idiots.

"Aw, come on, Valley. We're more than twice your age if you add our ages together," he smirked, making me roll my eyes heavily.

"Still not who I would let fuck me," I muttered, finally getting him off before I turned to look at the guy behind me.

Denzel, I think his name was, and although he was definitely one of the most handsome guys in college, I wouldn't let him get any closer than this.

"Get away," I hissed, and after he gave me some space with his hands up in the air to protect himself, I walked past him with a shake of my head.

"I'll fuck you one day!" I heard Cedric call out.

How embarrassing, I thought, letting out a harsh laugh. "Never in a million years," I muttered.

***

I found Kennedy sitting all alone at the big dining table with a drink in her hand and an upset look on her face.

I sighed, walking over to her and sitting down next to her. "Guess I shouldn't have left you alone," I said, reaching out to brush back a strand of her long, blonde hair.

"He said he would talk to me tonight. He's been dancing with other girls ever since we arrived and he didn't even say hello," she whispered.

"Who?"

"Reece."

"Keller? That Reece?" I asked, raising a brow and trying to hold back a laugh.

"Yes. God, what's so funny about that now?" she asked with a frown, giving me an angry look.

"Nothing...I just think you deserve better than Reece Keller."

"Then why would he ever tell me that he likes me?"

Because he's a teenager who's controlled by his damn dick.

I studied her face for a while, then decided that it was time for her to see what real men were like.

Not that there weren't great guys our age, but most of them were already in a relationship, and others just simply were too focused on school to date anyone.

"Come on, we're going to meet some nice guys you can have actual conversations with," I told her, getting up from the chair and pulling her up with me.

"We can't just leave. Where are we supposed to go?" she asked.

"I know a bar we can go to. Come on, Ken. It's gonna be fun."

"We're eighteen, Valley. What's there for us to do at a bar?"

"Hang out and watch men enjoy their beers. Maybe even get some fries and a nice iced-tea," I suggested, knowing we wouldn't get alcohol at that bar.

"I know the owner. He won't kick us out," I added.

She thought about it at first, then she nodded and got up with a sigh. "Okay. Let's go."

***

The bar belonged to a friend of Dad's from college, and although he wasn't allowed to, Dad often took me there when he wanted to have a beer after work.

I used to sit at a booth, drinking some type of soda and snacking on either salted peanuts or chips.

It wasn't the best place for a child to hang out, but I enjoyed playing with the cards they had laying around on the tables or coloring in the last few empty pages of a children's coloring book that the owner strangely had laying around in one of the drawers.

When we entered the bar, I looked around before pulling Kennedy toward the counter to greet Henry.

"Valley! What a nice surprise," he called out when he noticed me, and I smiled at him and walked around the bar to hug him.

"Hope it's okay if we hang out in here tonight. We came from a college party. It was boring," I told him, stepping back again.

"Yeah, go sit down. I'll get you both something to drink and some fries. How about that?"

"You're the best. Thank you, Henry."

I grabbed Kennedy's hand again and walked to the booth with her, and once we sat down, I looked around to see if there were any potential men for Kennedy to talk and maybe flirt with.

"So...now what?" Kennedy asked, looking around the bar a little unsure.

"Now we sit, eat, drink, and enjoy the music in the background until I find the right guy for you. What's your type?" I asked, knowing it always changed.

"Uh, I don't know. Tall, dark...very handsome. No beard," she told me with a shrug.

"How about tall, dark, and handsome and with stubble?" I asked, grinning at her.

"Where do you see that type of man?"

"Right over there." I pointed to a booth on the other side of the bar, sitting with another guy who I knew looked far too scary for Kennedy with all his tattoos.

"What if they're married?" she asked with worry in her voice.

"Guess we'll have to find out if they are first."

Henry brought us two drinks which looked like iced tea I always got when I came here, with a bowl filled with fries.

"Thank you, Henry. How's life been?"

"Oh, you know, hectic as always. Wife's been at the hospital for a few days last month, but she's back on her feet again. How's your father? Haven't seen him in a while."

"Dad's great. This is my best friend Kennedy, by the way," I announced.

He nodded at her with a smile. "Good to meet you, doll. You two have a great night. Call out to me if you need anything."

I nodded and watched him leave, then I took a sip of my drink and set the glass back down to get up from the booth.

"You're not going over there, right?" Kennedy panicked, and I grinned at her and winked.

"'Course I am. You'll see, a little company won't hurt. You need to get over Reece Keller."

She sighed and hid her face with her hands, mumbling something under her breath.

Without waiting for more of her inaudible words, I headed over to the booth where those handsome men were sitting, and when I reached them, both turned their heads to look up at me.

"Can we help you?" the guy with tattoos covering his arms asked. His weren't as pretty as Riggs's who pulled them off nicely. Riggs also had tattoos all over his chest, and I even spotted a few on his stomach when I gave him that blowjob and his shirt rid up.

"Not me, but my friend over there. She's just been...let's say dumped, and I wanted her to know that college guys ain't shit."

Before I continued, I looked at both their hands to assure there weren't any wedding rings, and when I couldn't see any, I smiled. "How about you come keep her some company?"

The guy with tattoos didn't look too intrigued, but I knew he was just trying to hide his interest.

"How about we give you some attention as well?" he offered, making me laugh softly.

"Of course, you can do that," I told him, turning to his friend with a smile. "She's a little shy, but if you talk to her long enough, she'll open up."

He looked over at Kennedy, then raised a brow. "How old are you girls?" he asked, asking a rightful question.

"Eighteen."

That was a good enough answer for them, and since they weren't too old, maybe in their mid-thirties, I figured Kennedy wouldn't be too timid tonight.

"I'm Valley, by the way, and my friend's name is Kennedy," I told them before they got up and grabbed their beers.

"I'm Mason, and this is Derrick," the one without tattoos said.

"Nice to meet you," I told them with a sweet smile, then I walked over to the booth Kennedy was waiting at.

"Kennedy, this is Mason and Derrick. They're gonna keep us company," I said, sitting back into the booth with Derrick quickly scooting in next to me.

Just what I wanted.

Mason to give Kennedy all his attention.

"How you doing, Kennedy?" he asked her with a gentle smile.

He was a more easy-going guy, whereas Derrick had a good chance of taking me home tonight.

But although I wouldn't mind spending the night with him, I couldn't get Riggs out of my mind.

He left a mark last night, and my knees were still shaking every time I thought about him.

So I decided that flirting with Derrick was as far as I'd go tonight.

**

It seemed as if Kennedy really liked Mason, and the more they talked and laughed, the closer they got to each other.

I knew it wouldn't take long for Kennedy to enjoy the attention of an older guy, and she even took the first step and touched his hand on the table, still holding on to it tightly.

"She's a sweet girl," Derrick whispered in my ear as he leaned closer, his hand on my thigh.

"She is. Your friend likes her," I pointed out, turning to look at him.

I knew he wanted to take this somewhere else, but I didn't feel like betraying Riggs, even though I had two men waiting for me later tonight.

I had to be home by midnight to get on my webcam and see first Frank, then Daryl.

"Something tells me you're the exact opposite," he murmured, his hand moving further up and pushing my skirt back.

"You wouldn't be too far from the truth," I admitted. "But I'm sorry I have to disappoint you, Derrick. Tonight's not a good time."

He looked upset, and the frown between his brows deepened at the realization that he was just sitting here so his friend could get it on with Kennedy.

"Can I at least get your number?" he asked, his voice hopeful.

"Of course you can," I replied, pulling out my phone which I had tucked between the waistband of my skirt.

"Maybe you can come over to my place sometime. Enjoy an evening on our own," he offered.

"Sounds great, Derrick. I'll call you," I told him. "Maybe you can drive me home? We can let these two enjoy the rest of the night," I said, winking at Kennedy.

She smiled, happy to have Mason all to herself.

They really looked great together, and if I were her, I wouldn't let go of Mason.

He seemed like a really good guy who wasn't just talking to her to have some fun.

"You two enjoy the rest of the night, all right? Take good care of her," I warned, looking at Mason.

"I will. Have a good night," he replied, turning his attention back to Kennedy.

I'd say that was a successful night.

She was comfortable enough to stay with him on her own, and after getting rid of Derrick, I could turn into the naughty little slut, my true self, once I was back in my room and in front of my webcam.

Chapter Fifteen

Valley

It's been a week since I've seen Riggs, but he stayed on my mind the whole damn time.

School has been a pain in the ass, and I had to focus on classes the whole week before Friday finally came around again.

It was the Friday my parents would leave to go to a spa retreat for Della's birthday, leaving me on my own for ten full days.

I was excited as I got home, and after putting my schoolbag away, I went to take a quick shower and change into something more comfortable, meaning yoga pants and a large sweater.

There weren't many days in which I wore an outfit like this, but since I didn't have to sit in front of the webcam tonight, I had the chance to turn lazy.

I walked downstairs to get to the kitchen, and when I passed the living room, I stopped by the old jukebox Dad once got for his birthday to turn on some music.

I loved old songs from the sixties up until the eighties, so I set the mood and went into the kitchen to cook something for dinner.

I was starving, and thanks to Della going grocery shopping for me this morning, we had the fridge filled with all of my favorite things.

Tonight, I would go for a broccoli salad with chicken breast and mashed potatoes on the side.

Quite the culinary gal.

I liked being alone in this big house, with music playing quietly in the background and the smell of delicious food filling the kitchen.

I had already planned the evening out, sitting cuddled up on the couch and watching a movie I haven't seen in a while, snacking on some chocolate and chips without anything to worry about.

Della and Dad thought I could use a few extra pounds, right? So why not try and gain some weight with unhealthy foods after a nice, filling dinner?

It was gone sooner than expected as my hunger kicked in right after I let the chicken breast cook in the pan, and my mouth wouldn't stop watering until it was ready to eat.

After finishing up dinner, I turned off the jukebox and got comfortable on the couch, pulling a blanket over my legs and then turning on the TV.

I chose the movie Burlesque, as Christina Aguilera was as confident in the movie as how I've always strived to be myself, and I thought I was doing pretty well, seeing as I wasn't lacking any confidence whatsoever.

The music in the movie was great too, and I often sang along to it in the shower, trying to move the way she did in the movie.

Halfway into the movie and I had already eaten a whole chocolate bar, a bag of chips, and was now onto my second chocolate bar.

Just what I needed, but I got interrupted by the doorbell ringing loudly.

I frowned and paused the movie to get up and walk over to the foyer, peeking toward the front door to see if I could recognize the silhouette of the person standing in front of our large door.

When I noticed who it was, a wide grin spread across my face, and I hurried to open up the door for my late-night guest.

"You're here," I pointed out, although it was intended as a question.

Riggs looks down at me with his dark, mysterious eyes, his fists pushed deep into his front pockets and his stance wide, almost as if he was ready to fight me.

He didn't say a word at first, but when I raised a brow at him, he finally spoke. "Wanna let me in?" he asked with a clenched jaw.

How could I ever say no to that?

He must've remembered my parents leaving, and the plan of me not going after him but letting him come after me worked out perfectly as well.

I stepped aside and let him pass me, and once I closed the door, he turned around to look at me again.

"Nice outfit," he muttered, sounding amused.

"Didn't think I would have a visitor tonight. If I had known, I would've worn something more revealing," I teased.

He didn't reply after that. Instead, he turned around and walked toward the living room to sit down on the couch without ever asking for permission.

Not that I wanted him to ask for it. At this point, he could've literally been doing whatever he wanted and I wouldn't complain.

Nope, wouldn't complain at all.

"Want something to drink? I know Dad has some red wine and champagne somewhere," I offered.

"Gin," he simply said.

Alrighty then.

I turned to head into the kitchen, then opened the pantry where Dad stored all of his alcoholic drinks next to Della's wide range of food.

I searched for the gin which took me a little while, but once I found it, I grabbed two glasses out of the cupboard and headed back to the living room.

"Anything else you'd like?" I asked, setting everything down on the coffee table and then pouring us both a glass.

"You're eighteen," he pointed out.

"So?"

"How often do you drink?" he asked.

I shrugged. "I've had champagne before," I told him, grabbing one glass and looking down at him. "What? Will you tell Dad that I had alcohol?" I challenged.

"No." His response was short and direct, and he reached for his own glass to take a sip of the gin.

I did the same, having to keep my face from grimacing because of its strong taste.

We were both quiet for a while before I sat down next to him, pulling my legs underneath me and holding the glass in both my hands.

"Is there a reason why you came here unannounced?" I asked.

He raised a brow at me again, letting out a chuckle. "Do *you* think there's a reason why I came here?"

I shrugged, knowing exactly why he came but wanting to hear it from him. "We haven't seen each other in almost a week and you blocked my number. You seem to be indecisive about me, so..."

"I'm not indecisive. I'm being careful."

"Careful?"

He nodded.

"Why?"

"Because despite me being in control over you most of the time, you've shown me just how fucking naughty you can be. It's unexpected, if I'm being honest, and if I hadn't kept my distance, I would've fucked up while your parents were in town."

So he waited to see me when my parents were out of town to...

"I'm not gonna fuck you tonight, Valley," he said, making my inner self pout.

"Then why are you here?"

"To show you what else I'm capable of. And for you to show me the same."

At least we wouldn't just sit here awkwardly.

I smiled and set my gin down on the coffee table, then got up from the couch. "Let me change into something sexier," I told him, ready to head upstairs.

He stopped me by gripping my wrist tightly, and after letting his eyes wander all over my body, he looked back into my eyes and said in a low growl, "You look sexy in whatever you're wearing, Valley. Sit down on my lap."

I opened my mouth to say something, unsure if he was being serious.

How sexy could yoga pants and a large hoodie be?

"Are you serious?"

"Straddle my fucking lap, Valley!" he ordered.

I quickly did, letting him pull me as close to his body as possible with both his hands on my ass.

My crotch pressed against his, and the already swollen bulge in his pants was not to miss.

"I want you to come on me by rubbing your pussy against my dick. I don't care how you do it, but you can't use your hands," he challenged, making me feel all warm and excited inside.

Now this was what I called a fun evening.

Would a college boy ever have this idea?

Probably not.

They'd immediately take off their and my clothes, put me down on the bed and fuck me for their pleasure.

Riggs was thinking of me in this situation, and I knew that if I only rubbed myself against him the right way, I would get to my orgasm.

I started to move my hips in small circles, trying to figure out how his cock was positioned in his pants.

He had jeans on which helped a little with the pressure against my pussy, but I wanted to feel more of him, so I placed a hand on his chest and looked back into his eyes.

"Will you at least take off your pants?" I asked, hoping he wouldn't torture me and not make me feel his cock through a thinner fabric.

He thought about it for a second before making me stand up again to take off his jeans.

I could see the bulge in his boxer briefs much better now, and I knew I would be able to feel it a whole lot better too.

He pulled me back onto his lap, making me straddle him again and placing his hands on my lower back.

"Go on," he nudged, leaning back and spreading his legs wider to get as comfortable as possible.

His cock was semi-hard, but the more I moved against him, the harder he got, and sure enough his length lied there with the tip peeking out from the waistband.

I smiled at the sight of the glistening drop of precum at the small hole on top, but since I wasn't allowed to use my hands, I looked back into Riggs's eyes and bit my bottom lip.

"Can I have a taste?" I asked him, knowing exactly what I wanted.

He moved his hand between us while I kept rubbing my pussy against him in circular motions, and when he brushed his pointer finger over the tip of his cock, he lifted it to my lips to let me lick it off.

"You liked swallowing my cum, didn't you?" he asked in a growly voice.

I nodded, pulling his finger into my mouth and sucking on it hard while his lips parted and his eyes watched me closely.

"If you're lucky, you're getting more today," he promised, making me smile and move my hips a little faster while pushing my pussy against him more.

"Fuck, baby...You have no idea how hard I'm gonna fuck you when the time's right."

I hoped that time would come soon, because as patient as I was, I didn't think I could wait for this for too long.

My pussy clenched every time my clit rubbed against his cock, hitting the right spot and sending sparks flying in my whole body.

He pulled his finger out of my mouth and cupped my jaw tightly while he moved his other hand up to my tits.

That's exactly where I wanted it, and he cupped one of them with his large hand, squeezing it gently over my hoodie.

"Keep rubbing that wet pussy against my dick while I play with those pretty tits," he told me, letting go of my jaw and lifting up my hoodie to uncover my breasts.

My nipples were perky and hard, ready for his mouth to cover them, but before he did, he pulled my hoodie off and threw it next to us on the couch.

A moan escaped me as I felt something deep inside of me build, knowing it wouldn't take too long to come right on his lap the way he wanted me to.

"So fucking perfect," he growled, cupping both my tits and squeezing them tightly with his rough hands.

They were the perfect size, and he didn't hesitate to start playing with them, pinching my nipples and pushing them against each other.

"Oh, yes..." I moaned.

I felt the need to close my eyes out of pure bliss, but I didn't want to miss a thing he did to my body.

Other than the night he pushed his fingers deep into my pussy, this was the only time he touched my body properly.

Sure, he did squeeze my ass a few times, but this was a step further, making me wish for more.

"Don't stop moving," he muttered, and I realized I was getting slower thanks to him distracting me with his hands.

He finally leaned in closer, his mouth covering my right nipple while he kept squeezing them in his hands.

I gripped his hair tightly, holding him in place as he started to move his tongue against my nipple, swirling it around the little nub and biting down on it rather harshly.

Another moan escaped me, but the rougher he was with me, the more I liked it.

His cock was throbbing against my pussy, and instead of a circular motion, I started to rub against his cock lengthwise, making sure not to miss an inch of his shaft.

He was long and hard, and I felt his tip was fully peeking out of his boxer brief's waistband.

I needed another taste, but for him to let me taste his cum again I needed to rub against him harder.

At this point, I wasn't even thinking about my own orgasm anymore

When he moved from my right nipple to my left, he looked up while I fisted his hair in my hands even tighter, pushing his face against my tit to show him that I needed more.

He chuckled, luckily letting me have what I wanted.

"Oh, God...don't stop," I begged, my vision slowly starting to blur as the tension inside of me rose.

Since I was holding him close to my tits, he let go of them and put both his hands on my ass to help me rub against him, pushing me tighter against him while his tongue kept teasing my sensitive nipple.

My body started to shiver and my hips slowly gave up after moving for so long, but with his help, I continued to rub my clit along his cock and finally reached the high I was aiming for.

A loud moan escaped me and my head fell back as the orgasm hit me hard, making me spiral out of control and stay way up for a long time.

I didn't wanna come back down and face reality, because there was a big chance of him leaving without letting me suck him dry first.

So I stayed right there for as long as humanly possible, feeling him twist and pull at my nipples a little while longer.

Yeah...I could definitely get used to the way Riggs played.

Chapter Sixteen

Riggs

I watched her lust-filled face as she slowly started to come down from her high, her hands tightly gripping my hair and her pussy still pushed against my hardness.

I made her work for her own pleasure, and she looked incredibly hot doing so.

My eyes moved from her face down to her tits, her chest rising and falling fast as she was still trying to catch her breath.

The tip of my dick was peeking out from the waistband of my boxer briefs, and I kept my eyes on it while I started to move her hips with my hands again.

I needed more of her, but I had already told her that I wouldn't fuck her tonight. It wasn't the right time or place, and before I would give her what she wanted, I had to build up to that moment until she wasn't patient anymore.

She liked the way I played, so why not keep it up a while longer?

Her tongue came out to lick along her bottom lip while I pulled her closer against my shaft to make sure I would stay hard, but that wasn't difficult with her on my lap anyway.

She was so damn pure, but she hid so much dirtiness inside of her which automatically pulled me in.

There were many pretty girls in this town, but none have ever piqued my interest and need the way Valley had.

She kept me interested enough to go after her, and if I wasn't careful enough, she'd one day be the one bossing me around.

"Open your eyes," I muttered, looking back into her face as she now moved her hips against mine without me controlling her anymore.

Her blue eyes had tears in them, but the look in them told me how good she was feeling.

The confidence never left them, which was another turn on.

I brushed the backs of my pointer fingers along her hard nipples, teasing and gently pulling on them before squeezing them between my finger and thumb.

A soft moan escaped her while she bit her bottom lip and kept her big eyes on mine.

"On your knees," I ordered, but instead of doing what I told her to, she placed her hands on my chest and leaned in closer, kissing me passionately and pushing her sweet tongue into my mouth.

Not what I wanted her to do, but her braveness had to be rewarded.

Just for a few seconds though.

I let my tongue dip deep into her mouth, licking hers and then pushing her away from me with an angry growl.

"On your fucking knees, Valley!" I barked, getting first a damn grin from her and then finally what I wanted.

I gripped a fistful of her hair when she knelt between my legs in front of me, and with my other hand I pushed my boxer briefs down my hips.

Her eyes flashed with need and hunger, but I didn't let her have it just yet.

"Tell me where you want my cum, baby."

I started to rub my dick right in front of her face, holding it tight in my hand and squeezing the tip with my fingers to intensify the feeling.

She moved her eyes to my hand, hungry for my dick and ready to suck on it. But first, I wanted her to answer my question.

"Tell me, Valley. Where do you want my cum?"

"In my mouth," she replied, her voice raspy and sweet.

Good enough.

I tilted my dick toward her lips but kept her in place with my hand still fisting her hair.

"You gonna suck on it hard, hm? Show me how much you want my cum, Val."

Her lips were parted and her tongue ready to lick another drop of precum off the tip.

"You want it?" I teased, watching the frown between her brows deepen as she realized how hard I was going to make this for her.

"Yes, Daddy," she replied with a devilish undertone.

I raised a brow and yanked at her hair. "What did I tell you about calling me that?"

But instead of letting her answer, I pulled her head closer to my dick, making her wrap her lips around it and pushing her head down until she had most of it in her mouth.

She gagged, tried to adjust to the sudden intrusion, but I kept her right there as punishment, not letting her move.

"You don't ever fucking call me that without my permission, understood?"

Wasn't really a question I wanted her answer to.

She knew she had to listen, and since she couldn't talk anyway, I kept her face pressed against my stomach with my shaft deep in her mouth.

I felt the back of her throat with my tip, and I moved her head around a little to try and get it even deeper.

She gagged again, pushing her hands against my thighs, fighting for some air, but how much fun would it really be if I just let her have what she wanted?

She had to suffer through this now, until her fucking face turned blue.

I kept her right there, not letting her breathe.

After struggling for a while, she finally calmed her body and relaxed, making me grin as her hands moved up to my stomach to caress it gently.

"Just like that, baby. Hold your damn breath and show me how good you can be," I murmured, loosening the grip in her hair a little and brushing along the side of her head with my thumbs while every muscle in her body relaxed.

"Fuck," I growled quietly, my own body tensing in response to hers. "This is how it will be from now on. You misbehave, I teach you a lesson. Seems like you're a fast learner."

Her fingers moved along the creases of my muscles, making sure not to miss one.

I liked this side of her when she surrendered and did what she was told, knowing there was no other way to get out of this situation.

And although I wanted to make her suffer more, I knew that if I didn't pull her head back soon, she would lose consciousness from not getting any air in her lungs.

I pulled her head back slowly without her making any sudden movements, and the second she was able to breathe again, she took a deep breath, her eyes on mine and strings of spit stretching from my dick all the way to her lips.

Her eyes were watery and she had shed a few tears, but the naughty little thing she was, she licked her lips and smiled, looking like a damn porn star.

One I would gladly fuck in front of a camera and show the world she was mine.

That's what she was.

I rarely claimed women, but this one was special and God forbid her sucking on another man's dick while I showed her how much fun playing games with a fifty-six-year-old could be.

She enjoyed it.

Of course she did.

"You're so damn beautiful," I muttered, pushing her hair out of her face and brushing along her full lips with my thumb. "You want more?"

"Yes, please," she quickly replied, eagerly looking at my dick.

"Put your pretty mouth on it again," I ordered, watching as she moved closer to wrap her lips around my hardness, immediately starting to suck on it with her hands at the base of it.

I leaned back again, holding her hair with one hand into a ponytail at the top of her head while she moved up and down along my length.

For an eighteen-year-old, she sure had a lot of practice, but just thinking about her with other men made me angry.

She was mine now.

I licked my bottom lip as she pulled my dick out of her mouth to lick along my length, from base to tip and then back down where she pulled my balls into her mouth.

She liked to experiment and show how much she knew about the male body and what they liked, and honestly...I wasn't mad at that.

Her finger in my ass surprised me, but it wasn't the first time a girl played around my back entrance while we fucked.

It felt nice, and so I let Valley even lick all the way down to my asshole while she kept rubbing my dick with one hand.

She wasn't afraid, but liked to explore.

Just what I liked, although I would've never expected such things from her.

"Use your finger," I told her, watching as she pushed her forefinger into her mouth to wet it and then place it at my asshole to slowly push it inside.

"Now keep sucking my dick, baby. I want to see my cum all over that dirty mouth of yours."

She grinned and moved further up to pull my dick back into her mouth, and since she wasn't going to tease me anymore after the lesson I taught her, I let her do whatever was needed to make me come.

"Use that tongue," I encouraged, feeling it twirl around my tip before she moved her lips further down along my length.

I let her do all the work, because once she has done enough, it would be my turn.

I'd fuck her until she screamed in agony, and I'd make her come so hard she would never forget how good an older man can make her feel.

I felt the tension inside of me rise, ready to explode and let her swallow my cum she so desperately wanted.

And to her luck, it didn't take too long until the first drop hit her tongue unexpectedly.

I gripped her hair again, pulling her head back just a little so she would keep my tip in her mouth while my body started to tense more and more.

A groan left my throat, and I pushed away her hands to rub my shaft myself to take control over it.

"Open up," I growled, and when she did, I couldn't hold back any longer.

A puddle of cum formed on her pink tongue while I released myself inside of her mouth.

Her pretty eyes stayed on mine the whole time with excitement flashing in them.

"That's it, baby. This is what you deserved tonight. You've been good," I praised through gritted teeth.

When the last drop hit her tongue, I kept stroking my dick and watched her while she knelt there with her mouth wide open and the puddle of cum on her tongue, waiting for me to allow her to swallow it.

I had other things in mind.

This wasn't over yet, and I knew whatever I would do, she'd like.

I let go of my now semi-hard shaft and placed two of my fingers on her tongue, letting some of the cum flow down her throat and some of it down her chin.

She swallowed to not choke on it, and I covered my fingers in my own cum before rubbing them against her tongue.

"This isn't the only body part of yours I want my cum on," I told her quietly, then I nodded upward motioning for her to stand up.

She did after I pulled my fingers out of her mouth, and when she was standing in front of me in those tight pants and no hoodie on, I ordered her to take them off and strip.

The good girl she was did exactly that, and when she stood there between my legs with her bare pussy right in front of my face, I lifted my hand and placed my two fingers between her folds, rubbing in my cum.

"I want it right here too. I wanna come inside of your tight, wet pussy," I told her, looking up at her.

Her eyes were hooded, and she held herself up with her hands on my shoulders, looking down at me and spreading her legs a little wider for easier access.

I dipped my fingers into her tight hole, stretching her while small moans left her lips.

She clawed her short but sharp nails into my shoulders, now closing her eyes as I started fingering her.

I kept my mouth shut for a while, making sure she wouldn't come while I rubbed my fingertips against her inner walls, smelling her arousal as I was sitting right in front of her.

So damn sweet, but I had to wait.

I had already gotten a taste of her pussy before, and she tasted so damn addictive.

"Please," she begged, her eyes closed and her lips parted. "Please make me come."

"No."

"Please, Riggs...I want you to make me come," she whispered, her legs slowly starting to shake.

Her pussy clenched around my fingers, squeezing them tight. But before she could reach that high she so desperately needed, I pulled my fingers out and pulled her back on my lap where her bare pussy pressed against my dick.

"Open," I ordered, my fingertips grazing her lips before she parted them enough to let my fingers in.

She sucked on them, licked both my cum and her juices off while her eyes stared back into mine again.

"Stop begging. I decide when you get to come, understand that?"

She gave me a small nod, then she moved her hips in circular motions again to tease me.

As much as I was ready for round two, I couldn't give it to her.

"I gotta go," I told her, placing my hands on her hips and pushing her off me again.

"So soon?"

I let out a harsh laugh. "I spent enough time here with you tonight."

I got up from the couch and pulled up my boxer briefs and pants while she stood there naked, not really interested in putting on her underwear or hoodie.

Not that I minded, but she was trying to get more out of this tonight when I told her there wasn't going to be more.

"Will I see you again soon?"

I buttoned my jeans and picked up my glass to empty the gin inside, and once I set it back down, I looked at her and nodded.

"Tomorrow night. Come by my house. Wear a swimsuit," I told her, then I left her standing there in the middle of the living room to get to the front door.

"Swimsuit?"

"Stop asking so many damn questions before I change my mind."

She had followed me, still naked, and now stood in front of me again with her nipples still hard and perky.

"Tomorrow night at eight. We'll have dinner and then we'll..." I stopped, not wanting to ruin what I had planned by telling her.

"We'll fuck?"

I let my eyes wander all over her perfect body once more before turning and opening the door without replying to her suggestion.

"Eight," I repeated. "And put some damn clothes on."

Chapter Seventeen

Valley

When Riggs invited me to come have dinner with him, of course I had to go all out on the outfit.

Like he asked me to, I wore a bikini underneath which was slightly too small for me, but since he has seen me naked already, I didn't think that would bother him.

If anything, it would make him want to take it off me.

I wore a tight dress similar to the one I wore at my dad's birthday party, but this one had a low cut out in the back.

I was punctual, even had a few minutes to spare which I spend in my car just staring at Riggs's house.

All the lights were on, but since the kitchen was hidden behind the large living room, I couldn't see anyone inside, thinking Riggs must've been in the kitchen cooking dinner for us.

By us I meant him, me, and his brother.

Garett, who I had to cancel for tonight as I couldn't turn down Riggs's offer to spend the evening with him.

Live action was still better than through a webcam, but what Garett didn't know was that he'd have someone to look at tonight.

So in my eyes, I didn't really cancel our online appointment.

When it was time to face Riggs, I got out of the car and walked over to the front door to ring the bell, and only a few seconds later, Garett opened the door with a wide smile on his face.

"Valley. Good to see you again."

He had already gotten ready for tonight, seeing as he wore a button up shirt every time I saw him on my screen, but he didn't look too disappointed.

"Hello, Marcus. How are you?" I asked, smiling back and passing him as he stepped aside.

"I'm very well, thank you. Nice of Riggs to invite you over now that your parents are on vacation, huh?"

"Yeah, very kind of him. Are you staying for dinner as well?" I asked, not wanting to assume anything although I knew exactly what was going on in his life at the moment.

"Oh, yes. I'll have dinner with you guys. But afterward, I'm going out to a bar. My date dumped me, so I'm going to look for someone else who can keep me company tonight."

Good for him, but the way he referred to me as a date rubbed me the wrong way.

I connected dates with feelings, which I didn't have for him despite all the things we've done together.

"Sorry to hear, Marcus. I'm sure you'll find someone who'd like to keep you company for the night."

"Hope so too. Riggs is in the kitchen. I'll be right with you guys," he told me.

I wondered if he realized that Riggs and I had gotten close before. Surely, he wasn't blind and noticed the way I was dressed.

"Okay," I replied, watching him leave and then heading to the kitchen myself.

Riggs stood there with his back turned to me, stirring something on the stove all focused.

He didn't turn around as I walked closer to him, and when I stopped right behind him, I wrapped my arms around his chest and placed my hands on it while pressing my body against his back.

"Did you miss me?" I purred, grinning like an idiot.

His body relaxed underneath my touch, and once he put the wooden spoon down on the counter, he turned around to look at me with dark, almost angry eyes.

Someone's in a mood, I thought.

"Everything okay?" I asked more seriously, but keeping my hands on him and pushing one of them into his hair.

"Everything's perfect," he muttered, lifting his hands and placing them on my lower back.

He let his eyes wander down my body, keeping them on my tits for a while before they met my own again.

"You look beautiful."

He meant it, even if his voice was monotone and lacking motivation.

Maybe he needed a little bit of that, and since I was good at getting him in the mood, I pushed myself up on my tiptoes and kissed his lips gently.

It came naturally, and he kissed me back while one of his hands moved closer to my ass, cupping and squeezing it just right.

Our tongues touched, slowly starting to move against each other in the most passionate way possible.

Never had he been this gentle with me, but just when I had that thought, he lifted his other hand and wrapped his fingers around my throat tightly.

He took my breath away in an instant, making me stop moving my lips while his tongue was still deep inside my mouth.

He explored it, even bit down on my bottom lip before leaning back and looking into my eyes again.

I couldn't talk or breathe, but who needed to do those things anyway when a handsome guy like Riggs was squeezing your airway shut?

"No teasing at the table. You wait until Marcus is gone, then you can go back to your usual self."

He meant my naughty-self.

"Think you can do that?" he asked in a low voice.

I nodded, still not able to use my vocal cords to communicate.

"Good. Go sit down."

He finally let go of me, and after sucking enough air into my lungs, I turned and walked to the dining table which was already set.

I had to give it to him.

For being an alpha, and an asshole for most of the time, he did have his life under control and didn't let himself go just because he was retired now.

I was positive he went for a run this morning, or did some workout in his home gym.

Either way, I liked where things with us were going.

I didn't expect him and I to fall in love and move in together, because quite frankly, that would only complicate things.

But I did like the thought of us seeing each other more often, even with my parents back from vacation.

They didn't have to know about us, and we could keep it our dirty little secret.

Yeah...I think I'd like that.

"Are you planning on staying for long, Marcus?" I asked, taking another bite of the food on my plate.

Riggs was a great cook, but as much as I enjoyed dinner, I finally wanted to be alone with him.

"I'm still trying to figure things out. I might stay until the end of the year and start over in the new one," he said.

"You won't stay here that long." Riggs wasn't just an asshole to me, but also his own brother.

"I told you you're allowed to stay for a few weeks, not four whole months."

The angel on my right shoulder told me to talk Riggs into keeping his brother here a little longer, but the devil on the other side made me keep my mouth shut.

"Right, then I'll be gone soon I guess," Marcus muttered, finishing up his dinner. "Do you need a ride home? I'm driving into town anyway," he offered, but I quickly shook my head.

"I drove here myself."

"Ah, right. Well, then." He got up from the table while Riggs and I were still eating, showing no manners whatsoever.

Sure, he wanted to hit the town and see if there's a woman waiting for him for the night, but he still could've waited for us to finish up instead of leaving in the middle of dinner.

Riggs didn't seem to mind and was probably happy he was leaving. "Bye," he muttered, and I smiled up at Marcus to wave at him.

"Have fun."

"Thanks. Probably won't have as much of it as I would've had with my initial date."

Aw, well...that's a nice compliment.

I smiled again and watched as he left the kitchen, then I turned to look at Riggs until we heard first the front door shut, then Marcus's car drive away.

"You could be a little nicer to your brother, you know?"

"You could just keep that mouth shut and let me handle him."

Rude.

Then again, there was nothing else I expected from him when he was in a grumpy mood like this.

I took the last bite and set my fork down to take a sip of my water, seeing as he didn't have anything other than alcohol around.

"Can I get a bit of the red wine?" I asked, pointing at the bottle and looking at him.

He shrugged. "If you can handle it."

"Handle it? It's just a little wine, Riggs. Maybe it will set me in the mood seeing as you're not helping much."

He raised a brow while I poured myself a little bit of the wine, and when I set the bottle down, he frowned at me.

"You know why you're here tonight. You should've come prepared," he told me.

"Oh, I am prepared for whatever fucked up and dirty shit you're up to tonight, but maybe you should lose that grumpy old man behavior and show me what you really want. All you're doing right now is making me want to go back home and use a dildo to make myself come."

He didn't like that at all.

Pushing himself back from the table, he got up and placed his hand on my throat, making me stand up and spill my wine all over the table.

Shit.

"Is that how you talk to me?" he growled.

There, was it so hard to turn into his usual self?

I bit my bottom lip to stop from grinning, and I shook my head to answer his probably rhetorical question.

He pushed my chair to the side and moved the plates and bowls on the table away to then lay me down on my back with him standing between my legs.

My heart started pumping hard in my chest, wanting him right there with his face pressed against my pussy.

To my luck, he knelt in front of me and pushed my dress up to reveal my bikini covered pussy.

A growl left his chest, and I pushed myself up with my hands behind me on the table to see what he was up to.

"You don't need this," he hissed, pulling down the tiny fabric and throwing it to the ground, leaving my pussy bare for easy access.

He pushed my legs apart and leaned in closer with his eyes still on mine.

He pressed his lips against my inner thigh, sending shivers through my body and making me reach for his hair to grip it tightly with one hand.

"Please," I begged, but that's not what he wanted to hear.

"What did I tell you about begging, Valley?"

I pressed my lips into a thin line to stop myself from sighing heavily, and when I didn't answer him, he let out a harsh laugh.

"Exactly. Keep still. This is what you deserve tonight."

He wasn't talking about an orgasm, that I knew for sure.

I didn't behave, and he was going to punish me again.

His lips moved closer to my folds, but instead of licking right through them the way he did once before, he let his tongue move along my inner thighs for a while, teasing and driving me insane.

I took a deep breath and tried to move my hips in a way to get his mouth where I wanted it, but the more I struggled to get it there, the more he teased.

I had to relax and let him do what he wanted, otherwise I would never get to experience my first orgasm caused by him.

The other times I had to work for it, which was nice either way, but I wanted to know what it felt like to come with his tongue flicking my clit.

Riggs pulled my legs over his shoulders and I kept them there as his hands cupped my ass to keep me in place.

Finally, and with his eyes still on mine, he let his tongue move through my folds, tasting every single drop of my juices.

"Oh, yes..." I moaned, gripping his hair tighter in my hand and pressing his face more against my pussy.

I didn't want him to leave anymore, not until he made me come which was exactly what he didn't want me to do and I had to admit that him keeping me from coming felt intense.

His fingers dug into my skin, making it hurt just enough to send sparks flying inside my body.

They were everywhere, and now that his tongue was licking my clit, I could finally relax a little and enjoy every moment of it.

Chapter Eighteen

Riggs

Those sweet noises and the way she kept my head in place to ensure I wouldn't move away made my dick jolt in my pants, needing to get some more space as it was starting to get tight in there.

She tasted so damn sweet, making me addicted to her.

But as much as I loved to play with her pussy, I still wanted to make her suffer by denying her an orgasm.

Her filthy mouth was what got us here, and the dining table wasn't where I had intended on fucking her.

Yeah, after thinking long and hard about it, I decided that I couldn't wait any longer.

I had to fuck her tonight.

Her juices were drooling down my beard but I swallowed as much of it as I could while I held her hips in place to stop her from squirming.

I could tell she was close by the way her face filled with lust, her lips parted, and her clit pulsated against my tongue.

That's right where I wanted her, and before her legs started to shake, I pulled away to see pure frustration wash over her.

"No, please, Riggs! Don't stop!" she cried, taking matters in her own hands and pulling her hand out of my hair to rub her clit and hope for the long-awaited orgasm.

"Don't!" I barked, gripping her wrist and pulling her hand away.

"Please," she begged again, trying to push her legs together and somehow cause friction between them.

It didn't work out, as only a few seconds later she looked defeated.

"Will you talk to me like that again?" I asked, pushing her legs apart again and holding on to her hips so she wouldn't move.

"No," she replied out of breath.

I licked her pulsating clit again, watching as her body jolted.

"And will you behave from now on?"

She hesitated on that, and I leaned back a bit to show her that I wasn't going to continue if she didn't respond.

"Yes, I'll behave," she whispered, her hand reaching for my hair again.

That was good enough, and I leaned in, with my eyes closed this time, to finish what I had started.

Her hips bucked more and more the faster I flicked my tongue against that little nub, and her fist in my hair pulled tightly at my hair to steer me the right way to the right spot.

"Oh, yes...please, don't stop," she cried, and without being an ass for once, I let her reach exactly what she aimed for.

Her head fell back, and although the orgasm hit her hard, she kept my head right there for me to continue licking her throbbing clit.

"God!" she whimpered, making me grin as now her body started to shake uncontrollably.

This was just as much torture as not letting her come, seeing as the feeling only intensified inside of her.

So instead of telling me to continue, she mumbled for me to stop.

"Riggs..." she breathed, trying to push me away this time.

She really needed to figure out what she wanted, but either way, I would do the exact opposite to show her who was in control.

I looked up at her with my mouth still covering her folds and swallowing every last drop of my saliva mixed with her wetness.

Valley had lost her strength, and her body was slowly shutting down while her brain fogged up from pleasure.

I had to stop before I couldn't use her for more tonight, so I licked through her folds one last time before standing up and leaning over her to kiss her passionately.

She was still in some kind of trance, and while I twirled my tongue around hers, I pushed her dress further up to cup her needy tits.

"More?" I murmured into the kiss, and she nodded her head while still recovering from what I just put her through.

"Tell me what you want," I said as I leaned back to look into her face.

Her cheeks were red in contrast to her pale skin, and her blue eyes looked more gray.

"I want you to fuck me hard," she whispered, still trying to catch her breath.

I moved my hands from her tits to her waist, then pulled her closer until her pussy pressed against my crotch with her legs spread wide on either side of me.

"Sure about that? You know I won't take it easy. Once I'm inside, I won't hold back, darling."

Valley licked her lips and shook her head. "I don't care. I want you to be rough with me."

Good.

I didn't know any other way to fuck.

My dick was hard already, waiting for me to pull it out of my pants to give it some space.

I was aching for her, and after quickly pulling off her dress and then her bikini top, I unbuttoned my pants and pushed them down along with my boxer briefs.

Rubbing my length, I watched her body squirm on the table.

It wasn't the first place I'd choose to fuck her, but I didn't feel like carrying her to the couch or my bedroom.

Not right now.

"Legs up," I ordered, watching as she lifted them straight into the air where I wrapped one arm around them and pressed them against the left side of my upper body.

I used my spit to wet my shaft before placing the tip at her entrance and pushing it in slowly, testing her tightness.

As much as I wanted to fuck her, I didn't want to break her on my first thrust.

Her eyes were wide as she felt my cock stretch her slowly, and once I was sure I could start moving, I pushed inside her in one swift move.

My right hand was on her hip, holding her down to stop her from moving too much.

"Fuck," I growled, remembering how good it felt to have my dick squeezed by a wet, hot pussy.

Valley felt incredible, like a warm glove hugging me just right.

Her face told me she was prepared for what was coming next, and to not make her wait any longer, I started to fuck her hard without showing mercy.

Valley's eyes rolled back and her hands gripped the side of the table tightly to make sure she couldn't get pushed back on it, but stay right there for me to thrust in and out of her with as much force as possible.

"This what you wanted?" I growled, showing her just how much energy an *old man* like me still had.

No way I would ever let her fuck another guy my age, or any other man on this planet.

She was mine now, and I hoped she realized that and wouldn't go fuck around with others.

Not that she did that anyway, but I had to show her that from now on, I was her only one.

I reached out my hand to cup one of her tits, squeezing it tightly and pulling at her nipple while continuing to fuck her hard.

"Eyes on me," I said, and she listened as always.

Her beauty added to the excitement inside of me, making my dick throb even more by just looking into those pretty eyes.

"Harder," she moaned, making me grin and grip her hip again, but in this position we were in, I couldn't give my all.

I pushed her legs down to one side so she had to turn slightly, allowing me better access to her pussy.

I placed one hand on her ass while pushing against the underside of her thigh, then I started to move my hips again to keep fucking her.

She clenched her walls around me, letting me know that she was already close. I was far from it though.

"Don't come yet," I muttered, lifting my hand and slapping her ass hard to make her feel something other than the orgasm building inside of her.

But who was I fucking kidding...this was Valley, and of course she only got turned on more by my spanking.

Her moans got louder with each thrust, and I focused on myself rather than her, wanting to fill her pussy with my cum.

I was holding back in a way, but also wanted to come already.

Valley must've noticed my indecisiveness, so she reached behind her back and toward my dick to cup my balls in her hand.

She knew how to drive me mad, and I let her do whatever was needed to release myself inside of her tight hole.

Her ass was bright red from my hips slapping against her skin, and while she continued to tug and squeeze my balls, the tension inside of me moved from my toes all the way up into my abdomen, where the orgasm exploded unexpectedly.

It was needed, because fucking her any longer would've become painful.

I emptied my load inside of her, watching as the cum oozed out between her folds and along my shaft.

Her breathing was just as heavy as mine, but since she didn't come yet, I pulled out and knelt in front of her again, spreading her legs wide and licking along her slit to get to her clit and start flicking my tongue against it.

I didn't care about tasting my own cum, and since it was mixed with her juices, it didn't taste half bad.

"Oh, yes!" she cried, pulling at my hair again and circling her hips to rub her pussy against my mouth.

"Please don't stop, Riggs. Make me come," she told me through gritted teeth, and luckily it didn't take too long for the orgasm to wash over her in an instant.

Her head was thrown back against the table and her back arched while I licked through her slit one last time before getting back up on my feet to watch her slowly come down from her high again.

I wiped my mouth with the back of my hand, then moved my hands along her sides to cup her tits to make her relax her body.

"This is how it's going to be from now on, Valley. I fuck you whenever I want to, wherever I want. And we will both come. I don't care how or when, but when I fuck you, I'll please us both," I promised her, making a small and exhausted smile appear on her lips.

Her eyes opened again, looking back into mine. "Okay," she whispered, her breath hitching in her throat.

I eyed her for a while until I had calmed down myself before pulling at her hands to make her sit up straight.

I cupped her face with both hands and leaned in to kiss her lips.

She placed her hands on my stomach, pushing my shirt upward and caressing my skin before nudging my shirt further up, wanting it off.

Guess it was only fair since she was naked already.

I broke the kiss and pulled my shirt over my head, then threw it on the ground and picked her up with my hands cupping her ass.

She wrapped her legs around my hips and I carried her through the living room to get to my favorite place in my house.

I had a heated indoor pool overlooking the city just like my bedroom, and normally I always wore my swimsuit to swim a few laps whenever I felt like it, but since the night didn't go as planned, I didn't mind getting into the warm water with her naked.

She squealed like a little child getting candy as she saw the pool, and while she bit her lip with excitement, I let her down on the border of the stairs leading into the water.

"I didn't know you had an indoor pool. This is amazing! And the view..." she gasped.

I grinned at how much a damn pool excited her, thinking it was the cutest shit I'd ever seen.

But we wouldn't just go for a swim in the pool tonight.

I wanted to fuck her again before taking her to my bedroom and doing it all over again.

"Get in," I ordered, grabbing my dick and stroking it slowly with my eyes still on her.

She smiled, taking a step into the pool and then diving into the water, submerging under the surface.

The way her dark hair flowed in the water made her look like a damn mermaid. Or should

I say siren, as those creatures were mostly known to kill men.

Valley was reckless, hell, even vicious, and just a look from her could kill but only in the best way possible.

I watched her come up for air and brush her hair back from her face with a bright smile.

"It's beautiful, come in!" she exclaimed.

As much as I wanted to stand there and watch her a little while longer, I wanted to touch her again.

Be inside her and fuck her right here in my goddamn pool.

Over and over again.

Chapter Nineteen

Valley

Sex in the pool was something I never really thought would be comfortable, but with Riggs, he made it just as hot as when he fucked me on the kitchen table.

I was on the stairs leading into the pool on all fours, with Riggs standing behind me, fucking me hard with his hands on my hips.

He pulled me back against him with every thrust, making me moan loudly because keeping it in was not an option.

It felt too damn good, and although I was starting to feel sore between my legs, I didn't want him to stop.

The burning sensation wasn't painful. Instead, it made me want him to slap and spank me again, show me exactly how rough he could be.

But with his cock deep inside of me, I couldn't talk much.

He took my breath away.

His hands moved from my hips to my ass, spreading my cheeks to then run his thumb over my asshole, teasing me.

I looked back at him with my eyes teary and lips parted, and when I saw him looking down at my body, I smiled at the admiration I saw flashing in his eyes.

A low groan left his chest and he stopped moving for a second to lift his hand up to his mouth and wet his fingers with his spit before placing them back on my slit, pressing his thumb against my tight hole.

I bit my bottom lip, knowing anything that had to with anal was something I would enjoy.

I watched him closely as he was in some type of ecstasy, his breath calm and controlled.

His cock was still inside of my pussy, pulsating and stretching me without him having to move.

"You like that?" he asked, keeping his eyes on my ass but knowing I was watching him.

"Yes," I told him, moving my hips to feel more of his finger against my entrance. "I love to be fucked in the ass."

Not lying about that, but up until this moment, I only had the pleasure of having one other dick in my ass, other than my dildos.

It's also been about a year since I last did anal, so I needed him to stretch and prepare me for his cock which is what he was already doing by slowly adding another finger while fingering my asshole.

I closed my eyes again, letting him do all the work.

He knew what he had to do to get his thickness all the way inside of me, so he took his time to make sure it wouldn't hurt too much when he entered me back there.

While he worked his fingers, he started to move in and out of my pussy again.

Just minutes before he had pulled me to the stairs and we were still on the deep end of the pool, he made me wrap my arms and legs around his tattoo-covered body.

He really did look incredibly handsome with all the different symbols on his skin, and although I didn't look at them too closely, I was sure I one day had the chance to ask him about each and every one of them.

"How does this feel?" he asked in a growl, pushing three fingers into my asshole now.

"It feels perfect," I moaned, opening my eyes again and looking back at him.

He lifted his gaze to meet my eyes, and when he saw how ready and willing I was, he pulled his fingers, then his cock out of me to press the tip of it against my back entrance.

I moaned again, relaxing my body and trying not to move.

"Fuck, baby...you're so damn tight," he muttered, trying to push further inside of me carefully.

It took a while until he was able to enter me fully, and although it didn't hurt me, I could feel him stretching me more and more.

I closed my eyes again, and once he was sure he could start thrusting into me without a boundary, he did just that.

From that moment on, I was in pure bliss, enjoying every second of him fucking me.

Coming from anal wasn't an option for me, no matter how hard and deep he pushed into me, but that didn't stop him from taking me out of the pool and into his bedroom, both of us still wet from the water.

He made me lie down on my stomach with my legs dangling from the bed as he stepped close between them to push his cock back into my pussy again and start pounding into me with no mercy.

Just how I liked it.

He wasn't as vocal as usual, but he showed me by his roughness just what he was thinking, and the longer I tried to hold back on my orgasm, the faster he moved in and out of me.

"Let go, Valley," he ordered, holding on to my ass tightly.

I was enjoying this far too much, and I didn't wanna come unless he did the same at the same time.

"Stop fucking holding back, Valley!" he growled, digging his fingers into my skin.

"No," I cried, reaching between my body and the mattress to cup my pussy and ease the aching.

He muttered something I couldn't understand, but he quickly showed me how unhappy he was by pulling out of me, turning me onto my back, pushing back into me and wrapping his hand around my throat tightly.

"I told you to come," he barked.

As much as I would've loved to tease him a little more, and as much as I enjoyed seeing him this angry, I finally let go, letting the orgasm hit me hard.

I threw my head back, closed my eyes and gripped the covers underneath me while my legs started to shake.

"Perfect...just like that, baby. Let go," Riggs growled, loosening his grip on my throat just a little to let me breathe.

Soon after, he stopped moving and I felt his cum fill me once again.

"Oh, Riggs," I moaned, reaching for his hand and tightening his grip again because, well...choking me was starting to become something I wanted him to do more often.

A low chuckle left him, and his fingers gripped my throat tighter again, and when he stopped moving, he stayed deep inside of me, not letting his cum flow out of me.

Instead, he leaned down to press his lips against mine, with his beard tickling my skin.

Kissing him started to feel normal, almost as if it was needed after his rough way of fucking me.

He was gentle, yet very determined.

But even though he was showing a whole different side of him in that moment, there was nothing changing between us.

He was still just a guy I liked to have fun with, and if I was being brutally honest, I didn't think there would be more between us than this.

Sure, he was a somewhat nice guy when he didn't act like a total asshole, but I was still eighteen. A relationship or even catching feelings for him wasn't an option.

Think again, Val.

No. He doesn't want that either, so why start hoping for something I knew would never happen?

His tongue moved against mine one last time before he stood up straight and finally pulled out of me.

But it wasn't over yet, because no matter what we did, there was always something more to do.

He looked down at his cock, then raised a brow at me with question in his eyes. I wasn't sure what he wanted at first, but when I moved my eyes to his still hard cock, I quickly realized what he wanted.

I got down on my knees, wrapping one hand around the base of it and then licking along his length to clean his own cum off it.

He watched me closely, his hand moving into my hair and whispering praises while I swallowed what was left on his shaft.

"Such a dirty little girl. You know exactly how to make me want more, hm? Damn tease," he muttered, making me smile.

To think that other girls my age were now partying at a stupid frat house while I let a fifty-six-year-old fuck me all evening long never made me think there was something wrong with me.

I did this because I wanted it, with no one forcing me to.

That's who I was, and it didn't make me a whore.

I was living my life, being a woman, pushing my boundaries and giving my body what it wanted.

But just because I was so open about my sexuality and all the things I liked to do, didn't mean I would push other girls to do the same.

It's their body, and they should do what they're most comfortable with.

When the last drop of cum was licked off his cock, Riggs pulled me back up on my feet and placed his hands on my lower back.

"You gotta go home," he told me, and I quickly nodded.

Staying here wouldn't be such a good idea, as Garett would come back home soon.

Besides, I couldn't imagine myself sleeping next to Riggs without a third, fourth, or even fifth round of fucking.

No way we could sleep.

I nodded, placing my hands on his chest and smiling at him. "Tonight was great," I told him, and his quick nod was enough of an acceptable answer.

We looked at each other for a while, then he cleared his throat and stepped away from me.

"Go get your clothes and get dressed," he ordered.

I pressed my lips into a thin line, then walked past him to get to the dining room where my clothes were laying.

Riggs had followed me to get his own clothes back on, and he started to clean up the table and kitchen.

When I was done getting dressed and putting on my shoes, I walked over to the kitchen and watched him for a while before talking.

"I'm leaving then," I told him, and he turned around to look at me.

"Got everything?" he asked, moving closer to me.

"Yes. Marcus won't know you undressed and fucked me all around the house," I said with a grin.

He chuckled and shook his head. "Not so sure about that. The smell of your wet pussy still lingers in the air."

Not a bad thing. Now he had someone to think of for the rest of the night.

He walked me to the front door and placed a hand on my waist, but didn't intend on kissing me goodbye.

Not that it was needed, but I wanted one last taste before leaving him.

I moved closer, placed my lips on his and my hand at the nape of his neck.

He was holding back at first, but soon eased into the kiss, pulling me closer against his body.

Our kiss was passionate and slow, but it didn't last for too long.

"Go home," he said in a low voice, moving back and opening the door.

"Goodnight, Riggs."

"Night," he replied, following me with his eyes while I walked to my car.

I felt different tonight, but as tired as I was, I couldn't think straight and see what was really happening inside of me.

Riggs definitely left a mark.

Chapter Twenty

Valley

"Did he at least kiss you?" I asked, my excitement going through the roof as Kennedy was telling me all about her and Mason.

She came by after school so we could study together, but we had done enough of that for now and since I still had the house all to myself, we wanted to put that opportunity to good use.

We already planned a dance party just for the two of us, then we'd order everything we wanted to eat, and then have a movie marathon for the rest of the night.

Kennedy's cheeks turned bright red, and while I put away my books, she fell back onto my bed with her hands covering her chest.

"Almost. He said he wanted to wait for the right time, but then he later texted me that it was incredibly hard for him to not kiss me," she told me.

I frowned. "Boring!"

"He's thirty-three, Val, and I'm the most inexperienced eighteen-year-old ever. I don't think I would've known what to do."

"You kissed guys before. It's not so hard, is it?"

"No, but don't older men kiss differently? I mean, I see it all the time in movies. Younger actors kiss so much differently than older ones."

Sure, you could tell by watching someone kiss if you'd enjoy kissing them.

"But if you never try, you'll never know what it's like," I told her with a shrug.

"True, but still…"

"Kiss me," I suggested, receiving a questionable look from her.

"What?"

"Kiss me and I'll let you know what I think of your kissing skills," I offered.

She studied my face for a while before her frown deepened but then disappeared again.

"Are you sure? Won't that make things awkward between us?"

"Ken, we're best friends since we're little. We've peed in a kiddie pool while sitting in it before. Doesn't get any more personal than that," I laughed.

She snorted and shook her head. "Guess so. Okay, at least you'll be brutally honest if I kiss like a drunk person."

I chuckled and nodded, then got on the bed with her and waited for her to sit up straight.

"Ready?" I asked, placing my hand on her thigh and moving closer.

"I think so."

"Relax, Ken. It's just a kiss."

She nodded and breathed in deeply before looking into my eyes and waiting for me to make a move.

I licked my lips and leaned in closer, moving my hand up to her cheek and cupping it gently before my lips touched hers.

Kissing girls was always a nice experience for me, although I hadn't done it in a long time.

Kennedy was shy, and I could tell she wasn't as relaxed as she seemed from the outside.

Instead of using my tongue right away, I let her ease into me a little more, and when she finally placed her hand on my thigh, I knew she wasn't totally lost when it came to kissing.

Her lips were soft and moved slowly against mine, and that was enough for me to know that she didn't suck at kissing.

I moved my lips against hers one last time before pulling back, noticing that she wanted more, quickly realizing how nice it was and turning bright red again.

"Wasn't so bad, huh?" I asked with a smile.

"No, it was...very nice," she admitted.

"I think so too. Mason will love the way you kiss. Maybe dare to do a little more. Use your tongue and just go for it. You'll see. The more you kiss someone, the more you understand what the other likes and dislikes, and sooner or later it comes naturally."

I got up from the bed and walked toward the door, but she stayed right there on the bed.

"Did anything ever happen that made you the person you are today?" she asked.

"What do you mean?"

"I mean...did something happen you never told me about? That need for an older guy's attention must come from somewhere."

Right.

Like other girls with daddy issues who needed an older man to act as their father because their own was never around.

Nothing against those women, and I surely wouldn't shame them for it.

But my need for an older guy just came from experience.

"I didn't live through any trauma, Kennedy. I just know what I want, and older men are who turn me on the most. There's really nothing wrong with that, and once you see past that, because I know you don't have daddy issues either, you'll see how great being with Mason really is. Just go for it without questioning everything. You like him, and he obviously likes you back. Get over your demons and enjoy your life."

She studied me for a while, then smiled. "And maybe that will make me as confident as you are, wearing it proudly and showing it off."

I shrugged. "Being confident doesn't mean you have to show it on the outside. As long as you're true to yourself. Now, let's go order something to eat because I'm starving."

***

The sushi, two burgers, and a side of fries was too much for Kennedy to handle, and so she fell asleep while watching our second movie of the night.

I didn't wanna wake her and tell her to come upstairs, as the couch was comfortable enough to sleep on, but I had to grab a blanket from my room as the one she already had over her wasn't warm enough.

I put the remote on the coffee table and let the fourth movie start, as I wasn't tired yet but wanted to hang out a little longer, eating the rest of the food we ordered.

I headed upstairs to grab my blanket which was big enough for two, and before walking back down, I checked my second phone to see if I had gotten any sweet messages from any of the men.

And, surprise surprise...Garett texted me asking if I had time for him tonight.

Well, seeing as Kennedy was out and probably wouldn't wake up again, I could easily sneak back into my room and put on a show for Garett.

I texted him back that I would be ready in fifteen minutes, then I quickly ran downstairs to put the blanket over Kennedy's body and then dashed back upstairs.

I locked myself in the room just in case she would wake up, then I turned on my laptop and set up the webcam to then change into something sexier.

The ski mask was what I pulled over my head last, making sure it sat right and didn't show unnecessary parts of my face.

When I was ready to accept Garett's call, I pressed the green button and he appeared on my screen with a bright smile on his face.

"I'm so happy to see you. I'm glad it worked out for you, Dove," he said.

Garett was naked already, rubbing his cock slowly and keeping his eyes directly on me.

"Of course. After leaving you hanging a few nights ago, I had to make it up to you," I purred, changing into my naughty self.

"Mhmm. I did go out that night and tried to find someone to spend some time with," he told me, as if I didn't know about that already.

"And did you find someone to keep you company?" I asked, starting to play with my bra strap to get his mind off our conversation and hurry things up a little.

"No. There was no one who could fill the void and need inside of me. You're the only one I was thinking of the past few days, Dove," he told me, his voice cracking and sounding defeated.

That's not how he seemed at dinner.

He definitely knew how to act around other people and not seem desperate.

"I'm here now, aren't I? What do you want me to do, daddy?"

For some reason, calling him that sent shivers down my spine but not in a good way.

The fact that Riggs, his brother, didn't like being called that made me dislike the nickname as well.

But Garett wasn't Marcus or Riggs's brother tonight, and I wasn't Valley.

I was Dove.

Riggs

Whatever sick and twisted shit my brother was doing in my guest room, I shouldn't have stood there for that long.

I also shouldn't have listened in on all the things he wanted that girl talking to him to do.

Lastly, I definitely shouldn't have gotten a fucking boner from hearing that sweet voice coming from Marcus's laptop.

It couldn't be her.

Marcus called her Dove, but then again...she called him *Garett*.

What the fuck is going on?

That voice nestled itself deep inside of my brain, not getting out again and making me clench my fists tightly while stopping the urge of pushing open the door and seeing for myself what was going on.

"Keep those legs spread wide, Dove," he ordered, which immediately made me angry.

If that girl really was Valley, she wouldn't get away with this shit easily.

I had to be careful though, as I had no proof other than the voice I was hearing.

But then, girls, especially cam girls one of which I assumed he was talking to, had to use those high-pitched and teasing voices to turn men on even more.

I listened closely, waiting for her to say another word.

"Like this, Daddy?"

Jesus Christ.

"Just like that, Dove. Fuck, I'm so damn close."

I had to leave.

"I wish you'd take off that ski mask," he then said, making me stop in my tracks and listen in a little longer.

Ski mask? What the actual fuck?

"You know I can't do that," she told him in a calm yet determined voice.

When Marcus let out a loud groan, it was finally time for me to leave and mind my own business.

It was wrong standing there and eavesdropping on my brother doing whatever the fuck he was doing in there, but that voice still stuck with me.

It reminded me so much of Valley, and I had to somehow find out if it's really her.

The time we spent together a few days ago was intense.

Never had I thought she would let me do whatever I wanted to her body, but everything I did, she took it like a pro and enjoyed every second of it.

Her liking anal was somewhat of a surprise, but there never seemed to be anything stopping her from having a good time anyway.

She's wild, very open when it comes to sex, and she's not afraid to push her boundaries and try new things.

So how strange would it really be for her to be a damn cam girl?

There were a lot of things I didn't know about her, but no matter what, I would soon find out.

Every truth comes out eventually.

Chapter Twenty-One

Valley

Della and Dad would come back in four days, and time without them was just starting to get fun.

Maybe I should talk them into going on vacation more often so I had the house to myself.

Although I didn't throw any parties for kids at my school, I still liked to have Kennedy over and do whatever we wanted to, eat what we wanted and maybe even drink some wine and talk about this and that.

It's Thursday after school, and I was getting ready in my bedroom to have Kennedy over again, but before I could walk into the bathroom to change into something more comfortable, my second phone lit up on my bed and I quickly picked it up to see which of the men was texting me.

I frowned at the screen as I saw Riggs's name on it, and the text underneath didn't sound like something he would ever send me.

I'm coming over in twenty. We'll have dinner.

First of all...he unblocked me?
Well, that's a surprise.

Can't tonight, I replied, not wanting to disappoint my best friend. Sure, it was Riggs, but Kennedy always came before any other man.

Tomorrow night. Don't make any plans, he texted back. I could sense how annoyed he was, but I wasn't going to put him first, no matter how much I wanted him back inside of me.

Riggs was like a drug, and after those nights we spent together, I was addicted.

He didn't respond to my text, so I put the phone down and continued with what I was about to do before Kennedy would arrive.

The fact that he wanted to have dinner with me again wasn't so strange, though we could skip that and go straight to fucking, as that's what his plan was anyway.

Why else would he want to come by?

As much as I liked thinking about him, I pushed all those thoughts aside and got ready for the night, getting into comfortable clothes and then heading downstairs to order food Kennedy and I agreed on getting.

***

Half an hour later, Kennedy was standing next to me by the kitchen counter, looking at the food that had arrived just minutes before.

"Think we got too much again?" she asked, reaching for the fries and eating a few.

"Maybe. I'll take the rest with me for lunch tomorrow," I told her. "Let's go eat."

We grabbed everything and brought it over to the coffee table and sat down on the couch.

"How are things with Mason?" I asked.

"Uh, good. He wants to see me on Saturday, but I'm not sure Dad will let me go out seeing as I spend most of the week here."

"Just tell him there's some type of quiz night on campus. I'm sure he'll let you go."

She shrugged and picked up the same burger she had last time, and I watched as she happily bit into it, not caring about anything in that moment.

Seeing as Dad and Della thought I was in need of some more pounds, I ate nothing but fast food since they were gone, but instead of feeling bloated, I somehow felt better than when I ate all those vegetables and fruits.

"Did I tell you that Reece texted me today?" she asked, looking at me with an amused grin on her face.

"You didn't. What did he want?"

"He asked me out, but I told him I was already seeing someone."

She was proud of that, her eyes sparkling with happiness.

"Good. He's not worth it. And Mason really seems like a nice guy. Did you get over the fact that he's older?"

She shrugged and took another bite of her burger. "I don't think about it much, but I'm sure when I see him again I'll remember and get nervous again."

"No, you won't. Just see him as a man. Age doesn't matter when he's a gentleman."

"So...is Riggs a gentleman?"

Easy question with an even easier answer. "Hell, no," I laughed. "Riggs is an alpha. So much so that there's no other man more alpha than him."

"Then why do you keep up with him when you can have any other man who would treat you like a princess?"

"Because I'm not a princess and never wanted to be one, Ken. The way he treats me is the way I want to be treated."

"Isn't that kinda degrading?"

Could be, if you weren't into those kinds of things.

"Riggs is not abusive and he doesn't do things to me I don't want him to do. I wouldn't let him touch me in certain ways if I knew he was doing it to hurt me. I like being fucked roughly, spanked, choked. That's who I am, and him doing what I ask him to doesn't make him a bad guy."

She thought about what I said, and after a little while, she smiled at me. "I know you're happy, but aren't you scared that you'll someday break from all of the rough things you let him do to you?"

I shrugged. "I don't know. But it's also not like I don't know where my limits are. If I don't feel like having sex, or don't feel like camming one of the men, I don't urge myself to. I know when to stop."

"Okay. That's important," she told me.

"Since we're already talking about him...he wanted to come over tonight, but I told him I didn't have time. So he'll be here tomorrow night," I explained.

"Lucky your parents aren't around. If I were Riggs, I wouldn't dare come here to sleep with his friends' daughter."

Well, Riggs was reckless, just like me.

I shrugged. "As long as they don't find out."

Besides, it was none of their business who I spent time with.

"I hope they don't."

***

"What have you been eating the past few days?" Della asked through the phone as I was walking through the hallway in school.

It was almost time for my first class, but she had to call this early and ask me about the food I was ingesting without them around.

"All kinds of things. Chinese, Mexican, Italian," I told her.

The hallway was empty, and I was the only one left who needed to enter my classroom.

"So you've been getting takeout most nights?" she asked, sounding slightly disappointed.

"Yes, hey, Della? I really need to go to class. I'm already late," I told her.

"Oh, yes. Your father says hello and we're excited to come back home on Sunday. Call me later, okay?"

"Yeah, sure. Enjoy your weekend. Bye," I said, hanging up the phone and letting out a heavy sigh.

"Miss Bentley," a stern voice called out just as I pushed my phone back into my backpack.

I turned to look at Mr. Trapani walking toward me, and with a sweet smile, I tilted my head to the side and waited for him to reach me.

"Good morning, Mr. T."

"Why aren't you in class?" He pushed his hands into his pockets, trying to look scary and intimidating.

He didn't have any effect on me at this point, seeing as Riggs was a man no one could ever top.

"My stepmother called. She's on vacation," I told him.

"Something wrong with Della?"

Right. I forgot that all my teachers knew my parents by name, since they all hung out at the country club like rich people did.

"No, she's doing fine. She was just worrying about what I'm eating, seeing as I can't cook."

That was a lie.

I knew how to cook, but I was too lazy to.

"Maybe you should learn how to cook. Far healthier than getting takeout every day."

I shrugged. "Maybe I should get cooking lessons by a true Italian. I love pasta," I teased, internally rolling my eyes at myself.

He chuckled and shook his head. "Maybe when you're older and not my student anymore. Go to class, Miss Bentley. And I hope you won't be late for mine after lunch."

I couldn't keep from grinning at his comment, and if Riggs didn't exist in my life at this point, I would've definitely flirted back even more.

"I won't be late. A presto, Signor Trapani," I told him, then I turned to walk to my class and get him out of my head quickly because he wasn't who I wanted to spend my thoughts on.

I'd see Riggs again tonight, and my excitement grew bigger minute by minute.

I sat down on my chair and pulled the books I needed out of my backpack while my physics teacher wasn't even here yet, so I didn't even have to hurry to get here.

"Val!" someone whispered loudly, and I turned to look at Declan sitting in the back with two of his friends whose names I didn't even care to remember.

I raised a brow to make him talk again.

"Come sit back here with us," he offered, nodding to the empty chair next to him.

"Never," I mumbled, rolling my eyes and turning to look down at my books again.

"Come on, Valley. Don't be such a bitch."

Nice.

I ignored him even when he continued to talk about me loud enough for the whole class to hear.

"He's a dick," the girl next to me said with a pitiful smile.

I looked up at her, remembering her name being Naomi, and shrugged her comment but most importantly her pity off my shoulders.

"I don't care what anyone in this school says."

"I wish I could do the same," she told me with a sigh.

"Why? You're not getting bullied or anything, are you?"

"No, but being as careless as you are is what most of the girls at this school thrive for. I even pulled up my skirt and opened a few more buttons to dress like you."

I looked at her uniform and sighed. "You don't have to be like me. That's never gotten anyone anything."

"But boys want you. And you reject them like it's nothing."

Naomi was naïve. Even more than Kennedy.

"Just...be yourself, okay?"

That's the best advice I could give her and any other girl at this school.

Chapter Twenty-Two

Valley

I was nervous to see him again, and while I waited for Riggs to knock on my door, I had already changed five times.

What the hell was I supposed to wear knowing he would rip my clothes off anyway?

I finally decided on a dress with a cutout on my stomach and a low cut at my cleavage.

It fit me perfectly, hugging my hips and breasts tightly.

Just as I was about to put away the clothes I decided not to wear, the doorbell rang and I walked over to the window to look outside where Riggs' car was now parked next to mine.

My heart skipped a beat, and I quickly ran downstairs to open the door and greet him.

"Hi," I said as he stood in front of me with a grumpy look on his face.

Someone's in a mood again, I thought, leaning against the door and looking up into his eyes.

"Wanna come in?" I asked as he didn't talk, and with a raised brow, he stepped inside.

"Hard day?" I asked, thinking that might've been the reason why he didn't talk.

"No," he growled, looking around the foyer and then staring back at me with a deep frown between his brows.

God, something was up but he wouldn't tell me.

"Want something to drink?" I asked.

Maybe alcohol will help loosen him up a little.

"Show me to your room," he ordered, pulling his hands out of his pockets.

Getting it on right away. Fine with me.

I rolled my eyes before turning around, but he didn't miss it.

His hand grabbed a fistful of my hair and he pulled me back against his chest with his lips close to my ear.

"Don't ever fucking roll your eyes at me again, understand?" he spat, pulling at my hair tighter and making me cry out.

"Yes," I croaked out, a little taken aback by his harshness.

I had gotten used to him being this bossy and rough, but this was different.

Something definitely was off, but maybe it was just something in his personal life I had no business knowing about.

We weren't that close anyway.

"Move," he growled, letting go of my hair again and then following me upstairs to my room.

I stopped in the middle of it, watching him while he looked around and let his eyes take in every inch of my bedroom.

He walked around slowly, staring at my laptop for a while before moving over to my bed.

His fingers traced my covers, then my pillow and lastly my bedside table.

"You're acting weird," I told him truthfully.

His eyes met mine again as he walked back toward the open closet door. "You think?"

"Yeah, and I'm not sure I like it."

He let out a laugh and shook his head, then he looked inside my closet and turned back around to look back at my bed.

"How many men have fucked you in here before?"

"None."

"Bullshit."

I raised a brow. "I've never had a guy over, Riggs."

He not only sounded but also looked jealous.

He stayed quiet again, moving to the other side of the bed now and making sure to check out every inch of it.

I kept my eyes on him and crossed my arms in front of my body, questioning what the hell he was doing.

"And virtually?" he asked, making me stand up straighter, pull my shoulders back, and lift my chin.

"What do you mean?"

Shit...where was he going with this?

I didn't have my webcam clipped to my laptop as I put it away every time I used it for homework or to write assignments.

"Have you ever talked to men on your laptop?" he asked, reaching for my pillow and lifting it slightly.

My heart was beating fast. My damn ski mask was right underneath the mattress, and for some reason I didn't get that he had already found my hiding spot, because when he turned around to look at me with the most infuriated look on his face, he was holding my ski mask in his hand already.

Shit! Shit! Shit!

"Wanna tell me what you need this for, *Dove*?"

I felt all the blood flow from my face, making me paler than I already was while my heart started to pump like crazy.

My throat clogged up, not able to speak anymore while he still held the ski mask gripped tightly in one hand while his other fisted at his side.

He was angry, looking scary as hell.

"Talk," he ordered, taking a few steps toward me while I stepped back but stopped as my back hit the door.

"I—"

"Not so vocal anymore, huh? Think you could get away with this? You let me fuck you while you make other men come through a fucking webcam?"

"How do you know?" I asked, my voice shaky and not at all confident.

Shit, he was furious.

He let out a harsh laugh and cupped my throat with the mask still in his hand, pressing it against my skin and making me hold my breath.

"You've been making my brother come for months."

I wanted to talk, and to my luck, he loosened his grip to let me speak. "I didn't know it was Marcus until I saw him at your house—"

"And you continued to make him pleasure himself while I had my dick sucked by you? Shit, darling...bold of you," he muttered, his face close to mine.

His fingers tightened around my neck again, and my eyes stayed on his the whole time while his stare got darker by the second.

He was quiet again, letting me know by his mood how angry he really was, but even with him knowing about me camming now, I couldn't help myself.

"Will you punish me now?" I whispered, my voice a hoarse whisper.

Something flashed in his eyes, and in one swift move, he pulled the ski mask over my head, gripped the top of it tightly and pulled me to the bed.

He pushed me to my knees and pressed his crotch against my face harshly, rubbing the hard fabric of his jeans against my skin.

"You dare to please other men when I should've been the only one. Did you think I would never find out?"

Honestly? No. I didn't think he'd find out. At least not this soon.

He pushed my face more against his crotch, letting me feel just how hard he already was.

I lifted my hands and cupped the backsides of his thighs to hold on to something, but just as I did, he pulled away and squatted down in front of me with his hand on my throat again.

With his other hand he adjusted the mask so I could properly look at him and have my mouth at the hole to breathe.

"And even now you're teasing me. You got some nerve, baby," he told me with a devilish grin on his face.

I couldn't help but grin as well. "Isn't a bad thing, hm?" I croaked out, biting down on my bottom lip.

He shook his head and let out a harsh laugh, then he let his eyes wander all over my mask-covered face. "I'm gonna punish you as

Dove tonight. Valley doesn't deserve this punishment."

I didn't care who he was gonna punish. It was my body he'd do all the things to, and I wanted nothing more than that.

My nervousness turned into excitement, and when he noticed that, he got back up on his feet and left me on my knees.

In an instant, he dragged me up on the bed and pushed my face against the mattress as his other hand left a burning sensation on my ass after slapping it hard.

I cried out but quickly decided that it didn't hurt but felt good, and after the second hard slap, I closed my eyes to turn the pain into pleasure.

"You fucking dare to play with me like this, and you get punished in return. I don't wanna hear one fucking whine tonight, understood?"

Another slap, this time to the other cheek.

"Yes," I moaned.

"Yes, what?"

I frowned. He didn't like to be called daddy, and he never wanted me to call him sir either.

But as reckless as I was, I decided on calling him the one thing he disliked to be called.

"Yes, daddy," I purred, and surprisingly, that didn't make him spank me again.

"Such a naughty little girl," he muttered, moving his hand over my ass to ease the pain, but seconds later his hands left my body and another electric sensation washed over me.

Riggs was strong, and it showed by how powerful his hands were.

"Think I will share you, huh? Fuck, Dove. You're mine, and I will burn that into your damn mind while I wreck you tonight."

That was a promise I hoped he would keep, because maybe that way I would learn not to be such a tease anymore.

Though, who would I be without being at least a little naughty?

"Please," I begged, wiggling my ass to get his hand on it again.

Riggs

I didn't spank her again, instead, I pulled her back down on her knees in front of the bed with her head tilted back and her eyes wide, looking up at me with pure ecstasy flashing in them.

She definitely didn't have any boundaries, but what I did next wasn't something I thought she would enjoy.

I wanted her to see just how dirty I could be and maybe scare her off a little bit to not intensify my addiction of her.

Then again, it's Valley who's kneeling in front of me, and it seemed no matter what I did to her, she enjoyed it.

I kept fisting the top of her head with one hand, gripping the mask and some of her hair tightly while I unbuttoned my jeans and pushed them down my legs, followed by my boxer briefs with my other hand.

Rubbing my dick and watching her closely, her eyes filled with need as she licked her plump lips.

"Open your mouth," I ordered, and the good girl she was, she did just that. "Heard you over the damn webcam, Dove. Talking to my brother and telling him how much you want him to drink his own fucking piss. Shit, darling...didn't think you'd be that nasty," I growled, seeing as the corners of her mouth turned up at the mention of piss.

Nasty bitch.
Just what I like.

"I want you to swallow. Don't move," I demanded, and seconds later, her mouth was filling up with my urine.

This little girl wasn't afraid to live out her kinks and fantasies, and with bright eyes, she started to drink my piss with no hesitation.

I was healthy, or else I wouldn't have made her drink it.

She also didn't swallow all of it, letting half of it flow down her chin and drop onto her cleavage.

I knew not to do things that could literally make her sick, or put her in any kind of danger.

We were living out our fetishes, sharing them with each other.

Nothing wrong with that, especially with her consenting to it.

"Dirty girl. Fuck...you really don't shy away from anything," I stated, emptying myself into her mouth, and when she swallowed the last drop, with some of it flowing down her chin, I pushed my dick inside her mouth to make her suck on it.

"Fuck," I groaned, letting her suck on my dick while I watched her closely.

Her eyes were on mine again, teasing the way only she could.

"You're gonna stop talking to my brother from now on. And to every other man who had the pleasure to see you in that fucking mask," I ordered, not wanting anyone else to see her naked anymore.

I hated the thought of my brother knowing what she looked like naked, but then, he met Valley, not Dove, and it was interesting how he didn't notice it was her by just looking in those big, blue eyes.

Then again, Marcus is a fucking idiot.

"You'll do what I tell you to, and you will only belong to me from now on."

I pulled my dick out of her mouth and let her catch her breath before helping her up on her feet and cupping her throat to take her breath away again.

"You're mine, and I'm the only one fucking you, do you understand?"

I could tell by her gaze that she didn't agree with that, but instead of letting her speak, I turned her around, pulled her against my chest and tightened my grip around her throat while I reached underneath her dress to cup her pussy.

She wasn't wearing panties, as if she ever did.

I started rubbing her clit and pressed my lips against the spot behind her ear, nibbling and licking and tasting her sweetness.

"I'm not asking you to stop seeing other men, I'm demanding it. If you want me, you'll stop talking to my brother and however many other men you talk to. I'll be the only one fucking you."

I didn't want an answer from her. She either listened, or continued to mess around with her damn webcam.

If she wouldn't choose me, I wouldn't show up anymore. We'd be over, with no other way of getting me back.

Whatever the fuck I was feeling, whatever I wanted to achieve with getting her to be mine, it was all new to me.

For now, I had to show her what else I was capable of.

What *we* were capable of together.

Chapter Twenty-Three

Valley

Giving up being a camgirl was never my plan. Not even for Riggs.

It was a way of making some extra money, to save it for when I needed it, and to not rip off my father and his heavy bank account.

I wanted to be independent when it came to buying things, and with camming, which was something I loved doing, I was able to do just that.

No matter how rough he was with me, giving up camming was not an option.

I couldn't tell him though, as he was still pressing down on my airway, not letting me breathe or speak while he continued to rub my clit.

It already started to pulsate heavily, and my knees were slowly giving in, but Riggs held me up with his hand on my throat.

The taste of his urine lingered on my tongue, but it wasn't bothering me as much as it bothered me the way he was ordering me to give up what I loved doing.

How could I ever tell those men that I would suddenly stop camming them because an alpha-hole demanded me to?

They'd be disappointed and mad, and I could easily lose my customers.

"You think you can play me like this, huh? You have no fucking clue how much I hoped for a moment like this. For you to fuck up to show you just how rough I can really be," he growled, his fingers still rubbing my clit.

He let out a harsh laugh. "This is what you signed up for, Dove. Let's see if you still want me after this. If you can still handle me."

For some reason, I started to believe that I couldn't.

His true colors were showing, and as aroused as I was by his rough way of handling me, my mind was slowly telling me that this was not gonna end well.

I started to feel lightheaded by the lack of air, and just as I started to see stars all around me, and the orgasm slowly creeped up on me, he pushed me onto the bed.

I turned to look at him, taking in as much air as possible while he stood there staring at me with dark eyes and a deep crease between his brows.

"Tell me, Dove—"

"Don't call me that," I hissed, wanting to somewhat tease but also gain control back.

"I'll call you whatever the fuck I want to call you. You've been showing that pussy to other men while you let me fuck you," he stated.

I didn't deny any of that, and it made me feel powerful, knowing he was jealous that he wasn't the only one.

This was getting messy really quick, and it wouldn't lead somewhere good. Yet...I was enjoying it.

I was sick, my mind twisted and perverted. Just like his.

Maybe that's why I felt such a strong connection to him.

He didn't judge me, didn't laugh at me for having all those kinks, and he pushed me to show them to him because he would profit from them just as much as I did.

Riggs was a real man, but I had to find a solution for his demands.

"I won't stop being a cam girl," I stated, but that's not what he wanted to hear.

He got on the bed and leaned over me, pushing my legs apart and pressing his knee against my crotch while his hand cupped my jaw tightly.

"And you dare talk back to me like that? Didn't you hear what I said? If you keep that shit up, I'll be gone."

That's what I didn't want.

I wanted to keep him, let him touch me, make me feel good.

I didn't like this ultimatum. Not one bit.

"Think I have to remind you what you'll miss out on if you choose those men over me."

He wasn't expecting an answer, but yet I whispered, "Yes, please."

He laughed, shaking his head and ripping the mask off my head, leaving my hair all wild and messy.

"You're a little freak," he muttered, but he didn't have to tell me. I knew, and I loved to push myself to test my limits.

His hand left my face for just a second before it landed flush against my cheek, burning just a little.

"I would've given you a way out, one last chance to think about what is coming next, but I don't feel like it anymore. This is what you deserve, and you'll like it no matter what."

I'm sure I would, and after another quick slap he pushed three of his fingers into my mouth, deep until they hit the back of my throat, making me gag.

"Not holding back. Not one fucking bit, and if you still feel like you can handle me and put aside those fuckers, you'll be mine forever."

It sounded like a dream.

Being his.

But he knew how much I wanted to have control over him as well, so I wasn't sure how that would work out if I did choose to be his.

There wasn't a way for me to tell him with him fingering my mouth to get his fingers wet, so I kept my eyes on his and let him do whatever he was up to.

Whatever it was, I wanted it bad.

"You're so damn beautiful. I'd give everything for you to be mine, baby. I can see past you making other men come, but only if you choose me," he muttered.

He pulled his fingers out, and with my saliva covering them, he placed them at my entrance and pushed them inside without a warning, moving them in and out of me hard and fast.

I moaned, keeping my eyes on his the whole time and reaching up to tug at his shirt, wanting him to take it off and show me his insanely handsome body.

But he didn't, and he continued to finger me as he pressed his forearm against my neck, taking away my breath again.

He added one more finger, pushing deeper inside of me and moving his hand faster and making another orgasm creep up.

He denied me the first time, which frustrated me at first, but I knew the more he denied it, the better my final climax would be.

"So damn tight. Wish I could fill both your holes at once," he groaned, making me tap his arm so I could speak.

He didn't let me though, and pulled his fingers out to taste them before placing them back on my pussy.

This time, he moved them to my back entrance, circling my tight hole before pushing two fingers inside.

It hurt at first, as he should've prepared me for it, but I was relaxed enough to push the pain aside and enjoy his way of pleasing me.

"I'm gonna fuck you right here. This tight hole feels so fucking good, baby."

I was getting lightheaded again, and I tried to keep my eyes open as he continued to choke me while his fingers brushed roughly against my inside walls.

"I have..." I croaked, not able to form a full sentence.

He raised a brow at me, and for a split second I thought he was going to continue choking me, but to my luck, he moved his arm to let me breathe.

"I have toys," I told him, which wasn't what he had expected me to say.

With a smug grin on his face, he pulled his fingers out again and moved away from me to let me get up.

"Show me," he demanded, and I quickly got up to grab the box from underneath my bed where I stored all of my sex toys.

When I put the box onto the bed, he told me to lay back down and let him see for himself, so while he went through all my toys, I quickly took off my dress, then leaned back against the headboard, massaging my nipple and clit to stimulate the tension and aching.

I watched him closely while he picked up the biggest dildo from the box, then a small vibrator and a blindfold.

Being blindfolded didn't seem appealing when I had the chance to look at his handsome face, but whatever he wanted to do, I'd let him do to me.

He put the box aside, mumbling something under his breath with his grin still in place, then he looked up and nodded to the headboard.

"Arms up," he ordered, crawling back onto the bed and moving closer as he let the other two toys fall between my legs.

I lifted my hands and already knew what he was up to, so I let him tie me up, tight enough so I couldn't move.

I was lying on my back now, him pulling me down by my ankles and then moving back up to grab the dildo.

He held it to my mouth, making me suck on it while he pushed it in and out.

"You're gonna keep those pretty legs apart at all times. If you move, you get punished."

I nodded, letting him push the dildo deeper into my mouth and holding it there for a moment before pulling it back out again.

He placed the tip of it at my pussy, pushing it inside me slowly and leaving it deep inside of me to grab the vibrator.

He moved, pushing my legs apart further and pressing down on my left thigh with his knee while his other pushed against my other leg.

No way I could move, and I knew what he was gonna do next.

"Don't you dare move," he warned again, turning on the vibrator and letting it trace the inside of my thigh before it reached my aching clit.

I looked down to watch his hand closely, and when he got closer to my clit, I held my breath on my own, knowing that first touch would send sparks through my body.

When it finally touched my clit, I bit my bottom lip and let out a suppressed moan before having to close my eyes out of pure bliss.

This is exactly what I needed, and I knew it wouldn't take too long for me to come. That's if Riggs would let me.

"Eyes open," he growled, but the way the vibrator made me feel wouldn't let me do what he said.

"Open your fucking eyes and look at me, Valley!"

So we're back to my actual name now?

Not that I cared.

I tore my eyes open and adjusted my hips to place the vibrator at the right spot, but Riggs knew exactly what I was trying to do, so he pulled the little toy away from my clit with a dark expression.

"I told you not to move," he growled.

"Yes, daddy," I whispered, fisting the blindfold wrapped around my wrists tightly.

The vibrator touched my clit again, and this time, he didn't pull it away.

Instead, he held it right there, making my legs start to shake quickly and my breath hitch while I tried to hold back an orgasm.

Riggs reached for the dildo still inside of me, starting to move it in and out of me, making it even more intense than before.

"Oh, fuck!" I cried out, not able to keep still.

And in an instant, he stopped moving the dildo and pulled the vibrator away again.

What a fucking tease.

"No, please...keep going," I begged.

"What did I tell you?"

"Not to move. Please, make me come," I breathed, lifting my hips and hoping to get my two toys closer to my pussy.

"Say it again," he demanded.

"I won't move. Please, I want you to make me come," I begged, finally feeling the thickness of the dildo back inside of me and the vibrator on my clit.

I relaxed and made sure not to move again, but I couldn't keep my eyes open anymore the way he wanted me to.

Shit, he couldn't have everything he asked for.

Not in this situation.

The tension inside of me rose, sending shivers all over my body and making me tense up again without me wanting to.

I had no control over my body anymore, and the harder and deeper he fucked me with that dildo, the louder my moans got.

"Don't stop," I croaked out, letting my head fall back.

"Don't come," he demanded, continuing to thrust into me with one of my favorite toys.

He didn't look too surprised when I pulled out the box, but I knew he was having lots of fun with my toys.

And quite frankly, I was enjoying being played with like this.

"Oh, yes...please," I begged again, and just as I was on the verge of letting go, he pulled both toys away from me, making my body shudder all over.

"You're an asshole, oh, God!" I cried, needing to push my legs together to ease the torture I was feeling in that moment.

Riggs only pushed down on my legs harder, making it feel so much worse.

He ignored me calling him an asshole, but that didn't mean he wasn't going to punish me for it.

In one swift move, he turned me onto my stomach and pulled my ass up in the air so I had to kneel while my head stayed on the pillow.

He had tied me in a way he could easily turn me on my back or stomach whenever he felt like it, which was very convenient for him, not so much for me.

I hated losing control, and in this very moment, he took all of mine away.

He pushed my legs apart again, moving between them until I could feel his hardness press against my ass.

"You need to be taught how to talk to an adult. You're fucking reckless, and you have been ever since this started. But I won't let it slip. Not this time," he spat, followed by a harsh laugh.

And from that moment on, the pain took over.

He started spanking me harshly, slapping his large hand against my ass and making it feel as if he was ripping off my skin.

It still felt good, and I tried to turn the pain into pleasure while he continued to spank hard.

"This is what you get if you keep being a fucking brat," he hissed through gritted teeth, and while tears stung my eyes, my skin started to burn like hell.

I wondered how red it already was, as with my pale skin, it was easy to achieve redness.

"Tell me to stop," he ordered, but I shook my head.

"No."

"Tell me to fucking stop, Valley!"

"No!" I cried, pushing back against him while he now squeezed my ass tightly with both hands.

"If this is really what you want, baby…tell me I'm yours."

"I can't…" I croaked, needing a little more time to catch my breath, and while I had that time, he pushed into me in a smooth move.

"I can't stop being a cam girl," I told him, which only made him angrier.

He started to fuck me roughly, continuing to spank me before thrusting into me.

"Be mine!" he roared, and knowing it would only make him angrier, I shook my head. "No."

"Fucking slut," he spat, now also slapping my thighs and lower back.

It didn't hurt as much as when he slapped my ass, yet I was sure he left marks.

I was already spiraling out of control, so I closed my eyes and let him continue with this blissful torture, making me moan and cry out in pleasure.

I didn't even care if I would come from him fucking me tonight, as long as he didn't stop.

I felt his cock throb inside of me, and the pulsating of my pussy only added to the intenseness of what I was feeling all throughout my body.

I was in a trance, feeling lightheaded without him having to choke me this time, and although I could breathe just fine, I didn't feel like it.

Not when he was about to come inside of me, and my body was slowly shutting down, not even bothering reaching a climax.

How he was fucking me was pleasure enough, so much so that I thought I didn't even need to be fucked anymore for the rest of my life.

This was enough, and I would remember tonight forever.

I've been quieter ever since he started to push his thumb inside my asshole, moving it rhythmically to his cock, but every once in a while I moaned, letting him know that he could go on longer, fucking and spanking me.

"I'm gonna say this one last time, Valley," he muttered as he stopped thrusting into me and reached forward to cup my tits with both hands and leaning over me from behind.

His lips were close to my ear, his breath tickling my skin as he spoke. "Be mine, or lose me forever."

How serious was he about this?

I kept my eyes closed and thought about it for a while before I couldn't help myself and shook my head.

"I can't," I whispered, knowing I would miss being Dove.

"She's part of me. I can't let go of her," I added, hoping he knew who I was talking about.

But my answer wasn't what he wanted to hear, and he immediately let me know what he thought about my choice.

He undid the blindfold tying me to the bed, then pulled out of me and turned me onto my back while getting off the bed himself.

I was exhausted and I felt defeated for the first time ever.

My eyes barely opened, and the pain grew now that my ass pressed against the mattress after his spanking.

He didn't speak, but his eyes told me everything he was thinking.

He wasn't happy about my response, and although he didn't look furious, he sure had anger built up inside of him, ready to explode and letting it all out on me.

Without another word, he kept his eyes on mine and rubbed his cock before pushing into me again, rough fucking me with no mercy and holding on tight to my hips to thrust even harder.

At this point, it didn't even hurt anymore, and I let him go at it like a wild animal, not caring about me anymore and only thinking about himself.

His groans got louder, and when I couldn't keep my eyes open anymore, I felt his body tense as he released his cum inside of me, with his cock pushed deep into my pussy.

He was leaving one more mark before disappearing, but no matter what he had planned, if he really didn't want to see me anymore after tonight, maybe I should've thought about it for a little while longer.

"This is over," he stated, pulling out of me and watching his cum flow out between my folds.

He placed his fingers at my pussy, rubbing them along my slit and then moving them up to my stomach where he rubbed his cum into my skin.

"You made your choice."

"Don't go," I whispered, trying to catch my breath as he moved his fingers up to my nipples.

"You chose them over me. This is it for us."

And there was nothing left for me to say to keep him here with me.

I watched as he lifted his hand to his mouth, licking his fingertips covered in his and my own juices before putting on his boxer briefs and jeans.

I felt weak, defeated, and I couldn't move.

My body didn't respond to my brain's demands anymore, and there was nothing else for me to do than lay there with my eyes on him.

He truly wrecked me, destroyed me the way he said he would, and now I had to watch him leave without being able to fight him about it.

That's not who I was, but I had to accept it for now.

"Go to sleep, Valley. You can't handle this side of me."

And for a moment, I fully believed him.

Chapter Twenty-Four

Valley

It took me exactly two hours until I had collected all my strength and found the motivation to get up from the bed.

My stomach was sticky, just like my pussy as his cum dried on my skin, and when I walked into the bathroom to look at myself in the big mirror, it took me a moment to recognize myself.

Not because of my smudged makeup or red cheeks from his slaps, but because of the way my eyes showed emotions I've never seen in them.

Regret was the biggest one flashing through them.

I felt lonely as well, thinking his words were meant seriously.

Shit...who was I kidding? Of course he meant every word he said, not wanting to see me again and whatever we had was over.

I let my eyes wander down to my breasts, then over my stomach and down to my legs.

My thighs were bright red, and when I turned, there were literal hand prints on my skin and all over my ass.

I moved my hand gently over it, suddenly feeling overwhelmed by the stinging I caused by doing so.

He's been rough with me, maybe even careless and reckless, but I didn't blame him for making me feel like this.

I pushed him, teased him to the point I made him do all those things to me, and it was my own damn fault making him behave like a wild animal who was let loose to hunt down and kill its prey.

Still, him taking a step back and closing the door on me because I didn't want to lose something I loved doing wasn't right.

And if he thought I'd let him get away with that, he was wrong.

I swallowed the thick lump in my throat and walked back into my room to grab my phone.

I couldn't be alone tonight, and Kennedy was the only one who'd understand what was going on.

Then again...there wasn't anyone else I talked to about everything that was going on in my life.

After sending her a text asking to come over as soon as possible, I walked back to the bathroom and placed my phone next to the sink to take a shower.

I needed to wash everything he did to me off my body to be able to think straight, but as hard as I tried to get Riggs off my mind, it wasn't possible.

My phone buzzed just as I was about to walk into my shower, and I grabbed it to check Kennedy's message, telling me she'd be here as quickly as possible, having to sneak past her dad.

She would never sneak out if there wasn't an emergency, and for some reason, she knew something was up.

I sent her a heart emoji and stepped into the shower to get all of his cum off my skin, then

I washed my hair and body before letting the water run down my body.

My thoughts were all over the place, but mostly stuck on the fact that I would have to fight to get him back.

That wasn't much of a problem, as I always got what I wanted, but as stubborn as Riggs was, there was only a slight chance I could reach my goal.

I wanted him back.

Wanted to be his while also living out my hobby of camming men and pleasuring them.

That's who I was, and I wouldn't let him take that away from me.

Not that easily.

***

Thirty minutes later, Kennedy had arrived with her pajamas underneath her coat, and we cuddled up on the couch with a blanket as I didn't want her to sit on the bed where I had let Riggs do dirty things to me.

Heck, even piss on me.

That was surprising, knowing there was seemingly nothing he didn't shy away from.

"Was he here?" she asked, playing with my hair while I leaned against her side, letting her cuddle me.

It was usually me being the one making her feel better, for example when she had issues with her parents, but right now, it was me needing support and love.

I nodded. "He left and took my soul with him," I muttered.

Kennedy let out a soft laugh. "Oh, boy. That bad?"

"I feel lost."

"Why, that's new. What happened? Did you argue?" she asked.

"No. We fucked. Well, he fucked me hard to the point I couldn't move for two hours," I frowned, turning my head to look at her.

"He knows about me webcamming."

"Oh, no..."

"He probably heard his brother when he was webcamming with me, and when he came by, he wanted to see my room. Then he snooped around my things and found the mask, calling me Dove."

"Oh, shit."

Yeah, same.

"Wait, he didn't punish you or anything, right? Did he hurt you?" Kennedy asked, looking at me with wide eyes.

"He did, but not in a way you think," I said, not able to keep in a chuckle. "I liked it. A lot. It seems we have the same kinks. Same way of enjoying all kinds of sexual experiences."

"Then why are you so sad?" she asked, her voice gentle and filled with worry.

"Because he doesn't wanna see me again. Not unless I drop Dove."

She didn't respond at first, and after brushing through my hair for a while, she sighed. "Can I be honest with you?"

"You *have* to be."

"Right. Maybe you don't need her anymore. I don't know what he wants, or what you want from him, but it doesn't seem right for you to spend time with other men, seeing them naked and them seeing you naked while you have a guy in real life who's willing to...uh..."

"Fuck me. We never talked about what this between us is, which for me is just fun. Sure, I like him, but I don't think he as a fifty-six-year-old wants to have an actual relationship with an eighteen-year-old," I sighed.

"Have you asked him that?"

"God, no. He'd probably laugh at me."

Kennedy shrugged. "You'll never know if you don't ask. If he says he doesn't want you to see other men, making him look like he's jealous, I don't think he's just in it for some fun."

She had a point there, but it was Riggs we're talking about, and that man was a huge wall of alpha-man.

Not sure he would let someone in that way, especially at his age.

"He doesn't wanna see me again. At least that's what he said."

"But that doesn't hold you back from going to his home and talking to him," she pointed out.

"No, it won't. Still...I think I have to think about it first. If I give those men up, who knows how upset they'll be? And what if this thing with Riggs doesn't work out? Then I'll stand here all alone."

She shook her head and smiled. "You've told me about those men before, and I think they're desperate. So...maybe tell them you'll take a break because of family issues. Things like that happen all the time. Didn't you tell me about a porn star getting back into the industry after five years, and now she's one of the best known porn stars ever?"

That made me laugh. "Yeah, that's true. But I'm not a porn star. Those men pay a subscription to see me, and when I'm gone, they'll find a different girl to have fun with."

"You don't know that. Jesus, who are you and where did you bury my best friend?"

She pushed me away from her gently, making me sit up and look directly into her eyes.

"You're confident, strong, and the most badass woman I've ever met. How is this bringing you down to your knees? He's a man. You've never taken any shit from a man before. At least not the ones you told me about. How much different can this one be?"

I smiled at her words, but as true as those words were, she had no clue how different Riggs was.

"He has this intense way of just...being. His presence makes me shiver, and his touch melts me. No matter what he says or does, sexually or not, he makes me feel a way I just can't explain."

Kennedy studied my face for a while before grinning, and I already knew what she was about to say.

"No, Ken. I'm not falling for him," I muttered.

"I'm not saying that," she laughed, then shrugged. "But maybe you're starting to feel something for him. At least it's a start."

I shook my head at her. "Being with Riggs won't be possible anyway. My parents would kill him and lock me up in my room until I'm forty."

Besides...I thought this was moving a little too fast.

I still had to get my shit together, collect my thoughts and figure out what the fuck I wanted from Riggs.

"So what? You have to give it a chance. You've got nothing to lose. You're young and beautiful, and if he doesn't want you that way, you'll still be the Valley I've always known."

She was right, now I just had to burn that into my own damn mind and believe it.

"Did we just switch roles? Normally, I'm the one whining."

"I'm not whining. I never whine," I laughed. "He's just one hell of a man, maybe even too much for me to handle at times."

"Well, you need that. Maybe that will stop you from being so naughty all the time. Especially in school," she grinned.

I rolled my eyes at her and got up from the couch. "I need a burger. And pizza. And chips.

Wanna stay here overnight? I could use your company."

She looked at her phone and thought about it for a while, then she muttered something and nodded. "Sure. Probably risking going out with Mason tomorrow night, but I'd do anything for you."

"Tell your dad you're here with me to keep me company. It's scary in a big house like this all alone," I said, winking at her.

"Yeah, right," she laughed, shaking her head but tapping a message into her phone to send to her father.

I needed her to distract me today so I could clean up all those thoughts in my head.

I had no idea how soon I'd see him again, but I knew I wanted to so bad.

***

We spent the night doing what we did best. Watching movies and eating fast food.

And tonight, we were wild enough to open a bottle of wine and drink it without using glasses.

We deserved it, and it *definitely* made me stop thinking about that asshole.

The huge, tall, so damn muscular and handsome man who did things to me I couldn't explain. His roughness and rudeness, his way of touching and fucking me.

All those things I desperately wanted and needed.

Yeah, I wasn't thinking about Riggs and the way he made me feel anymore.

Nope, no way.

Chapter Twenty-Five

Valley

"Valley, we're back!" I heard Della's voice call out from downstairs, and I looked at the time on my phone, wondering what took them so long to get here.

It was almost nine p.m., and I patiently waited for them to come back from vacation to finally have a real meal.

Even if I loved fast food, I could use something healthier for once. Maybe some broccoli salad and a nicely seasoned chicken breast.

I got up from the bed and headed downstairs to see Della and Dad take off their coats as I reached the foyer.

"Did you have a good time?" I asked, hugging her first before letting Dad pull me into his embrace.

"It was wonderful, relaxing. The house looks surprisingly clean," Della pointed out, her tone mocking.

"I cleaned. Vacuumed and wiped the floors. Well, here, in the living room, kitchen, and my room," I told her, not even lying about that.

I had a headache after deciding to drink by myself last night, as it seemed that thinking with alcohol in my blood was much easier for me.

But drinking wouldn't become an addiction, so I wasn't worried about that.

I had made up my mind about Riggs anyway.

At least I thought I did.

"That's nice of you. Did you eat? We had something at the hotel before we came here," Dad said, letting go of me again.

I looked up at him and shook my head. "I thought we'd eat something together. I can make some pasta though."

Dad nodded, then grabbed both suitcases and walked toward the stairs. "How was school last week? Any important tests I need to know about?"

I followed him upstairs while Della walked into the kitchen to inspect every inch of it. She wouldn't be happy about any splashes of tomato sauce or anything else on the counters.

Lucky me, I never cooked.

"No, no tests. But I'll have one next week. I've studied hard for it, and I'm ready to take it," I told him.

We walked into their bedroom, and while he opened the suitcases to unpack, I sat on the bed and watched.

"You seem tense for coming back from a spa vacation," I pointed out.

"Della and I fought on the way here. Well, it was more a discussion than a fight. She wants me to stop working."

I tilted my head, not finding that a horrible idea at all. "What's holding you back from finally retiring?"

"My law firm. I don't have anyone to take over. I don't want anyone to take over. Not until I'm too old to go back to work."

"Hm...but if you wait that long, who's gonna make the decision when it's finally time to let someone else take over?"

"I will. Just because I'll be old, doesn't mean I can't make a valid decision."

Touché. But still...

"You work too hard. I have to stand behind Della on that. Didn't your doctor once tell you to be careful because you already have high blood pressure?"

"Yeah, so?"

I raised a brow. "That could lead to a stroke, and to be honest with you, I'm not ready to lose my dad because he didn't want to listen to his loved ones."

"I won't have a stroke, and I will continue to work. Go eat, then head to bed. It's getting late, Valley."

I sighed and got up from the bed, walked over to him and kissed his cheek before heading for the door. "I'm just looking out for you. Good night, Dad."

"Valley?" he called out as I turned my back to him, and when I looked at him again, he continued to talk.

"You look different," he said, letting his eyes wander down all over my body.

Maybe it was the large sweater I had on, or the old sweatpants I haven't worn since my freshman year of high school that I chose to pull out from the darkest corner of my closet.

Maybe it was the way I felt. Lonely, pushed aside.

And all that because of Riggs.

I missed him and his harsh touch, but I still didn't feel like seeing him. Or telling him exactly how I was feeling.

"I had a fun week without you two. Maybe that's why," I teased, making him shake his head at me and chuckle.

"Good night, Dad," I repeated, and without waiting on his response, I went back downstairs to make myself something to eat for the first time in the past week.

"Would you like for me to cook you something?" Della offered.

"Oh, no. That's okay. You must be tired," I said, smiling at her.

"Okay. Has Kennedy been over this week?"

"Yeah, a few times."

"And did you have boy over?"

I raised a brow.

No, I had a *man* over.

"No. Would that have been a problem?" I asked.

"Oh, no, not to me. Your father was making speculations," he explained.

Of course he did. "Only Kennedy. We had takeout a few times. She slept here too," I told her with a smile.

"That's nice. So you weren't all alone the whole week. Have a good night. I'll see you tomorrow morning," she said, cupping my cheek gently before heading upstairs.

Luckily, none of them would expect me to start something with a close friend of theirs.

***

"You don't look like yourself," Kennedy said as I stepped out of my car in the school's parking lot.

"I don't feel like myself," I muttered.

This morning I woke up with a major hole in my chest, feeling as if my heart had been ripped out.

Never had I felt anything like this before, and it was all Riggs's fault.

"You're gonna put on quite a show today with that outfit on," she pointed out, looking at me as if I was a whole other person.

A monster of some sort.

I chose to wear black tights with my skirt, and I buttoned up my shirt so no cleavage was showing. I also put on the jacket and buttoned it at my waist.

"I'm uncomfortable," Kennedy said, still looking at me confused.

I sighed and closed the door, then grabbed my backpack from my backseat and locked the car before passing her and walking across the parking lot.

"I'm still me. I'm just trying to figure things out."

"By not showing as much skin as you usually show?"

"Yes. To see if I can go a day without the attention of men," I stated.

"And you're doing this because..."

"Because Riggs has taken up too much space in my head the past two days and I need to be clear about him."

"I honestly didn't expect that. I thought you'd just keep on living and be yourself, show him that you don't take any of his bullshit."

I shrugged. "I'm still me. Just without all the naughtiness."

"So you think you and Riggs could turn into something serious?" she asked, walking next to me as we entered the building to get to our lockers.

"I'm trying not to get my hopes up, but I wanna see what it feels like not being the center of attention for once. And not spending evenings making men come through a webcam."

"Have you been talking to him again?"

"Riggs? No. He blocked me again. So when I know what I want, and if I want it from him, I'll show up at his door. No matter if he wants me to or not."

"Sounds like a plan. But there's something you need to know about the attention thingy..."

We stopped at our lockers and I turned to look at her while I opened mine. "What's that?"

"You have a beautiful face, and as many eyes as your body attracts, your face can do the same."

I rolled my eyes. "Not at a school like this. These boys are idiots and only have eyes for boobs and asses. Because if they would look at the girls' faces at this college, they'd see how beautiful all of them are. Including you."

She studied me for a while, and a small smile appeared on her lips as she took in my compliment.

"Okay, you maybe have a point there. But you doing all this for Riggs means you do have feelings for him."

"I don't know what I feel for him other than some type of anger for just leaving me laying there on the bed after rough-fucking me like a beast. Other than that...there's a ball of confusion inside of me."

"That's not necessarily a bad thing,"

"Not sure about that," I whispered, grabbing my notebook and closing the locker to then lean against it.

"I want today to be over," I mumbled.

"Already? School hasn't even started, Miss Bentley," Mr. T. said as he stopped next to us with his hands pushed into his pockets.

I looked at him, letting him take in the new me for today, before he spoke again. "Bad day?"

I smiled, but it didn't meet my eyes. "A little bit," I replied, rolling my eyes internally and pushing myself off the lockers.

"We should head to class," I told Kennedy, hoping Mr. Trapani would leave me alone.

If it weren't for Riggs, I would've unbuttoned my jacket and shirt for him to see more.

But I was different today, with my reason for it slowly fading and starting to sound ridiculous.

"Good idea," Mr. T. said, and so Kennedy and I started to walk away from him, but I didn't get far as he pulled me back by grabbing my wrist.

"If there's something you need to talk about, you know where my office is," he said, keeping his voice low.

I looked at him and wanted to sigh heavily, letting him know that today was not the day.

"I'm fine. But thank you," I told him with another smile before I freed myself from him and followed Kennedy to our first class.

"What a creep," she whispered, making me laugh out loud and change my mood at least for a little while.

***

Stephen was one of those men who liked to talk while I sat in front of the webcam and listened to his worries and thoughts.

Tonight, although he wouldn't be my first choice when I turned on my webcam, I needed to see and talk to him.

He wasn't a very sexual person, but he enjoyed having deep conversations, so maybe he could help me with my little problem concerning Riggs.

I was waiting on him to appear on my screen, and once he did, a wide smile spread on his face.

Stephen's sixty-one, the oldest out of all the men I met through my website but definitely the sweetest.

He was like a granddad, one I never had, which also led me to not wear the ski mask when I was camming with him.

It was strange at first, as I did leave my mask on throughout our first few chats, but when I was certain there was no way he could ever spread pictures of me on the internet, since he wasn't good with any electronic devices, I decided to take the mask off.

He was definitely someone I considered a friend, no matter how weird it was.

"Hello, sweetheart," he said in the gentlest voice ever.

"Hi, Stephen. How's your day been today?" I asked, smiling at him and getting more comfortable on the bed.

I had cuddled up underneath my blanket with my laptop on my lap and a tea on my nightstand.

"Oh, it was wonderful. I went for a walk and had dinner at a nice restaurant. The usual. How are you doing? You look sad," he pointed out.

"I'm not sad...just frustrated. I think I need your advice," I told him.

"Tell me all about it, sweetheart. I'll help as much as I can," he promised, making me smile.

"I'm afraid I might have to stop camming," I told him after releasing a deep breath.

"Did you meet someone?" he asked, clearly happy about that thought.

"Well, it's complicated. He's...a family friend and he's given me this ultimatum. If I want to be his, I'd have to stop being a cam girl."

"And you're not sure you can give it up so easily?"

I nodded. "It's what I love doing. I also love talking to you and I don't wanna give that up either," I confessed, no matter how boring some nights with him were. He warmed my heart, as he didn't have anyone else to talk to.

He was lonely.

"You don't have to think of me or any of those other men if that guy is who you really want."

"So you're saying I should just give this up and run to him?"

"I'm saying you should try and compromise," he told me with that knowing undertone every adult seemed to have.

But compromising was never my thing. No matter what there was to compromise about.

"What's his name?" he asked.

I sighed, the thought of him making me feel all weird inside. "Riggs."

"I've never seen you like this before, Dove, and that Riggs guy seems to have left quite an impact on you. If he gives you all the things you want, why don't you give him a try?"

I frowned. "What if it won't last long? And what if all these other men suddenly disappear?"

"Then they weren't here for you but for the show you put on for them. One thing is for sure...if you leave for a while but come back even years later, I'll be right here, ready to talk to you again," he stated.

I smiled at his sweet words, making me feel appreciated and adored. "I don't think I would stop talking to you, Stephen. Just the guys who want to see me naked."

He chuckled and waved his hand. "You do what you feel is right, okay? No one owns you."

Not yet.

But once I made my mind up, Riggs definitely would.

Chapter Twenty-Six

Valley

A few days had passed, and while I was dressing like my usual self again, I still didn't feel the way I should have been feeling.

A big chunk was missing, and my need for his rough touch was growing bigger by the second.

I had to see him again, so I decided to lie to my parents, tell them I would be going to Kennedy's house to study, while I did a whole other thing.

I was driving to Riggs's house, not knowing if he was home but taking the chance that he was.

There was also a big chance that Marcus aka Garett was still at his house, but even with him there, I had to show Riggs exactly what I wanted.

Him.

All of him.

I had already told most of the men I least cammed with that I would most likely be gone for a while for personal reasons, and that was kinda true.

Maybe Riggs was what I needed.

But although I communicated that news to them, none of them have unsubscribed to my website.

Maybe they had to think about it before making a decision, but either way, I was grateful none of them sent me a hateful message.

I took a deep breath and tried to go back to my usual self. The Valley who's strong-willed and gets what she wants, and when I parked in front of his house, I stared up at the house with determination.

Only the downstairs lights were on, and I was positive Garett was gone as his car was nowhere to be seen.

Good. This made things a whole lot easier.

I got out of the car and tugged at my dress, straightening it and making sure no wrinkles were showing.

I decided on a black dress with a low cut in the front and back. It hugged my body tightly, showing all my curves.

This is it, I thought. *I'm going to tell him what I want and he'll easily take me back.*

When I reached the front door, I took a second to go through the things I wanted to tell him, and once I was prepared to see him again, I pushed the doorbell and stepped back.

It took a few seconds for him to open the door, but once he did, I almost melted at the way he looked.

He was in his loungewear, his hair brushed back and his beard trimmed to perfection. His hands fisted at his side as his eyes met mine, and he didn't dare to move them down my body to inspect my dress.

"What?" he spat, obviously very happy to see me this Wednesday evening.

"May I come in?" I asked, brushing a strand of hair back and out of my face.

"No."

I raised a brow. "Huh?"

"No. Leave," he growled, making my blood boil in that very instant.

"Seriously? I'm here to talk. Let me in," I urged, but instead of stepping aside, he started to close the door on me.

"You will *not* shut the door in my face, Riggs!" I fired back, taking a step closer to him.

Why was he acting like an asshole?

Maybe because he is one.

"Why are you here, Valley? Didn't I make myself clear that night?" he asked with a deep crease forming between his brows.

I mimicked his expression. "You really thought I would let it end like this? God, you really don't know anything about me," I laughed with a shake of my head.

"You made your decision. There's no reason for you to show up here unannounced," he spat.

I wanted to slap him.

Kick him in the balls and make him suffer for talking to me like this.

Sure, I told him I wouldn't give up camming for him, but that didn't mean I couldn't change my mind about it.

"Let me in so we can talk about it," I offered, crossing my arms in front of my body to show him just how serious I was about this.

I had already dropped a few men because of him, and if he'd let me in, I was sure I would do the same with the rest of them.

Even Garett.

"Go home, Valley," he pushed, not up for a confrontation.

"Don't tell me you're over me already. You fucked me. You showed me the real you, and now you expect that I just leave and never return again?"

"Go, before I call your father," he warned.

"Do you really think I'm here without a damn reason, Riggs?" I asked, ignoring his threat. "Do you really think I would show up here just to get a rise out of you?"

"Don't know you any other way," he muttered.

"Where would that get me after all those nights you showed your true colors to me? You don't really wanna push me away, and you damn well know it."

I was frustrated with myself but mostly with him.

"Where'd you get the nerve to be such a dick?" I spat, trying to turn my anger down a notch.

Even without any neighbors close by, my voice definitely could be heard at the houses down the street.

He stared at me for a while, and if my eyes weren't deceiving me, I saw the corners of his mouth turn up slightly.

So this was amusing to him?

Was he just playing hard to get?

"Go home, Valley," he repeated, this time in a calmed, gentler voice.

I snorted and almost stomped my foot on the ground.

"Fine. We're playing by your rules again. But there's one thing you're forgetting, Riggs..."

I stepped closer to him, poking my finger into his chest and looking up at him with narrowed eyes.

"This game isn't over," I whispered, moving my hand down to cup his crotch and squeezing it tightly.

"Not until I say it is."

But not even that made him rethink his choice of not letting me in. He pushed my hand away, took a step back and nodded toward my car.

"Go."

And so I did, already planning a way to get back at him for this.

Feisty.

Just how I liked my women, and Valley was no fucking exception.

I watched her drive her car out of my driveway, and when she was gone, fully infuriated and angry at me, I couldn't help but laugh at her energetic and almost provoking way of coming here to tell me what she thought about this whole situation.

She was different in a good way, and although I had been rude to her once again, we both knew things between us weren't over.

I needed a little more time after what I put her through last Saturday night, and although she enjoyed everything that I did, I wanted to give her time to reflect on it.

If she was one-hundred percent sure of her choices.

She wasn't when I asked her the first time to be mine, but seeing her show up at my door in an insanely tight and sexy dress, determined to get me back showed me exactly that.

She wanted me and I wanted her, but if she let me have her, she'd have to be sure about all the things I would put her through.

The way I was on Saturday wasn't the harshest I could get, and even if there didn't seem to be any limits for her, I would definitely show her that at some point, even she had to take a step back.

I walked back into my kitchen where I had been for the past half an hour to cook dinner, and even before Valley came by I had been thinking about her.

Wondering how she was doing and if I hadn't hurt her too badly that night.

She seemed overwhelmed after I came inside of her, and her body needed to rest just like her mind to take in everything we did.

Certain kinks weren't looked at as normal ones like maybe having daddy issues, but even that got frowned upon.

Even if a girl did go through trauma when she was little.

If there's one thing I hated on this planet, it was the way people just couldn't ignore things they disapproved of.

That's why I accepted Valley the way that she was, and that's also why we could live out our fantasies without judging each other.

Hell, bodily fluids connected to sex were never my thing, up until a day I suddenly started to like it.

But even before that I didn't shame people who enjoyed that shit.

Who knew my own damn brother was one of those people?

No matter what it was, no matter what you liked in life, there were always closed-minded people who judged. And those exact people were ones I didn't have time or patience for in my life.

Valley wanted to get a second chance to answer my question I asked her multiple times that night, and what kind of asshole would I be to not give it to her?

In the end, I was getting older, and who knew if there's another beautiful, strong, and confident girl out there wanting to live out her desires with me?

There were things I felt for Valley I never felt for another woman before, and although it only seemed as if I wanted her for the sex and my own pleasure, Val could be the one I wanted to settle down with.

Only if she wanted the same, because at eighteen, she had her whole damn life ahead of her.

I focused on the food I was cooking, but every now and then I thought of her parents, my friends, finding out about what their daughter has been doing behind their backs.

That could get messy, and knowing Andrew, he wouldn't approve of me being with his daughter.

Maybe not so much because of our age difference, but more so because of me being his long-time friend.

It would be immoral in his eyes, and I could already imagine him being angrier at Valley than me, because she was irresponsible for flirting and throwing herself at an older man.

It was all up to me to make sure he wouldn't disown his daughter for getting what she wanted, because as much of a tease Valley was, this wasn't all on her.

I played with fire and let her burn me.

Heavily.

Chapter Twenty-Seven

Valley

"Valley, are you ready? Guests will be here any minute!" Della called out from outside my bedroom, knocking at my door while I looked at myself in the mirror, making sure I looked good for tonight.

This was exactly what I needed.

Della inviting friends and family on a Saturday night to celebrate her birthday which was last night.

To be exact, I needed Riggs to be in my house to continue my quest to get him back.

He'd be here with us as well, and it was the perfect opportunity for me to put on my best dress, highest heels, and most beautiful makeup to show him what he'd miss out on.

"Coming!" I called back, leaning in to get closer to the mirror and wiping my thumb along my bottom lip to perfect my wine-red lipstick matching my exposing dress.

I had curled my hair and pulled it back into a low, messy ponytail so Riggs would have something to grab on to if he did decide that I was what he wanted.

I had no doubt about that, but he was being stubborn and an ass, showing off how much of an alpha he really was.

Walking over to my bedroom door, I opened it and didn't expect Della to still be standing there.

"Is there something you need?" I asked, closing the door behind me.

She let her eyes wander all over me, and with a sweet smile, she shook her head. "I wanted to see you before we headed downstairs. You look beautiful," she complimented, hiding her disapproval of either my heels or the dress.

Maybe even both, but I ignored it.

"Thank you. You look gorgeous," I replied, rubbing her upper arm before walking toward the stairs.

"I've invited a few of my girlfriends from college and they're bringing their daughters. They are around your age so maybe you can talk to them and make new friends," she suggested.

I didn't have time to make new friends, and I also didn't need any more.

I had Kennedy, who by the way was really hitting it off with Mason and having another date with him.

Good for her. She deserved a nice guy like him.

"I'll see what I can do," I told her as we reached the foyer to see Dad sitting on the couch, reading a newspaper.

"Andrew, look at how beautiful your daughter looks tonight," Della said, changing the subject.

Dad turned around and put the newspaper down, then smiled at me but kept half of his stern facial expression.

"You both look wonderful. I'm the luckiest man alive," he told us.

I smiled at him and walked over to the couch, leaning down to kiss the top of his head and immediately tasting all the hair gel he had used tonight.

"And you're the most handsome man I've ever seen," I told him, totally lying about it since Riggs was the literal definition of handsome.

Dad chuckled and got up from the couch to then pull Della into his arms, congratulating her once more for her birthday yesterday.

"It's gonna be fun," he promised her, and as they kissed, I turned to walk into the kitchen where three catering staff members were standing, waiting for guests to arrive.

Those were the usual ones Dad hired for parties, but I never had much to do with them.

Tonight, I decided to talk to them to make them feel welcome in our home as they always looked so tense.

"How are you this evening?" I asked, smiling at them and seeing their confusion as to why I was talking to them.

"Very well. Thank you, Miss Bentley. We're happy to be here," the woman on the far right said with a heavy, eastern-European accent.

"Have you had something to eat already? You know you can always come back here and take a little break if you need one," I offered.

"Thank you, Miss Bentley," another one of the women said, and the second my father walked in, their bodies tensed immediately.

I hated the impact Dad had on most people, but I hated it the most with people who worked for him.

"Ready? Guests arrived," he said, meaning for them to take their trays and head out of the kitchen.

They did, and I smiled at them to remind them of what I had said seconds before.

"Did you invite Kennedy?" Dad asked.

"No. She's on a date with someone she met a few weeks ago. But Della said her girlfriends will bring their daughters so...that'll be fun."

"Oh, don't be like this, Val. You'll have a great time. Get something to eat, drink, and talk to people."

I would, while teasing Riggs and making sure we would never break eye-contact.

I sighed and nodded, then walked out to the foyer to greet our first guests who I've never met before.

Della's friends and their daughters were nice, and there was even one who looked like she was right up my alley.

Sexy, a tease, and with a resting bitch-face.

Maybe I would make friends tonight.

"You're Valley. I've heard about you before," one of the daughters said with a smug grin on her face.

"And you are?" I asked, taking in her beautiful dress which did make me jealous for a second.

"Payton."

"And where did you hear about me?" I asked.

"At school. I think it's your cousin who goes there too. Beatrix, I think is her name."

I nodded, puckering my lips. "Small world," I said, taking a sip of the champagne I had grabbed from the kitchen counter.

"So...are you one of those girls who keeps on looking at other girls with that judgmental look until they leave or is that just how you look?"

Where'd she get the audacity to talk to me like that?

"I was gonna ask the same," I replied, staring back at her until neither of us could contain a laugh.

Yeah, this chick was exactly like me.

"Want a smoke?" she asked, but as much as I would've enjoyed to go outside and do all the things my parents would hate to know about, I had to pass as I saw Riggs walk into the house as handsome as ever.

"Not right now. How about I let you in on a little secret, P?"

"Love secrets," she grinned, watching me closely while I followed Riggs with my eyes.

We were standing a little further away from the others, next to the stairs where no one could hear us talk.

"See that man over there with the slicked back hair and white beard?" I asked, nodding in Riggs's direction.

Payton looked toward him and nodded, then she frowned and looked at me again.

"Don't tell me you're into that guy..."

"Oh, I so am. He fucked me a few times, but he's avoiding me and I wanna get back at him. You could help me," I suggested.

"How?" she asked, slowly changing her mind about it.

"You can't hide how dirty you are, P. I can see it in your eyes that you're just as naughty as I am. Okay, maybe not as naughty...but you wouldn't mind acting like you're into me for the night, hm?"

She stared at me for a second, and the way her eyes glowed told me that she was into the idea.

"So...you wanna make him jealous with me?" she asked.

"Yeah. I wanna see how he reacts. What do you say?"

She shrugged. "As long as my mother doesn't see."

I laughed and shook my head at her. "Don't worry about that. Della would have a stroke if she saw me with another girl."

I grabbed her hand and pulled her through the kitchen to get a better look at Riggs who was now standing next to Dad in the living room, a glass of Gin already in his hand.

"How old is he?" she asked, starting to seem interested in Riggs herself.

"Fifty-six," I quickly replied, keeping my eyes on him while he talked to Dad.

"He's handsome."

Yeah, no shit. "He's mine," I made clear.

She laughed and held up her hands. "Relax, girl. He's all yours. I have a boyfriend."

"Yeah?"

"Well, we've been dating for month. Not sure where we stand."

That's what bothered the shit outta me about guys my age. They had no clue what they wanted, always saying *we'll see where things take us*, and the second they find another girl to fuck, they drop you.

Riggs made it clear he wanted me. Only me.

Then I made the mistake to reject him and now I had to fight to get him back.

When he turned his head and met my eyes, I kept my eyes on his as I moved my hand from Payton's hand to her hip, pulling her closer to me.

He was as serious as ever, not showing any other emotion and staring into my soul like there was nothing else he was good at.

"What do you want me to do?" she asked quietly, noticing Riggs staring at me.

"Nothing yet."

"Well, that's no fun," she muttered, leaning against the counter and drinking a sip of her drink.

That was enough staring for now, so I turned to Payton and moved my hand to her waist, grinning at her.

"What? You wanna make out right now?" I asked with a laugh.

She shrugged and laughed as well. "Would that be too weird?"

"No, but I don't want him to think I'm trying to get a rise out of him." Though, that's what he probably always thought.

I looked back to see if Riggs was still watching us, but he had vanished just like Dad.

I stepped away from Payton, emptying my glass and grabbing another glass from the counter.

She studied me for a while, moving her eyes over my dress again before sighing. She really wasn't bothered by me using her as bait, and who knows? Maybe we would really have a fun evening and become friends.

Riggs

All evening long she had been hanging out with another girl, touching and hugging her, dancing and rubbing herself against her friend while making sure I always saw what was happening.

She was doing this to anger me, show me how much she hated the fact that I pushed her away, but that's what she deserved.

It was her punishment for rejecting me the first time.

Yeah, I did miss her touch, her body, her full lips around my dick, but as much as I had to suffer, I wanted to make her suffer just as much.

I was standing outside in the backyard with Andrew and some of the men still left, waiting on their wives to finish drinking champagne and talking about shoes and clothes.

We all had something to drink in our hands, and I was finishing up my third beer as I watched Valley walk over to the lounger near the pool house with her friend.

She was a big ass tease tonight, showing off her legs, curves, beautiful face and hair, and I'd be lying if I'd say she wasn't turning me on just by being in my presence.

She looked fucking incredible, and I didn't think she could get any hotter tonight. But then she sat down on the lounger, her friend next to her, and their arms wrapped around each other as their heads moved closer.

Was no one else seeing this?

Shit, I had to turn my back to them just like the other men.

But I didn't, because when their lips touched, I needed to know how far they'd actually go with their dads standing only a few feet away.

Valley's dark red lips moved slowly against the other girl's, sensually and passionately in a way only she could.

Was I hallucinating?

No, my dick could easily tell apart reality from fantasy, and the show they were putting on for me was one-hundred percent real.

My dick was throbbing already, and when Valley's tongue moved along the other girl's lips, I had to clear my throat and get myself to look away.

When I was about to do so, Valley's eyes opened while she continued to kiss her, with her hand cupping the girl's jaw gently to take control over her.

Shit.

What a dirty little fucking slut.

It was revenge which lingered in her eyes, and even with the dim lights in the backyard, I could tell she was enjoying this.

Me watching.

Me not being the one kissing her.

And me not being hers.

Things needed to change, and although my heart was racing, for whatever fucking reason, I stepped away from the group of men I was listening to and walked back into the house.

Valley had reached her goal of making me angry, but the way she did it was what infuriated me the most.

Reckless.

The only word I could use to describe that naughty little girl.

Chapter Twenty-Eight

Valley

Safe to say Payton enjoyed making out with me while I made sure Riggs saw everything, because she asked me for my number and offered to hang out with me sometime soon.

I clearly left quite the impression on her, but as hot as our kiss was outside on the lounger, I didn't think we'd make plans anytime soon.

She lived a few towns over, and I liked to have my friends close enough to see them in less than ten minutes when needed.

I promised her we could keep in touch by texting though.

She left with her mother and some other guests half an hour ago, and since Riggs was nowhere to be seen, I figured I had made him so mad that he left the party early.

Wouldn't be surprised if that's the case, because the way he stared at me while I made out with Payton to get on his nerves, he sure wasn't happy.

Though, he definitely enjoyed the show we put on, and if I weren't mistaken, there was lust in his angry eyes.

I walked into the living room with a sigh, then smiled at the remaining guests still drinking and eating, and talking with Della.

"I'm going upstairs. Tired. Enjoy the rest of the night," I told them, rubbing Della's shoulder before they all said good night.

"Night," I replied, and without bothering my father and his friends still standing outside, I walked upstairs to get to my bedroom and replay everything that happened tonight from the teasing to the making out with Payton, and Riggs's sudden disappearance.

Guess I won a point tonight, and defeated him at his own game.

But the game was far from being over.

A sharp pain ran from the back of my head down into my body as my hair got pulled back forcefully.

I hit my back against his hard body as he pulled my head back with his hand wrapped around my ponytail, and simultaneously muffled my cry with his other hand pressed over my mouth.

He wasn't gone, and my excitement rose without hesitation.

My heart was pumping fast, making my chest ache in a way it never did before, and also making me nervous for some reason.

"Walk," he growled, his voice deeper than ever, rougher.

I blinked a few times to make sure I wasn't just imagining this, but the way he gripped my hair and sent sparks of pain down my spine assured me that this was reality.

I started walking into my room, and once we were both inside, he closed and locked the door behind him with the hand he had covered my mouth with.

"Think you can get away with this? Kissing that girl while eye-fucking me?"

Out of all the times he acted this way, his voice had never been this dark.

With his hand still wrapped around my ponytail as if he was holding on for dear life, he turned me to face him with his eyes filled with rage.

Shit, he was really mad, and for some stupid reason, that's exactly what I hoped he'd be.

"You proved your point. You want me. But that doesn't mean you have to act like a fucking slut, making out with another girl to fuck with me," he grumbled, his jaw tense and barely moving as he spoke through gritted teeth.

Had I pushed him too far?

Even if...this was what I wanted, and now I'd have to pay for what I've done.

"What are you gonna do about it?" I croaked, wanting to sound more powerful instead of weak.

I wasn't suffering through this, but I sure sounded like I was. I liked this side of him. One of the biggest reasons why I wanted to be his.

This is what I needed. A man who didn't hold back and put me in my place when I acted like a brat.

It was what I've always wanted, and Riggs was the only man who's ever made me feel this way.

Complete.

He made me who I really was, no matter how sick and twisted it might've been. I loved being claimed, spanked, fucked hard, and hell...even degraded.

That's who I was, and Riggs brought out all the best in me.

A harsh laugh made his chest vibrate, and since he was still holding on to my hair, I couldn't move and had no other option than to look into his eyes.

"What am I gonna do about it? I think at this point you should know what's coming, darling," he growled.

He moved his left hand up to cup my jaw tightly, and he pressed his fingers against my cheeks, leaving marks without having to slap me.

"I'm gonna fuck you until you can't think straight anymore. Harder than the last time," his threats sounded like promises to me, and I needed them immediately.

I was about to reach up to grab his wrist, but he turned, making me face the door as he pushed me against it with a loud thud.

"You will not touch me tonight and I don't wanna hear one fucking word coming out of your mouth," he spat, pushing his knee between my legs from behind and wrapping his hand tighter around my throat to cut off my airway.

His right hand moved to my stomach, lifting my dress and then cupping my pussy to rub it roughly.

"Think we've been through this too many times, Val. This is my game, and we play by my rules. And there's no way you will be the one winning in the end."

At this point, I believed him.

I surrendered, even if it was against everything I stood for.

"This cunt is mine," he growled into my ear, his breath tickling my skin. "Say it, Valley. Tell me who this cunt belongs to," he ordered, rubbing his fingers against my clit and circling it while sending sparks of pleasure through my body.

"You...my cunt belongs to you, daddy."

"What did you say?" he asked, and I knew calling him daddy only made him angrier.

His fingers tightened around my throat, and at this point, I couldn't breathe anymore.

"Is that what you wanna call me while your father is downstairs?"

I nodded as best as I could, then closed my eyes to focus on not losing consciousness.

"You won't until I tell you to. Open your mouth," he demanded, and I did because there was literally nothing I wouldn't do for him.

He lifted his left hand from my pussy to my mouth, pushing three wet fingers inside and making me suck on them while I tasted myself.

"You're gonna do exactly what I want you to while you keep quiet so no one will hear you."

I nodded again, getting some air into my lungs as he loosened his grip for a second but immediately cut off my airway again.

He pushed his fingers deep down my throat, but while he choked me, there wasn't really a gag reflex I was feeling.

Maybe this way he'd get his dick even further down my throat.

Just the thought of that excited me, and I squeezed my legs together tightly as he continued to finger my mouth and wet his fingers.

"You're gonna get punished tonight. Harder than last time, and we both know how that ended," he said, his voice amused.

Could I handle more than last time? I had almost passed out from the intensity of what he did to me, but then, last time I was upset about a few things.

I had a clear mind tonight, and I wouldn't let him tear me down the same way.

I wanted to feel everything without being on the verge of losing myself in the torturous but so damn pleasurable things he did to me.

Tonight would be different, and I'd stand my ground to hold on to him for as long as possible.

He pulled his fingers out of my mouth and placed them back on my pussy, moving them through my slit and finally pushing them into my tightness, all three of them at once.

I moaned, but he quickly muffled my sound by covering my mouth again, and when he stepped back to pull me with him, I went willingly.

We stopped in front of my bed where I lifted one leg onto it to make it easier for him to finger me, and when he was sure I wouldn't let out another sound, he placed his right hand on my inner thigh to hold my leg up there steadily.

"I'm gonna fuck your cunt and your tight little ass until you can't take anymore."

Again, something I hoped for but would fight against to keep my eyes open and get the full experience.

I started to move my hips in small circles as he continued to push his fingers in and out of me, making my body tense and shiver at the same time.

"Wet fucking cunt. And it's all mine," he growled, pulling my legs apart further and making sure I wouldn't move them.

I leaned back against him to relax my body while he made everything inside me tense. He knew exactly how, and he did it so well.

"Want another taste?" he asked not waiting on an answer before holding up his fingers covered in my juices to my lips, making me pull them into my mouth again.

I licked and sucked, cleaning them perfectly and swallowing my own taste while keeping my eyes closed.

"On the bed," he ordered, but as I was about to get on the bed, he lifted me up with his arms underneath my knees and neck, laying me down so my head was dangling from the edge of the bed.

My dress had ridden up to my waist, leaving my pussy bare. I wanted him to see more though, so I pulled my dress up, exposing my tits and pulling it off entirely and letting it fall to his feet.

I moved my gaze up to see Riggs standing over me, getting rid of his belt and then unbuttoning his pants.

He was looking at me with his deep, intense stare, showing me how serious he was about punishing me.

When his pants and boxer briefs dropped, his cock was where my eyes went in an instant as he started to rub himself right there in front of my face.

Blood was already flowing into my head, making my temples throb.

He still had his belt in his left hand, but instead of hitting me with it like I had imagined, he wrapped it tightly around my throat, holding it at the nape of my neck while he moved closer to brush the tip of his shaft along my lips.

"Make no sound," he reminded me, but that would be difficult anyway with his belt around my neck.

I opened my mouth, but he pulled back when I did.

"Shut that mouth," he muttered, waiting for me to behave to then brush along my lips again.

His precum rubbed into them, and I had to stop myself from licking his tip to get a taste.

"Open," he finally said, and I did so he could push his hardness into my mouth as deep as he could get in the position I was.

His belt tightened around my throat, making me hold my breath and keep my eyes closed as he started to move his hips to thrust in and out of me.

I surrendered to him in that very moment, letting him fuck my mouth as hard as he wanted.

I kept my hands at my side, gripping the covers underneath me to not get pushed back but stay right where I was.

Riggs

I didn't care about the people downstairs, or the possibility of getting caught, but what I did care about was Valley realizing that this was what it will be like after this night.

I was gagging her with my dick, pushing it deep down her throat while tightening my belt around it.

The sight of her on her back, showing off her beautiful body with my cock in her mouth was so fucking erotic, making me throb and wanting more.

"You're a damn goddess," I praised while treating her like a slut.

To ensure she wouldn't pass out, I pulled out of her mouth and looked down at her, watching as her eyes slowly opened.

She took a deep breath, coughing, then staring up at me with eyes filled with need and lust.

She wanted more, and I was determined to give her just that.

I let go of the belt and cupped her head with both hands, pushing my dick inside her mouth again and pumping in and out with more force and speed now.

"Take it like a fucking good girl. Don't move. Don't make a sound," I growled, continuing to move my hips fast until she needed to take another breath.

I didn't let her, pulling her head against me as tight as possible while the tip of my shaft touched the back of her throat, making her gag again.

"Don't fucking move!" I spat as she lifted her hands to push against my thighs, which only resulted in me pushing against her more.

Fighting back wouldn't help, and she had to learn to let me do whatever was needed to punish her in a way that would benefit us both.

My dick was harder than ever, but I wanted to hold on to my climax for as long as possible.

Hell, maybe even until someone caught us.

After seconds of pressuring her to keep her mouth around my shaft, I finally pulled out, watching her turn onto her stomach and coughing while her saliva mixed with my precum dropped to the floor.

"You're not taking it like a good girl, baby. Do I really need to get rougher?"

Of course she nodded, showing me how much she could take.

I fisted a handful of her hair and pulled her up so she'd kneel on the bed, then I cupped her jaw with my other hand to make her look at me.

"Answer me with words, Valley," I ordered.

"Yes, daddy," she croaked, dark tears rolling down her rosy cheeks.

She looked hot with all that makeup running down her face. It made her look like a mess, but that's what I wanted to see when I made her head spin to the point she couldn't think straight anymore.

Chapter Twenty-Nine

Valley

I've said this before, but tonight was different.

He was showing me yet another side of him, an even rougher, more intense one which I quickly adjusted to.

There was nothing left he could do that surprised me anymore, and whatever he'd want from me, I'd give to him with no hesitation.

"Your toys. Take them out," he ordered, and when he let go of my hair, I bent down to pull the box from underneath my bed.

He grabbed it and took the lid off, pulling out the vibrator and setting the box aside again.

"Turn around. Ass up," he demanded, pushing the button to make the vibrator do what it did best.

I turned around on all fours, with my ass sticking up into the air as he gripped my hips to pull me back against him.

His shaft slid between my folds, teasing me as it throbbed against me.

"No sound," he muttered before sliding into my pussy without any warning.

I muffled my moan by covering my mouth with my hand and I closed my eyes to ease the stinging sensation from his sudden movements.

"Fuck," he growled in his deep voice, moving the small vibrator along my skin before he stopped right above my clit.

"So fucking tight. Squeeze my dick with that wet cunt, baby."

I tried to focus on my body, to do what he told me to and simultaneously enjoy myself while he thrusted into me with his thickness.

I circled my hips to try and get my little toy right where it felt good, but he pulled it away and slapped my ass. "Don't. Fucking. Move," he spat, slapping my ass again before stopping his own movements.

"Do you really want to show those people downstairs what's going on up here? Because that's what I'll do if you don't fucking listen to me!"

Another threat, another challenge.

"Maybe," I purred, looking back at him with a naughty grin.

"Cunt," he murmured on the verge of losing it because of me, but he controlled himself and pushed my head back against the mattress with enough force to make me cry out.

He started fucking me again, harder and faster this time.

People finding out I was fucking Riggs would quickly turn into a disaster. It would be catastrophic, but that didn't stop me from provoking the chance of getting caught.

I was eighteen, old enough to make my own decisions, and fucking Riggs was the one thing in my life that fulfilled me in a way nothing else ever has.

So I moaned, loudly, as he continued to thrust into me while his hands gripped my ass tightly.

The vibrator was still in his right hand, and I felt it vibrate against my skin, making me want him to move it closer to my asshole where it would stimulate some of the intense sensation.

But he didn't, and he also didn't seem to care about me making too much noise anymore.

"Oh, yes, daddy...harder," I begged, pushing against him with every single one of his thrusts, making him push deeper into my pussy.

He wasn't talking, but the growls and groans he let out had a sort of angry undertone. Not that all the other times he fucked me sounded any different.

I was slowly falling back into that known trance he often put me in, but right before I could let myself fall and let him take over my body again, I heard heels clicking in the hallway, coming our way.

"Shit," I whispered, reaching back to make him stop moving.

Suddenly, I wasn't feeling so brave anymore.

"Valley, sweetie...what are you doing in there?" Della's concerned voice called out from outside my room, and I looked up at Riggs, both breathing heavily.

There was something mischievous in his eyes, something challenging.

He pulled himself out of me, and for a second I wondered if he'd really go as far as opening the door and exposing himself—us.

Instead, he held the vibrator to me and nodded toward the door. "Tell her you're playing with yourself," he challenged, making my eyes widen at his words.

"Sweetie, is everything okay in there?" She must've heard me, thinking I was in pain or whatever, but what Riggs wanted me to do would change the way Della saw me.

She had no clue who I really was, what I did when I locked myself in my bedroom at night.

"Go," he hissed, and I quickly took the pastel teal vibrator out of his hand to then walk to my bedroom door and unlock it while Riggs stepped right next to me, hiding from our somewhat unwelcomed guest.

I looked up at him with worry in my eyes, but he nodded and waited for me to open the door just a crack, keeping him hidden as I peeked out to look at Della.

"Everything's okay," I told her, placing my left hand on the side of the door with the vibrator pressed against it. I had turned it off, because letting it vibrate against the door would only make a loud, unpleasant sound.

Della's eyes widened as she took in my makeup-smeared face, and her confusion quickly turned into shock as she realized what I was holding.

"Oh, I..." she started, moving her gaze along the small crack to inspect more of my body. There wasn't much to see though, as I was standing with my body hidden behind the door while leaning over so only my head was visible.

And to make matters worse for me, Riggs reached between my legs and started rubbing his wet fingers along my slit, making me press my lips into a tight line.

Asshole, I thought, trying to focus on Della instead of his fingers rubbing my clit.

"I'm sorry. This is embarrassing," she said, her cheeks turning bright red.

I understood her embarrassment, but there was no way she didn't do the same when she was my age.

What girl didn't pleasure herself?

Okay, maybe there were some, but did she really expect that I wasn't one of those girls who did?

She's seen me walking around in my clothes, right? She must've had some speculation that I wasn't as much of a saint as she hoped I was.

I stared at her, hoping she would finally move her feet and leave me alone before the orgasm starting all the way down in my toes had a chance to move further up.

He was doing this on purpose, circling my clit while I awkwardly stood there with Della, unsure of what to do.

"A little," I replied, but I didn't have any intentions of hiding the vibrator.

"I'm so sorry," she said again, turning around and placing her hand over her mouth before walking back downstairs.

I immediately locked the door and turned to look at Riggs, slapping his chest to show him how stupid of him it was to tease me like that right in front of my stepmother.

"You're an asshole!" I hissed, shooting him an angry glare.

But he didn't care what I called him, or if I was mad. He picked me up with his hands on my ass, my legs wrapped around him as he walked back to the bed and threw me onto it as if I was some kind of toy.

"Her little girl has to grow up sometime, doesn't she?" he smirked, fisting his shaft and stroking it while moving his eyes along my body.

"Come here," he then ordered, and as angry as I was, I needed him to finish what he started.

I moved to the edge of the bed with my legs spread wide as he knelt in front of me and started to kiss the insides of my thighs while pushing them further apart.

I set my vibrator to the side, watching him as he moved his lips closer to my clit and finally started to flick his tongue against it.

"Oh, God..." I mumbled, keeping my eyes on him the whole time.

His tongue moved fast, and it didn't take too long for him make that well-known feeling creep up on me again.

My legs started to shake, and to add to it all, he pushed two fingers into my pussy, moving them fast and rhythmically to the flick of his tongue.

My body tensed, and I reached down to grab fistfuls of his hair and pull him closer to keep him right there.

My toes curled as I felt the orgasm slowly hitting me, and while my clit ached against his tongue, my pussy clenched around his cock.

"Oh, yes!" I croaked out, moving my hips while he continued to lick my clit until I spiraled out of control.

It didn't last long though as he moved away and pulled me down onto the floor in front of him, cupping my face with one hand and the back of my head with the other.

He kissed me, letting me taste myself on his tongue as he circled it around mine.

Even with him being this rough and dirty, I couldn't deny the feeling he made me feel in my chest.

I needed more of him and didn't wanna be just his little toy. I wanted him, and if he meant it like I did, then I wanted to be his too.

His girl.

When he broke the kiss again, he looked into my eyes and studied me for a while before making me open my mouth again, spitting into mine and then standing up to stand over me.

I kept his spit on my tongue, leaning my head back and watching as he put one foot onto the bed while holding on to my hair and stroking his cock with his other hand.

I knew exactly what he wanted without him having to tell me, and with his asshole right in front of me, I licked it to stimulate him, knowing men liked it just as much as women.

"Fuuuck," he growled.

There was nothing he could ask me that I wouldn't do, and while I continued to lick around the rim of his tight hole, I cupped my tits and pulled at my nipples.

"So fucking dirty," he muttered, but then he moved after a while to pull me back up onto the bed.

He spread my legs again, reaching for the vibrator while sliding back inside of me and holding my little toy to my clit without a warning.

His other hand moved to my neck, squeezing it tightly as he started to fuck me.

There wasn't much coming from him, but everything he wanted to say I could easily read from his eyes.

So many emotions ran through them, and I kept my eyes right on his to not miss a single one of them.

My moans weren't as loud as they were before, because quite frankly, my body was starting to shut down again.

In a good way, especially after that orgasm he let me have.

His groans were muffled as well, and I wondered how he was gonna leave my room without anyone from downstairs being suspicious about where he had been for so long, but that wasn't my problem.

His cock throbbed against my tight walls, and it didn't take too long until he started to choke me to the point I couldn't breathe anymore.

I closed my eyes, not able to keep them open while trying to reach another high thanks to the vibrator on my clit.

"Don't come," he muttered, but that wasn't possible.

I needed another release, and the longer he kept my toy right there, the more intense the feeling inside of me became.

Just as I thought I could spiral out of control once again, he pulled the vibrator away, making me look at him.

"No, please," I begged, placing my hands on his arm. "Make me come."

He only let out a harsh laugh and squeezed my throat again, thrusting into me with more force until he released himself inside of me.

I was mad at him for not giving me what I needed, but then, there wasn't anything else I had expected from him.

I couldn't forget that he was still punishing me, and once he emptied his cum inside my pussy, he groaned and pulled out of me before kneeling down between my legs again.

"Please," I begged again, needing him to give me my release as well.

He started to lick my clit again as his cum flowed out of my pussy, and he kept pushing my legs apart to stop me from moving.

Everything around me started to look blurry, but I kept my eyes on him and squeezed his hands cupping my tits tighter as I tried to keep my mouth shut.

His eyes met mine, and with the intensity inside of them, there was nothing left for me to do other than come.

I covered my own mouth with my hand, arching my back as he continued to make me ride on that wave of pleasure until I reached the top and fell over the edge once again.

It hurt, but it felt so damn good.

Everything he did to me was addictive, and the emptiness I felt after his mouth left me was leaving a mark and bruising me on the inside.

I laid there for I don't know how long, but when I finally opened my eyes again, he was standing there, putting on his jeans.

His beard was sticky from his own cum, and once he put on his shirt, he walked into my bathroom to clean himself up.

I needed a second to sit up, but when I did he was already back in my bedroom, buckling his belt and giving me a look I wanted to burn into my brain.

"Come here," he demanded.

I got up from the bed and walked the few steps toward him, letting him cup my face with both hands and brushing my cheeks with his thumbs.

"Say it."

"I'm yours," I replied, knowing exactly what he wanted me to say.

He tilted his head to the side and looked to my lips. "Say it again."

"I'm yours, Riggs. All yours," I said, pushing myself up onto my tiptoes and kissing his lips as if it was what I needed to survive.

I gripped his shirt tightly in my hands to keep him there, and he gripped fistfuls of my hair at each side of my head to assure me he wasn't letting go.

Not yet.

Our tongues moved against each other, twirling and dancing in a sensual way. In a way I never had imagined was possible but it filled my heart with so much love.

A low growl made his chest vibrate, and he slowly pulled back, giving me one last kiss before looking back into my eyes.

"Rest. I'll call you," he promised.

I nodded and stepped back to let him adjust his clothes once again before he unlocked the door and left me standing there.

My heart was pounding in my chest, my knees still shaking, and when he was out of sight, I finally took a deep breath to come back down to earth.

He didn't leave me standing there feeling empty, though my mind still needed time to get back to how it was before.

I couldn't think straight, but I did know one thing...

Riggs is my man, and I would fight for us no matter who'd stand in our way.

Chapter Thirty

Valley

Riggs had made a quick escape after leaving my room last night, because when I walked downstairs into the kitchen the next morning, Dad asked me if he had said goodbye to me.

He must've left without showing his face again after our time together.

Della was standing by the stove, cooking some eggs and bacon while Dad and I waited, me tapping my fingers on the counter and trying my best not to make things awkward.

Clearly, Della's thoughts were probably all over the place, wondering if she had seen correctly last night.

"You two are awfully quiet this morning," Dad said, placing his hand on my lower back and grabbing his cup of coffee with the other.

"Oh, I'm still tired. I was up late last night," I told him.

"Why? Couldn't sleep?"

"Yeah, there were a few things keeping me up and not letting me sleep. Uh, school stuff," I lied.

"Do you need help with anything? I know Riggs's brother left town but I'm sure I can find someone else who can help you," he suggested.

"No, that's fine. It's an assignment I'm writing. Not really something anyone can help me with."

Della turned with the bacon and eggs on a plate, but she avoided eye-contact with me.

"Everything okay, darling?" he asked her, but she simply nodded and passed us to get to the dining room.

"Breakfast's ready," she announced, sitting down and immediately grabbing a piece of toast and smearing butter on it.

I smiled up at Dad to assure him everything's fine, then we sat down and started eating as well.

"Anything fun planned for today?" Dad asked.

"Not really. I might ask Kennedy if she wants to come over if that's okay."

"That's fine with me. I'm taking Della to the country club later today for a round of golf and maybe dinner."

I nodded, not feeling the need to go with them as I didn't like that place much. Besides, most of my classmates would be there too, as they spent most their time playing golf or tennis while hitting on all the pretty staff-members.

I looked at Della as she cleared her throat, and unexpectedly, she spoke. "Does Kennedy do things like that too?"

Raising a brow, I waited for her to clarify what she was talking about, but it soon occurred to me.

"Do you mean pleasure herself?" I asked, not letting this turn into a conversation where we'd beat around the bush.

Della's breath caught in her throat, shocked at the words I chose which could've literally been worse.

"Valley," Dad warned with a stern look which turned into confusion. "Why are you asking her this, Della? We're eating breakfast."

I kept my eyes on Della to challenge her to talk, but she was quiet, unsure how to tackle this.

I sighed and looked at Dad, hoping he wouldn't feel too uncomfortable about what I would say.

"She knocked on my door last night because she must've heard me while I was pleasuring myself. I'm eighteen," I stated.

Dad didn't react to what I said, thankfully, but Della shook her head and laughed.

"I didn't do that when I was your age. Where did you even get that...*thing*?"

"It's a vibrator, Della. And it's not wrong to use it when you have the need to."

"It's disgusting," she spat, surprising me with her words just as much as Dad.

"Della, please! She's eighteen."

Didn't expect him to react this way, but I was glad he didn't shame me like Della did.

"How long have you been sexually active?" she asked.

I knew that whatever she believed in didn't accept things like this. Sex when you're not married was a sin, and having a boyfriend was frowned upon if you didn't keep that boy for the rest of your life.

"Want the truth?" I raised a brow at her, waiting on an answer. "Because I don't think you can handle it."

Her jaw dropped and she slapped her hands onto the table with a shake of her head. "Young lady!"

"Jesus Christ, Della, stop it! Let her live. She's not getting into trouble."

Exactly, and even if...it would be my life we're talking about.

"It's not okay. It's unholy," she mumbled.

"I'm not trying to be a saint," I muttered back, standing up from the table with a heavy sigh.

"I'll have breakfast in my room. I don't feel like sitting here, getting shamed for something so damn natural."

Neither of them said a word, and I grabbed my plate with the eggs and bacon on it, put two slices of bread on it as well before heading upstairs and letting everything I said dwell on her.

I wasn't born into a religious family, and as much as I respected other's beliefs, I hated when they had to rub it in your face.

Della did it passive aggressively, which was even worse.

Once I reached my bedroom I closed the door and sat on my bed, pulled my laptop closer and put on a random show on Netflix to watch while eating breakfast.

I didn't leave the table to calm myself down, but to let her rethink her way of judging me. It wasn't okay, and if she didn't see it the same way, I didn't think there would ever be a way for us to be like before again.

Della was a mother to me ever since my real one left, but I would've expected a little more from her.

More acceptance of who I was. Who I was turning into.

***

"Wanna talk?" Dad's voice broke through my thoughts, and I turned to look at him as he stood in the doorway, looking like a professional golfer.

I shrugged, sitting up and pressing the space key to pause the show I had been watching for the rest of the morning.

It was almost noon, and Dad had gotten ready to go to the club.

"She grew up in a very religious family, and being open about sexuality or even just thinking about it is a taboo topic," he explained.

"Yeah, I know."

He sat down next to me on the bed, sighing and placing his hand on my leg. "I'll try to talk to her when we're on the golf course, but she's pouting like a little kid right now."

I smiled. "I'm sorry if I made you uncomfortable, Dad."

"Oh, you didn't. I figured you weren't sexually abstinent. I'm glad you're exploring your own body. I know how hard it is to do that, especially in college."

If he only knew...

"Well, I'm glad you're not mad. Will you meet a few friends at the club today as well?" I asked to change the subject.

"I'm not sure who will be there, but it will be fun. Sure you don't wanna come along?"

"Kennedy's coming over later. Thank you though." I smiled at him and kissed his cheek before he got up from the bed.

"Sounds good. Have fun you two. I'll see you tonight."

"Bye," I replied, watching as he left and then turning back to my laptop to continue with the show.

***

"That's straight out of a porno," Kennedy laughed after I told her the story about how Riggs fucked me up here while we had guests downstairs.

"Yeah, now that I told you all that, I could've easily set up my camera and filmed it all," I said with a grin.

We were lounging on my bed with the laptop between us and some random movie playing.

"But enough about me. How was it last night with Mason?"

Her cheeks turned red in an instant, and I smiled at her, knowing she had a great time.

"It was amazing. He took me out to the bar where we first met, then we had something to eat and went for a late night walk. It was wonderful."

"Did you kiss?"

"Yes…"

"And?" I grinned from one ear to the other.

"It was perfect. He kisses like a God and I almost swooned because it was so beautiful," she gushed.

"I'm happy for you, Ken. Do you have any more dates planned?"

"Yes. He invited me to his place next week and we'll cook together. I'm excited. I think I'm already falling in love with him."

She deserved to be happy, but her talking about all those things normal couples did made me wonder if I would ever do things like that with Riggs.

He didn't seem like the kind of guy to take someone out for dinner, or cook for them.

But that's not what I needed when I could get all those other things from him.

The sex, with all our dirty needs and wants.

"You deserve everything and more, Ken. He's lucky to have you, but if he fucks up, I'll let him know he messed with the wrong girl."

Kennedy smiled and reached out to grab my hand. "Thank you for everything. I know him because of you, and I would've never thought we'd hit it off so well. So...thank you, Val."

I smiled back and squeezed her hand, then lifted it to kiss the back of it. "Anything for you, Ken. You know that."

She'd be my lifelong friend, no matter where life would take us after college.

We still had three years, and after that, we'd see where life would take us.

"Did Riggs call you yet?" she asked, changing the subject and turning onto her side to look at me.

"Nope, and I'm trying not to check my second phone all the time to see if he has unblocked me yet," I sighed, still holding her hand in mine and playing with her fingers.

"Maybe he needs some time. I can't imagine him not calling you after everything you two did."

I shrugged. With Riggs I never knew.

He was hard to read.

"Hey, can I ask you something?"

"Shoot."

"If I wanna try things...sexually...should I just tell Mason or see where things go?"

I grinned at her question. "It's best if you're open about whatever you two do. Let him know what you want, and you'll see that he'll even let you take control."

"Is that what makes you so confident? Having control over men?"

"That's definitely something that makes me feel powerful. You'll see, not everyone's the same. Don't think too much about it. That won't help."

"God, I'm so lucky to have you. I'd be lost without you," she said, moving closer to me and hugging me tight with her head resting on my chest.

I wrapped my arms around her and kissed the top of her hair. "Love you, Ken," I whispered, thankful to have her by my side as well.

Chapter Thirty-One

Valley

A few days had passed, and Riggs still hadn't called.

As nervous as I was that maybe he changed his mind and didn't wanna see me, I tried to play it cool and focus on school rather than on him.

There was still this ache inside my chest which I had to figure out what kind of ache it actually was, but it didn't take me long to realize that I was missing him.

All of him, and I needed to see him soon or I'd go crazy and make up all those stupid and non-sensical reasons why he didn't call me as promised.

"Damn, you look like you just got slapped," Kennedy said as she stopped in front of me.

I was blankly staring into my locker, my mind stuck on Riggs instead of getting ready for my last class.

"I feel like I got slapped," I muttered, grabbing my biology book and closing the locker.

"Need some chocolate?" she asked.

"No, I need Riggs. I think I'll go to his house to see what's up."

"Tonight?"

"After school. He should be home anyway," I explained, hugging the book to my chest and sighing.

"Sounds like a plan. Ready to go to class?"

I nodded, but as we started to walk down the hall, Cedric and his friends stopped right in front of us with stupid grins on their faces.

"Can I help you?" I asked, my brows raised.

"Maybe. Do you offer your service only for older guys, or are we allowed to subscribe to you as well?"

I frowned at him. "What are you talking about?"

"Oh, no," I heard Kennedy whisper, and I immediately realized what was happening.

Shit...

But, how?

"How'd you find out?" I asked, my mood getting worse by the second.

"Isn't too hard to hack into this town's system and find websites created around here when your father works as a security analyst. Kent's big on encrypting and all that stuff too, you know?"

"Fucking great," I muttered, taking a step toward them to hopefully pass them and leave.

But they wouldn't let me.

"How's this not making you angry?" he asked amused.

It was making me angry, but I didn't care that they found out about my secret. I wasn't going to let them turn this into something big.

"And what if I send the link to all my friends? Maybe even your father? It's easy to find his email address on his business site."

Those were empty threats. At least I hoped they were.

"Just leave me the fuck alone, Cedric," I spat, trying to pass him again.

He grabbed my arms and pushed me back against the lockers with his friends moving in on us to form some type of wall to protect us from the other students walking down the hall.

I heard Kennedy struggle to get to me, but those boys wouldn't let her.

"Here's what we'll do, *Dove*," he whispered, his face close to mine. "You'll let me fuck you, and I will not send that link to your father."

What. A. Dick.

I stared back at him and shook my head. "Is this how you get girls to sleep with you? Threatening them? Is that really the best you can do?"

"No, it's only you I have to be like this with. How come you open your legs for those old, disgusting men but you won't let a guy like me show you a good time?"

I didn't answer him, not wanting to make him cry. "Don't be childish and take no for an answer for once. You're making a fool out of yourself," I told him, keeping my voice low this time.

He was still pinning me against the lockers, but the second he heard Mr. Trapani's voice, he showed just how big of a coward he was and quickly let go of me as his friends also stepped away.

"What the hell is going on here? Did he hurt you?" Mr. T. asked with a concerned look on his face.

I rubbed my upper arm and shook my head. "No, no one can hurt me," I stated, shooting Cedric one last glance before leaving with Kennedy right by my side.

"He's such an asshole. I'm sorry they found out. Do you want to go home?" she asked, rubbing my back while I was determined to leave school early.

"You stay here. I need to go talk to Riggs."

"Are you sure?"

"Yes, Ken. I'm sure."

"Miss Bentley!" Mr. T. called out as he followed us to the exit, and when he reached us he frowned at me.

"Is there something you'd like to talk about? I have time. We can go to my office."

I shook my head. "I'm leaving."

"You have one more class, Miss Bentley. Follow me to my office," he offered, but I was hesitant.

"Mr. Fanning will send an email to your dad if you miss his class," Kennedy reminded me in a worrying tone.

I knew he would, but I didn't really care.

"We have ten more minutes before class starts. Let's talk," Mr. T. said again, and I finally gave in.

I hated the thought of Cedric sending Dad that link, but even if I could stop him from seeing it, this town talked, and someday the truth would come out anyway.

"Fine."

"I'll see you in class," Kennedy said, rubbing my arm before leaving.

I followed Mr. Trapani into his office and sat down in one of the chairs in front of his desk.

"I've sent Cedric to the principal. Wanna tell me what's going on?"

I crossed my arms in front of my chest and looked to the side, trying to get rid of my anger quietly. "He's not taking no for an answer and he's harassed me for not having sex with him multiple times. He's threatened me before," I said, sounding like a damn snitch.

"And what's the threat?"

I moved my eyes to him and raised a brow. "Do you really wanna know?"

"Yes."

I rolled my eyes and leaned back against the chair. At this point, did it really matter if I told him the truth or not? "I'm a cam girl. They somehow found my website and now he wants to fuck me and in exchange he won't send the link to my father."

He didn't look as surprised as I hoped he would, but then...I guess Mr. T. had always known I wasn't just a regular student at this school.

"Can you delete that website?"

"Yes, but I'd need to go home to do that."

He clicked his pen too many times, making me nervous. "Cedric's with Mr. Thompson and he'll stay there until school's over. He's got a few more classes than you do, so you will have enough time to go back home and make that website disappear."

He watched me closely, let his eyes wander all the way down to my skirt and back up to my eyes.

Looks from men other than Riggs really didn't do much for me anymore, and I waited for him to talk again as I didn't have anything to say.

"You're not lying to me about the camming thing, right?"

Jesus, why would I expose myself like this otherwise?

I frowned at him.

"All right, all right. I'll make sure he won't have his phone until his last class. Go, and don't think about it too much, okay?"

As if it were that easy.

***

I drove directly to Riggs's place after my biology class was over, and although I could've easily gone home to take down my website, I didn't want to surrender Dove so easily because of Cedric being a total fucking asshole.

That website was what kept me going for the past two years, and giving it up because of him being petty that I didn't want to fuck him wasn't worth it.

I knocked on the front door, rang the bell multiple times and even kicked it to let out my anger before I would let it out on Riggs.

The door swung open and he stood there with an angry glare. "What the fuck are you trying to achieve here?"

I crossed my arms and blew a heavy breath out of my nose. "We need to talk," I stated.

"You should've called first," he said.

"No, you should've called! You told me you would but you didn't, so now I'm here to talk. Let me in."

Instead of putting up a fight with me, which would've been a mistake in the first place, he stepped aside and watched me closely as I walked inside with my arms still crossed.

"What's wrong?" he asked, sounding more concerned than he ever has before.

"Some kid at my school found out about my website, and he's threatened to send it to Dad if I don't have sex with him."

He raised a brow at me and closed the door. "You still have that website up?"

I told him I would stop camming, but that didn't mean I would delete my site and lose everything I built up on there.

Luckily, all pictures other than the banner on the page that could be seen once you clicked on the link were hidden from non-subscribers, and only had access with a password they'd receive from me personally once they added a credit card to pay.

"It will stay up, but that doesn't mean I will keep on camming."

"That's not how this between us will work."

"But this isn't about us right now!"

"Then why the fuck are you here?"

He had a point, but there was nowhere else I wanted to be while feeling like shit.

"Because I wanted to tell you about it before Dad locks me up in my room until I'm old enough to be passed on to a retirement home."

He studied me and sighed, pushing his hands into the pockets of his jeans. He looked good with his hair pulled back into a low man-bun I've never seen on him before, but I liked the way it looked on him.

His hair had grown quite a bit, and his beard was starting to hide more and more of his face.

"You should really get rid of that website then," he suggested.

We've never had a conversation like this.

An honest and somewhat calm one where we were trying to figure things out together.

It was nice, and for some reason, it calmed my nerves while my heart still beat like crazy.

I looked away and furrowed my brows, not wanting to accept the fact that deleting the site might be the best resolution.

I still had about two hours until Cedric would get his phone back from Mr. Thompson, but those two hours weren't made for me to think about it too much.

"Dove's a part of me. I can't just get rid of her, Riggs."

"You're not getting rid of her. She doesn't just exist on your laptop screen, Valley."

"How do you know?" I muttered, receiving a challenging look from him.

"I know because I see her every damn time I fuck you. Every time you suck my dick and every single damn time you stand in front of me looking like a goddess. You are Dove, Valley, and if you want this to work, you'll delete that site."

His words warmed my chest and I wondered if it was really him saying all those things.

It wasn't in his nature to talk without making any growling sounds, but this time it was different.

He meant every word he said, and he showed me in that very moment that he was serious about us.

I stared at him, not able to speak or think straight.

This man had shown his true colors in the past few weeks, but even more of them right now.

He wasn't always this rough, harsh man, but there was something soft deep inside of him that only showed when he truly wanted it to.

"Come here," he ordered with his hands still in his pockets, but when I stepped closer, he pulled them out to wrap his arms around my waist, pulling me onto my tiptoes while I put my arms around his neck to hold him tight.

His embrace was something I've never felt before from him, but it was loving and warm, making me drop all those bad thoughts I had thanks to Cedric.

"Get rid of the site but not of Dove," he said, his voice deeper and darker this time.

I closed my eyes to take in every single moment of this, not wanting to let go.

My heart was pounding in my chest, just like his was, showing me that we were feeling the same.

I was falling for this man, despite all the things standing against us.

I leaned back to look into his eyes with my hands cupping the back of his head and my body pressed against his.

"If I delete the site, you have to promise me this—whatever this is—will last."

I needed to know, because if he would only want me for a short period of time, I didn't care if the whole town found out about my website.

I'd continue camming, add some more customers and make a damn living from it.

He chuckled and moved his hands from my lower back to my ass, cupping it and squeezing it gently. "I'm getting old, darling. You're it for me, and there's no time left for me to find a girl who treats me like a king."

I smiled at his words, feeling all the butterflies in my stomach go wild.

"And I know you'll treat me like a queen," I whispered back, biting my bottom lip to hold back a grin.

"A fucking naughty one at that."

I laughed, feeling my happiness grow inside of me by the second.

Yeah, this man was it for me, and I wanted to scream it from the top of my lungs to show the world that no matter how old you were, you could be with whoever you chose to be with.

Chapter Thirty-Two

Riggs

I decided to go home with her and watch her get rid of that website she spent so much time on in the past.

It sure was hard for her, but I was a jealous piece of shit and knowing she could someday get bored with me and turn to those men bothered the hell outta me.

We arrived at her house and found that Della wasn't home either, probably out getting groceries or something while Andrew was at work.

"Do you want something to drink?" Valley asked, still holding on to my hand as we walked through the foyer.

"No, I want you to shut that website down."

She sighed, and although we had an intense moment back at my place with her promising me to be only mine, she still had to right the thought of Dove not being part of her life anymore.

Valley let go of my hand as we walked upstairs and into her room where I sat down on the edge of the bed while she grabbed her laptop from her desk.

The webcam wasn't attached to it like it had been the last time I was in here. "When's the last time you put on a show for someone?"

She sat down on the bed next to me with her legs crossed and her laptop on her lap. "A few days ago," she mumbled, typing something as she kept her eyes on the screen.

"Was it my brother?"

"No."

"What did he make you do?" I asked.

She raised a brow and looked at me. "Do you really wanna know?"

"Would I ask if I didn't want to?" I shot back.

She shook her head and looked back at the screen. "He wanted me to play with my toys while he either pissed on himself or rubbed his cock," she told me.

There were really no more boundaries between us, and everything she ever did in the past were things I wanted to know about.

Maybe there were things I didn't know she liked.

"Did he ever made you drink your own piss?" I asked, getting an annoyed look from her in return.

"Is this really what you wanna talk about while I'm shutting down a website I worked so hard for?"

"Answer the question."

"God, no, he didn't."

I was making this whole situation so much worse for her, and I wondered why I couldn't be kind for once.

My asshole-behavior pushed her over the edge at times, but never had she been this annoyed with me.

"Need help?" I asked, looking at the screen and watching as she logged into her own website where she was able to edit everything on it.

She shook her head and let out another sigh before clicking on a tab with all kinds of actions.

I watched her closely as she didn't move anymore, staring blankly at the screen and holding her laptop tightly in her hands.

Her agitated face filled with worry and confusion, probably wondering if she was doing the right thing.

This shit really meant a lot to her, and just because I was a selfish fucking bastard, didn't mean I had to take away the one thing she was so proud of.

Still, she had to get rid of the site to make sure that little piece of shit wouldn't send the link to the whole goddamn town or hack his way onto the main page.

No matter how proud she was about this, I couldn't let him expose her at such a young age.

It would ruin her time in college, no matter how much she loved being a cam girl.

Yet…I wasn't thinking about what could happen if I took this one thing away from her. One thing that made her truly happy.

"Don't," I said as she moved the cursor to the words *permanently delete page*, and she quickly looked up with confusion flashing in her eyes.

"What?"

"Don't delete it."

She gave me a strange look and laughed. "Why? Cedric will send the link to everyone."

"Yeah, and he can do so once you're out of college. Pause the page."

She frowned, not sure if she should believe what I was saying. "I don't understand...you said you don't want me to ever go back to camming..."

"I didn't say that, Valley. I said I don't want you to cam while you're with me. Pause the page so you don't lose any of those damn customers, but you have to promise me not to go on it while you're with me. I don't fucking care what you do when you decide to leave me for another guy who's not too old to fuck you, but for as long as you're mine, no one else can have you."

She studied me and kept frowning, letting my words sink in until she realized I was not messing with her.

"Are you sure?"

"Hell, pause the fucking page before I change my mind back," I grumbled, and she quickly clicked on the one option that would let her still get back to what she loved doing when I wasn't around anymore.

She let out a deep breath and put her laptop aside, then I pulled her onto my lap, cupping her face and brushing back her hair.

"Relax. Your father won't find out. You're the only one who can access the page right now," I assured her, studying her face closely as she kept her eyes on me the whole time.

"And even if, you know you'd fucking own it, Valley. Did you ever care about what others think about you?"

"No," she muttered with concern still lingering in her eyes.

"Then stop worrying about it. If it comes out, don't let anyone tell you what you're doing on the internet is wrong. Hell, they'd probably be jealous knowing you can attract men online who pay you good money. You know how many girls do this shit for free and never get anything out of it? Even some damn porn stars don't get paid enough."

She knew damn well that she was confident enough to fire back if anyone ever called her any names for being herself, and I hated seeing her like this.

Defeated and unsure of herself.

"This isn't you, Valley, and now that there's no way your site can be seen or looked up by anyone anymore, I want you to push all those thoughts aside and put a smile on your face."

Valley

I swallowed the lump that had formed in my throat to then take a deep breath and nod at his words, knowing that he was right about everything.

Shit, Mr. Trapani knew about the page, but that didn't bother me. So why the fuck would it be an issue if anyone else, even Dad, would've found out about it?

Good thing I didn't have to deal with it anymore. Not right now.

"You're right. I'm sorry I'm acting weird. Guess I was worried something bad would happen."

"It won't. Relax and stop thinking about it. That little fucker's got nothing on you now. What's his name?"

"Cedric Cortez," I replied. "What are you up to?"

"Nothing," he said, placing his hands on my thighs and caressing my skin with his thumbs. "Have we calmed down a bit?"

I nodded. "Yeah, I'm better," I told him honestly, though I was still furious about the way Cedric treated me back at school.

Riggs's eyes moved from mine down to my uniform, taking it in carefully until they stopped at my skirt.

I knew what was coming, but I was all for a change of subject at this point.

"I wanna fuck you in this uniform," he told me in a low voice, making me shiver and push all those worrying thoughts aside to make space for him.

I moved my hips on top of him in slow circles, feeling his shaft in his pants grow bigger with every movement.

"God, you're so fucking beautiful, Valley," he muttered, pushing my skirt further up and moving his hands to my ass, cupping and squeezing it tightly.

I smiled at him, my admiration for him growing.

Before today, I never let my feelings show in his presence, unsure of what he'd think, but now that I knew I was his, I had to show him how he made me feel.

I pushed my hands into his hair, undoing his bun and letting his hair fall out of it so I could curl my fingers around it and hold on tight.

He leaned in to kiss me, and I quickly took over by licking along his bottom lip to then dip my tongue inside his mouth and taste more of him.

He groaned, pushing my crotch against his while I kept moving on top of him.

Our kiss quickly turned into a hot make out session, with our tongues dancing with each other and our hands moving all over each other's bodies.

His cock was getting hard in his jeans, and thanks to my skirt not being in the way, I felt it throb against my pussy.

I moaned softly as he kept squeezing my ass and helping me circle my hips on top of him.

"Take this off," I ordered, pulling at his sweater.

But as he broke the kiss to do what I asked him to, we both froze as we heard the front door open.

"Shit!" I muttered, quickly getting up from his lap and running out of my room and to the stairs.

Della walked into the house with bags of groceries in her arms, her eyes immediately looking up the stairs.

"Hey," I said out of breath, answering the question that was written all over her face. "Riggs is here. He helped me with my laptop. It didn't work right," I lied.

She looked skeptical, and when Riggs stepped next to me with his hair pulled back into a bun again, Della smiled.

"Oh, hello, Riggs. Does her laptop work again?" she asked, not looking back at me.

Guess she was still upset with me.

"Yeah, it works just fine now. I'm leaving," he said, looking at me and then walking down the stairs.

"So soon? Andrew is coming home early from work, and I was thinking of cooking dinner already. Why don't you stay?"

Yes!

I stood at the top of the stairs, waiting for his response.

He stopped before he could reach the bottom step, and without turning to look at me, he nodded. "I'd love to. Thank you, Della."

I smiled, but I couldn't show my happiness.

Sure, she just interrupted our make out, but I loved having him over for dinner, and I could use some of his company after everything that happened today in school.

"Valley, why don't you come set the table?" Della suggested.

"I'll be right there," I told her, taking another look at Riggs before heading back into my room to collect myself.

My body was aching for him, but I guess we'd have to wait for another time to continue what we had started.

Chapter Thirty-Three

Valley

"Why isn't your car outside? Did Valley pick you up?" Della asked Riggs as I was setting the table while they stood in the kitchen.

"Yeah, she came by my place to ask me if I could come over and help. She doesn't have my number," he explained, lying directly to her face.

I had to bite back a grin. I liked this side of him.

"I'm sure she will drive you back home after dinner," Della said, making it sound like a punishment for whatever reason.

Little did she know I'd totally give Riggs a well needed and deserved blowjob.

"I will," I said, grinning at Riggs while he shook his head with a smirk on his face.

"How's life now that you don't work anymore?" Della asked.

"Great. I'm thinking about working on a few things around the house to keep me busy."

"If you ever need help with gardening, I'm really good at it."

"I know. I'll definitely come back to you about it sooner or later."

That is, if by then this thing between us hasn't come out yet. Della would be the first to disapprove of me being in a relationship with a much older man.

But Dad I wasn't so sure about.

Not after the way he took the fact that I was sexually active and had sex toys lying around in my bedroom.

They were still good friends, and maybe that would help make the relationship between Riggs and I okay.

For now, him and I still had to make it official.

The front door opened and Dad walked in, looking tired and stressed.

I ran to him to hug him, kissing his cheek and hopefully making him feel better. "Hi, Dad. How was your day?"

He patted my back before I leaned back to look at him. "Hello, sweetheart. It was a long day but I made it out alive," he joked.

"Riggs is here," I announced, and together we walked into the kitchen so he could greet his wife and friend.

"Good to see you again, Riggs. You doing okay?"

"Yeah, hard day?"

"As always. I'm starting to take into consideration what Della suggested," Dad said, chuckling at the idea of finally retiring.

"Think that wouldn't be such a bad idea," Riggs said.

"Can't stop right now. Important things are happening. Had to fire two employees and am now searching for a new one," Dad sighed, turning to look at me again. "You're not interested in working at the firm for a few hours after school, are you?"

"Uh..." I actually thought about it, but I knew that wasn't anything I'd enjoy. "I don't think so. I'm busy with school, and I don't wanna fall behind."

"Oh, you're a smart girl, Valley. I'm sure it won't be so bad taking up a small job like that to help your father. Maybe you'll take over the firm one day."

"No," I answered, frowning at her.

"Why not?" she challenged, and I was starting to think she was trying to mess with me on purpose.

"Because I'm not studying biology in college for nothing."

"And where will that get you?"

Jesus Christ...

"There are many things she can do after graduating with a biology major. I'm sure she'll find the right thing," Riggs said, defending me from her.

"Whatever," she mumbled, turning back to the stove and making me roll my eyes.

"Ignore her," Dad whispered into my ear before he pointed to the stairs. "I'll go put away my things and be right back."

When he left, Riggs nudged my side and winked at me, making me smile again and remember his words he told me earlier.

Others couldn't do or say anything to me. I was confident in who I was, what I wanted in life, and who I wanted to be.

***

Dinner was over quicker than expected, but it was Riggs who seemed eager to leave after finishing his dinner and emptying his beer.

I was sitting next to him, my hand on his thigh underneath the table while he rested his on mine.

"Wanna go home?" I asked, turning my hand so our palms faced each other's, and I slid my fingers through his to hold on to him.

"Yeah, I think it's time for me to go home. Thank you so much for dinner, and I'll invite you guys over sometime soon."

We all got up from the table and walked over to the front door, and while they all said goodbye, I checked myself in the mirror to see if my uniform was still looking good.

"Drive safe, Val. I'll see you in a bit," Dad said.

"Oh, actually...I have to stop at Kennedy's. She needs help with some homework and since I'm driving by her house anyway, I told her I'd stop by."

Another lie, but I was becoming good at them.

"Fine, let me know when you leave her place."

I nodded, smiling at him before leaving the house with Riggs who had a knowing look on his face.

"Naughty little thing," he murmured, making me grin from one ear to the other.

We got into the car and I pulled out of the driveway to head to his place, and because we couldn't keep our fingers away from each other, he reached over to me and cupped my pussy, making me spread my legs so he had easier access.

"You kept your uniform on. Do you have any idea how hard you make me without even touching me?"

I had a little bit of an idea how I made him feel, which made me feel powerful.

"You deserve to be fucked tonight, and I want you to keep that uniform on while I do so."

I licked my lips and kept my eyes on the road, my hips moving at the touch of his fingers on my clit.

"I can smell your sweetness from here. Shit, baby, you're so fucking wet."

He pushed his fingers into my panties to slide them through my slit and then hold them up in front of my lips for me to taste them.

I wrapped my lips around them, licking and tasting while I gripped the steering wheel tighter.

If he kept teasing me, I'd have to stop the car on the side of the road.

Luckily, the drive to his house wasn't too long, and when I pulled up into his driveway, we both got out quickly.

He was faster, walking over to my side and pressing me against the door with one hand on my throat and the other on my waist.

His lips crashed onto mine, immediately deepening the kiss and letting me know how much he wanted me tonight.

I moved my hands to his chest to grab onto his sweater, making sure I wouldn't collapse as my knees weakened, but after a deep kiss, he lifted me up and threw me over his shoulder, making me laugh.

"Riggs!" I squealed, slapping his ass while he walked to the front door to unlock it.

He didn't say a word as he walked down the hall to his bedroom, and when we got there, he let me fall back onto the bed with him crawling over me.

He kissed my neck and cupped my tit while holding himself up with his other hand propped up on the side of my head.

Moaning, I moved my hands into his hair to undo his bun again, needing to tug on it the way I knew he liked.

"Mine," he growled, and I nodded in response.

"Yours. I'm all yours, Riggs."

He kissed a trail from my neck down to the top of my tits, sucking and nibbling on the sensitive skin and then unbuttoning my shirt to gain access to my needy nipples.

They were aching already, as every other body part of mine was ever since we made out in my bedroom earlier.

His groans got louder as I pulled at his hair, and I reached between us to rub his cock through his jeans.

This time, it didn't seem as if we were fighting for who had control over each other, and we both were eager to get naked and fuck in a way we've never had.

This time...we both knew there were feelings involved, and I wanted to feel every single one of them before I had to leave him and go back home.

His cock was rock-hard, and I unbuttoned his jeans as he pulled one nipple into his mouth, sucking on it while he played with the other one.

"Take them off," I said, tugging at his jeans and waiting for him to do what I asked him to.

He got off the bed and pushed them down his legs, getting rid of his boxer briefs as well before taking off his sweater to stand there in his full glory.

His muscles flexed underneath his tattooed skin, and I smiled when I noticed a small tattoo on his left hip hidden between two bigger ones.

"Since when do you have that?" I asked, sitting up and placing one hand on his stomach and the other on his hip to brush along the small dove.

"When I was twenty. I forgot about it up until the day my damn brother called you Dove," he said, keeping his voice low.

I looked up at him in awe, thinking that was one hell of a coincidence.

"That night I knew you were mine. It's stupid, I know. And I don't believe in shit like that. But this time I did."

I stared up at him like a little kid staring at a lit-up Christmas tree, eyes filled with happiness and amazement.

He placed his hands on either side of my head and brushed back my hair gently, not breaking eye-contact and silently showing me how much he meant those words he just said.

My heart was full, and when I looked back at the tattoo, I leaned in to kiss it.

I had no words, feeling as if they weren't needed at this point.

When he fisted my hair with both hands, I looked back up and smiled, then he leaned in to kiss me and push me back onto the bed.

He deepened the kiss as he leaned over me, and I wrapped my hand around his cock to rub it while he finished unbuttoning my shirt and exposing my tits more.

He had pushed my bra aside already, and although it wasn't too comfortable, I didn't feel like taking it off.

Riggs wanted to fuck me in my unform, so I would let him.

This side of him was new, but as gentle as he was right now, I knew he wouldn't hold back while he was inside of me.

My heart couldn't stop pounding, and when he broke the kiss, he finally pulled my panties down and settled himself between my legs with his hand around his shaft now.

"You're so damn gorgeous, baby. I'm not letting you go. You're mine, and I will show you each fucking day that you belong to me."

I was starting to love his promises, no matter how harsh or aggressive they were.

He meant it, and that's what mattered most to me.

"Show me," I whispered, cupping his face with both hands and feeling the tip of his cock rub against my entrance.

"I want you to show me."

With one swift move he slid into me, stretching and filling me in a way only he could.

I moaned, throwing my head back as he started to thrust in and out of me with force, keeping his promise and making me feel whole.

As much as I loved his rough side, and the way he punished me when I was being naughty and misbehaved, I loved this new side of him he was showing me almost as much.

Chapter Thirty-Four

Valley

"You look happy today," Kennedy said as she stopped next to me by my locker, and I lifted my gaze from my phone to look at her with a bright smile.

"I am happy."

It's been a few days since Riggs and I unofficially made it official. We both knew being together would be difficult if it someday came out to the public, but for now, we enjoyed this little secret and kept it to ourselves.

I could already sense my parents getting mad at me, and even Riggs, because our age difference wasn't the only thing that could seem immoral.

Riggs has been friends with Della and Dad for years, even before I was born, and considering how strict Della can be, I'd expect her to freak out and call me all kinds of names.

"Did he unblock you?" she joked, making me laugh.

"Yeah, believe it or not, but this isn't my second phone. He said he wants to be the only man texting me dirty things, so I shut off the other one."

I still received messages from some of the other men, mostly dick pics and videos of them stroking their cocks. But as much as I missed camming already, I was content with my life and having Riggs by my side.

"Well, I'm happy you're happy. Can you believe us both being in relationships at the same time?" she asked, leaning against the lockers.

"The fact that we even have boyfriends is what's surprising," I said, grinning at her.

"We should go on a double date. Maybe go to a bar or something. A nice restaurant," she suggested.

"Not sure Riggs would be up for that. He's a selfish old man who likes to keep me hidden from the world when he has the chance to."

"Aw, come on...I'm sure he can give up his possessiveness for one night."

I doubted that.

"I'll see what I can do."

I looked back down at my phone and finished typing the text I was about to send him.

He wanted me to come over after class, and I agreed to go once I did my homework so I wouldn't have to worry about it over the weekend.

See you soon, handsome, I texted, watching as the *typing* bubble popped on his side of the chat.

Can't wait, he simply replied, and I could literally hear his deep, growly voice.

"Did you hear anything from Cedric since that day he threatened you?" Kennedy asked, and when I looked up I noticed why she mentioned that douche.

He was walking toward us, his face stern but his walk unsure.

"What does he want now?" I mumbled, turning with my head high and waiting for him to stop in front of me.

"Can we talk?" he asked, his voice as annoyed as ever.

I shrugged, waiting for him to continue.

He sighed and looked around, then leaned in closer so he didn't have to talk too loudly. "I don't know what the hell happened but I'm sorry your page got deleted. Kent was the one playing around with it, so it's on him."

I frowned.

"Huh?"

"Jesus, your website. I was the only one who had the link to it, and I don't know how he got it or found it, but the page's gone now."

I was confused at first, but then I realized that he had no idea I was the one pausing the page to make it unavailable for anyone.

I looked at Kennedy who knew all about what Riggs made me do with my website, and even she looked confused until she realized what was going on and had to hold back a grin.

Just play along, Val.

"Yeah, that's kinda rude. But I guess now you can get rid of that link yourself," I suggested.

"I wasn't going to send it to your dad, you know that, right?"

My frown deepened. "I'm sorry?" Was I hearing correctly? "Then what were all those fucking threats about?"

Cedric rubbed the back of his neck and shrugged, looking like a little boy who just got caught stealing candy.

"Come on, Val. I was just messing with you. I got a proper beating when I got home that day, and the principal is making me stay every day after school for the rest of the semester."

I looked past him and saw Mr. Thompson standing outside his office with his arms crossed over his chest and a deep crease between his brows.

Mr. Trapani was standing next to him, and I sighed, knowing this apology didn't come from Cedric himself.

I looked back at him and raised a brow. "Just stop being a fucking idiot, all right?" I suggested.

He shrugged. "I'll try. I'm sorry. And I'm sorry about your site. Really would've loved to see what you were hiding on there."

I flicked my middle finger against his forehead in response to his yet again inappropriate words, and Kennedy laughed as he stepped back like a hurt little lamb.

"Jesus, I'm sorry, Valley. I won't talk about it anymore, and I didn't tell anyone about it. Only the boys know, but I will make sure they keep their mouths shut as well."

"Good. Now, leave. I don't wanna see your face anymore," I said.

He looked back at Mr. Thompson, and once he gave a nod of approval, Cedric left.

"What an asshole," Kennedy muttered.

"Couldn't agree more."

"Miss Bentley! My office." I sighed as I heard Mr. Thompson call out to me, and I shut the locker with a roll of my eyes.

"I'll see you in class," I told Kennedy, then I walked across the hall to his office where they were already sitting in their chairs.

I closed the door behind me and walked over to the empty chair next to Mr. T., and when I sat down, both of them cleared their throats.

"Go ahead," Mr. Thompson told Mr. Trapani, and I turned to face him with a questioning look.

"I had to tell him about it or else he couldn't issue any consequences. But know that your...hobby is safe with us."

At this point, I didn't care about who knew, since there was no evidence to prove I was a cam girl.

"Anything else?"

"Yes," Mr. Thompson said, making me turn my head and look at him. "I wanted to congratulate you on how well you're doing academically. All your teachers are satisfied with your homework and assignments, and you somehow managed to pull that A minus in Chemistry into an A plus. We wanted to reward you, as we think you'll be one of our best students ever. Not even your father had such perfect grades."

I smiled, because as wild as I seemed on the outside, I was proud of myself for being smart, even kicking some of the nerds' asses in most classes.

"This is a hundred-dollar gift card for you to spend in whatever store or restaurant around town," Mr. Thompson said as he pushed the card over to me on his desk.

I knew about those gift cards. People could purchase them at the town hall, and mostly were gifted at Christmas or Birthdays.

It was a great gift when you didn't want to worry about what to buy for someone, and this way, you could choose how to spend that money.

I smiled at him and reached for it. "This is great! Thank you so much," I said, proud of myself for everything I've achieved so far.

"You're welcome, Miss Bentley. Now, go to class. Don't wanna ruin your perfect attendance."

"Nope, and I won't. Thank you again," I said, standing up and smiling at both of them before leaving the office.

I guess telling Mr. T. about it wasn't such a bad thing after all, and now they had a few more things to dream about at night because of me.

Too bad Mr. T. didn't have a chance with me anymore, now that I belonged to Riggs.

I headed into class and sat down next to Kennedy as she looked at me with a concerned look. "Everything okay?" she asked.

"Yeah, everything's perfect. Life's perfect," I assured her with a smile.

She smiled back and rubbed my arm, and sure enough we had to focus on our teacher while I tried my best not to grin like a fool, sitting there and thinking of my man who I'd see later tonight.

***

"Where are you going?" Dad asked as I walked through the foyer with my backpack filled with my pajamas and overnight things.

I stopped in my tracks and turned to him, seeing his and Della's eyes on me, looking curious as ever.

"Kennedy's. We're having a sleepover," I said, highlighting my lie with a sweet smile.

"When will you be back tomorrow? Your uncle has invited us to the country club to have dinner with them. Riggs will come too," he explained.

"He will?"

"Yeah, at least that's what he told me. He's been busy the past few days."

Yeah...making me come and fucking me in every room of his house.

"Okay, I'll be home around lunch time."

"Make sure to eat breakfast in the morning because I won't cook anything for lunch tomorrow as we'll have a big dinner at the club," Della announced.

"Okay. Good night you guys," I said, waving at them and then heading out the door to get to my car.

I couldn't wait to see Riggs again.

The drive to his house didn't take too long, and after parking next to his car, I got out of mine and rushed over to his front door.

I knocked three times, then stepped back and waited for him to open it while I tucked my hair behind my ears to get it out of my face.

I chose to wear a pleated skirt, similar to my school uniform but with a black, long-sleeved shirt on top, feeling as confident and sexy as ever.

The door swung open and Riggs stood there in his dark gray sweatpants and a white shirt which fit him perfectly.

"Hi," I greeted, biting my bottom lip to hide my excitement.

Riggs, on the other hand, didn't care about showing his emotions for once, which I kinda liked instead of him being grumpy all the damn time.

"Hey, gorgeous."

I stepped closer to wrap my arms around his neck, and he pulled me tight against his body with his arms around my waist, kissing the crook of my neck.

"I missed you," I whispered, even if it hasn't been too long since we've seen each other.

He was always on my mind, and my addiction to him grew each day, making it hard to go one day without him.

"Getting cheesy now?"

I laughed. "You're an ass. You missed me too," I pointed out.

"Yeah, I did," he mumbled, kissing the sensitive spot underneath my ear and then nibbling on my earlobe.

"Gonna let me in?" I asked, leaning back to look at him again, and he nodded before letting go of me and stepping aside.

"Did you eat?"

"Yeah, I had dinner," I replied as I entered his house, and before I could ask him if he'd eaten yet, he picked me up and threw me over his shoulder again. I kinda liked this new way of him carrying me to bed.

I laughed, letting my body relax and dangle over his shoulder while he walked down the hall to his bathroom.

Guess he had something planned, because as we entered the bathroom, there were white rose petals all over the room, making me look up and open my mouth in awe.

Riggs let me down slowly, immediately taking off my backpack and setting it aside while I looked around to take everything in.

"Wow..." I whispered, staring out the big windows overlooking the whole city. "This is beautiful," I told him, turning to look at him now.

"You like it? Thought I'd show you that I can be romantic," he said, which only made me laugh out loud.

"Keep trying to convince yourself about that, big guy," I teased, but I did think this was a side of him I'd love to see more often as long as the fucking stays just as rough.

"Shoes off," he ordered.

And we're back to normal, I thought, quickly taking off my sneakers and pushing them closer to my backpack on the floor.

I knew the meaning of white flowers, and one aspect of them contradicted who I wasn't.

Innocent.

Then again, white roses also symbolized new beginnings, which Riggs and I were definitely going through one of them at this moment.

He moved closer to me, his hands cupping my face as he leaned in to kiss me, and while our lips moved against each other's, I placed my hands on the hem of his shirt to tug on it, needing him to take it off.

His kiss was deep and passionate, and when I moved my hands underneath his shirt to brush along his muscles, he growled and fisted my hair in his hands tightly.

As much as I loved being in control, I wanted to let him take over tonight. At least for now.

He moved, making me step back and stop as my back hit the sink behind me, and when his hands left my hair, he picked me up to lift me onto the counter next to the sink.

I wrapped my legs around his hips, pulling my hands out from underneath his shirt again and placing them on either side of his neck to keep him close as his tongue brushed against mine.

I could feel his shaft harden against my crotch, and he held me close with one hand cupping the back of my head while the other grabbed my leg above my right knee.

My heart was pounding again, and I wished I were more open about my feelings toward him, wanting to tell him just how he made me feel even when he wasn't around.

I fell hard for him, and I knew he did the same for me, but saying those three words were a big step neither of us wanted to take. Not yet, but hopefully very soon.

I moved my hands into his wavy hair and tugged on it close to his scalp, making him press his hips against mine harder and let out another groan as I deepened the kiss with my tongue dipping further into his mouth.

The more time I spent with him, the more I realized our age difference. Not because I had lived fewer years on this planet than he had, but because of our bodies.

Whenever my soft skin rubbed against his, or his hands moved along my body, the roughness made me shiver all over again, and the wrinkles I felt whenever I caressed his face reminded me of the first time I realized I was into older men.

Something about them, especially Riggs, made me feel safe and protected, but it was the confidence and strength he radiated that made my body tingle most.

Again, it wasn't something most girls related to, but I didn't care about them. Riggs was the only man that mattered, and there was no one in the entire world who could tell me I couldn't be with him.

Chapter Thirty-Five

Riggs

I broke the kiss to press my lips against her neck while pulling back her hair and making her tilt her head to the side, and while I nibbled and licked all the way from her ear to the top of her tits, Valley cupped my cock and started to rub it through my sweatpants.

I had a few ideas for how to fuck her tonight, but I decided to go the unexpected way.

It wasn't like me to take things slow, and I knew Valley was slowly going crazy while I took my time to discover every single part of her body all over again.

I loved her curves, her tight waist, her beautiful long legs which held me close while they were wrapped around my hips, and I loved her hands, showing me with every single touch how much she loved what we did.

I've had many women in my life before, but none had ever touched me the way Valley had.

No one compared to my girl.

They didn't even have a chance.

"Daddy, please..." she begged, but I knew damn well she had no clue what she was begging for.

"Say that again," I challenged, cupping both her tits with my hands now and squeezing tightly as I looked back into her eyes.

She stared back at me, her eyes wide and filled with lust, just how I liked to see them.

"I need you, daddy," she croaked out, her hands fisting my hair tightly.

She didn't have to tell me that, but hearing her call me daddy made my dick jolt every damn time.

I loved it, and the more she said it, the more I wanted her to continue calling me that.

Lifting her shirt, I exposed her tits as she wasn't wearing a bra. Another thing I loved about her, and hoped she'd never change.

Once I got rid of my own shirt as well, I cupped her tits again and leaned in to pull one of her nipples into my mouth, circling my tongue around it while squeezing the other.

Her soft moans got louder as I sucked harder on it, and when I let it pop out of my mouth, I moved to the other and licked it before giving it the same attention.

Her hands were still in my hair, tugging and pulling and sending bolts of lightning right to my dick.

"More," she begged, trying to push my head down. But I wasn't done with her tits yet.

I massaged them while I was sucking on her hard nipple, not getting enough of her.

Her tits were perfect. Not too big but just the right handful, and the longer I played with them, the more sensitive they got from my touch.

She bucked her hips and pressed her crotch harder against mine before moving them in slow circles, rubbing her pussy on my hardness.

"Fuck," I growled as she moved one hand between us to cup my dick, squeezing it tightly and pulling at my balls now that it was easier for her to access them through my sweatpants.

"I'm really trying to be good, Valley, but you're making it so fucking hard."

"I don't want you to be good. I want you to fuck me like the first time. Please, daddy," she begged once more, and that was it for me.

Guess she really didn't like this side of me, but I happily changed into the rough motherfucker I've always been.

My hand wrapped around her throat to choke her hard, but that didn't faze her much anymore, so I squeezed harder until her breath caught in her lungs, not able to let it out and having to hold her breath.

There had been a reason why I wanted her in my bathroom, but I was contemplating taking her to my bed and fucking her merciless, as that's what she wanted me to do.

"And I hoped you'd drink my piss again tonight," I said in a low voice, seeing her eyes light up as she heard the word piss.

Dirty little girl...just how I liked it.

She tried to move her head, most likely wanting to shake it while I kept my fingers tightly around her throat.

"Or am I mistaken?" I asked, placing my other hand on her pussy underneath her tiny skirt.

A choking sound came out of her, and I let her take a breath for a quick moment while rubbing her clit which—surprise, surprise—wasn't covered by panties.

"I want it," she told me, catching her breath before I tightened my grip again.

"Show me how much you want it," I challenged, but it didn't take her long to make me step away from her.

Her hand squeezed my balls hard, making it hurt instead of feel good which made me take my hand off her pussy and slap her cheek hard enough to make her jump.

"Starting to be reckless again, huh? On your damn knees!" I ordered, letting go of her and watching as she got down from the counter to kneel in front of me.

"Yeah, open that mouth. You're a fucking slut and you already know what to do, hm?"

Talking to her like that had an interesting effect on her, and there was no sign of her not liking it.

She loved being called all kinds of things, but if she'd have the choice, she'd want me to call her a slut every time we'd fuck from now on.

I pushed down my sweatpants, exposing my dick as I wasn't wearing boxer briefs, and her eager eyes immediately dropped to my length as I palmed it and started to stroke it right in front of her face.

"Tell me what you want, Valley."

She licked her lips and swallowed hard. "I want your piss in my mouth," she told me in a soft purr which always made my dick jolt.

"I wanna taste it. Swallow it," she added, placing her hands on my thighs and moving closer.

I fisted her hair at the top of her head and pushed her back, not letting her get what she wanted so easily.

With her head tilted back against the cabinet, I stood over her and made her pull my balls into her mouth.

"Argh, fuck..." I groaned, continuing to rub my length while she sucked and licked my most sensitive body part.

And the tease she was, she licked her way down to my asshole, wetting it before pushing her finger inside of it.

She was brave enough to do so without my permission, but at this point, I couldn't give less of a fuck.

I pulled back and pushed my dick into her mouth while she kept playing around my backdoor and making me throb while my tip hit the back of her throat.

"Keep those pretty eyes on me, baby. Fuck...you're so damn gorgeous," I growled.

I pulled out again, and as she looked at me, the first few drops of piss filled her mouth.

She was so damn young, and for her to be into this kinky shit was like hitting a fucking jackpot.

I loved seeing her swallow my piss, and although most of it flowed out of her mouth and onto her tits, it made this whole experience hotter.

"You like that, huh? God, baby...you're so damn perfect."

When I was done emptying myself in her mouth, I pulled my dick out before pulling her up and making her wrap her legs around my hips again as I carried her to the bed.

I didn't care how dirty my sheets got. Changing them would be worth every second after tonight.

"I want you dirty, Valley. Show me you belong to me."

I sat down on the edge of the bed and made her straddle my legs while I easily slid inside her wet pussy while my other hand cupped her ass.

She steadied herself with her hands on my shoulders, and once she got used to my length again, she started to ride me as if she hadn't done anything else in her life before.

I pulled her skirt up in the back, reaching around her to slide my fingers through her slit from behind and wetting them before pushing one finger into her ass the way she did to me before.

I had other intentions than using just my finger, and for that I had to start preparing her for it.

"I'm gonna fuck this tight pussy first, and your ass is next," I muttered as she kept riding me.

As I was impatient, I needed to hurry up and get her tight hole ready for my dick, and once I pushed two fingers inside it with her still on my dick, I stretched her by pushing apart both fingers.

"Oh, God!" she cried, throwing her head back and closing her eyes as I continued to finger her until she stopped moving on top of me.

That was the right time for me to turn around and let her down on the bed, making her turn onto her stomach with her legs dangling down on the side of the bed.

I quickly leaned in to lick through her slit, wetting her asshole a little more before pushing my tip against it, letting her adjust to the thickness of my length.

She was good at enduring the pain I caused, but this was different and could cause more pain than even she could handle.

"So fucking tight. You're a good little slut for letting me fuck this tight asshole," I praised.

It didn't take long for me to slide into her, and once inside, I let her take a few breaths before I gripped her hips on both sides and started to fuck her hard.

Her cries were mixed with pleasure and pain, and the way she pushed back with every single one of my thrusts made me move faster.

"That's it, baby. Show me how hard you want to be fucked."

I reached around her to place my fingers back on her clit, and it was already pulsating as much as it would when I licked and sucked on it.

"Such a good girl," I praised, reaching for her hair with my right hand and wrapping it around my fist, pulling on it every time she met my thrust.

I continued to rub her clit, and it didn't take too long for her legs to start shaking and her cries turn into muffled sounds as I pressed her head against the mattress.

"I'm gonna come in this tight hole, baby. Keep clenching it around my dick," I challenged, and as always, she did.

I was close, and instead of holding on to it and pushing back an orgasm, I needed to let go before I'd be the one not having enough strength for round two and three later on.

She was staying here the whole night, and fucking once wouldn't do it.

My orgasm snuck up on me as I let go of her hair and slapped her ass hard, making her cry out again and her clit throb with excitement.

"Make me come, Valley."

She moved her hand between her legs to reach for my balls, playing with them and intensifying everything I was feeling inside.

"FUUUCK!" I groaned, slapping her ass again before thrusting into her one last time and staying buried deep inside of her while my cum filled her asshole.

My body shuddered in response to hers, and when I finally caught my breath again, I pulled back slowly, moving into her one last time before letting all my cum ooze out of her.

I watched as it flowed down her aching pussy, and since I wasn't going to let her suffer tonight, I made her turn onto her back and knelt between her legs to play with her clit until she came as well.

The taste of my own cum didn't bother me, and as I licked through her slit, I tasted her sweetness just as much.

I moved my gaze to hers, watching how her face relaxed as I pushed two fingers back into her ass.

"Oh, God," she moaned, gripping my hair, keeping me right there and making sure I wouldn't leave without letting her reach an orgasm.

I flicked my tongue against her clit, watching her closely, and only seconds later, her eyes closed as it hit her all at once.

Her whole body shook, legs squeezing my head and her hands pulling my hair, almost ripping it out.

She calmed down after a few seconds, and I moved up to kiss her, letting her taste not only me but herself on my tongue.

"Mine," I muttered, needing her to burn that into her brain and never forget about it.

"I'm yours," she replied in a whisper against my lips, deepening the kiss shortly after while we both came down from our highs.

***

It's been years since I last slept with a girl next to me, but having Valley wrapped in my arms was what I wanted to get used to from now on.

After our long night of fucking, she collapsed and fell asleep with no more strength left in her body.

Even I was overwhelmed and completely ruined because of her, but I wouldn't wanna have it any other way.

I had opened my eyes more than once in the past few hours, making sure she was still here with me and hadn't left without saying goodbye.

For some reason, I was scared she'd suddenly disappear, leaving me empty and alone, but to my luck, this girl stayed in my arms without moving and breathing so calmly I could barely hear it.

As wild as she was when she was awake, which I loved about her and was one reason why she was mine, I liked her this way almost as much.

Calm and serene, without a naughty mouth teasing me in the most inappropriate situations possible.

I brushed through her hair, keeping my right arm wrapped around her shoulders while her face was buried deep into the crook of my neck.

Our legs were tangled underneath the covers, and her hands were clasped close to her chest, almost as if she was trying to protect herself.

Her soft skin felt amazing underneath my touch, and when I placed my left hand on the side of her face, she turned her head with her eyes still closed.

The city lights lit up my bedroom enough to see her beautiful face, and when she mumbled something, barely moving her lips, I tried to figure out if she was talking to me or in her sleep.

I didn't wanna wake her up, so I kept quiet and brushed along her cheek gently as she furrowed her brows slightly, looking so damn adorable.

"Your Dove," she whispered, this time clearer, but there was no way she was awake.

I smiled, kissing her forehead to make that frown go away. "You're my Dove. My *Valley*," I corrected myself.

This, the calm version of herself, wasn't Dove, because that naughty little thing never looked so angelic as Valley did right now.

"And I'm yours. Forever," I whispered, pressing one more kiss to her cheek before falling back asleep, knowing she'd still be here when I woke up in the morning.

Chapter Thirty-Six

Riggs

The country club was a place I liked to spend time at when I was younger, but now that I had retired, this didn't feel like the place for me.

People here talked a lot of shit, and although meeting my old friends was nice, I wouldn't come back here if it weren't for Andrew's invitation.

Now that I had Valley by my side, all I wanted to do was lock her up in my room and fuck her ruthlessly until we both collapsed.

Once again, over and over.

Last night was one of those times, and when I saw her walk toward me by the country club's entrance, I couldn't help but grin at her unsteady and shaky walk.

Maybe fucking her that hard was a mistake last night, knowing we'd both be sitting at the same table with most of her family tonight.

She looked incredible in that dark green dress covering not even half of her body, and the velvety texture hugging her upper body tight made me want to fuck her in it.

Her long legs weren't covered in tights, and their smoothness made my fingertips tingle with excitement to touch them.

She smiled at me from across the room, a hint of naughtiness in her eyes as she said hello to her uncle while keeping her eyes on mine.

With my hands pushed into my pants' pockets, I waited patiently for her to reach me, and in the meantime, I took in all her beauty from head to toe.

How the hell did I get so lucky? And it was mostly her pulling me closer to her.

"Glad you could make it," Andrew said as he stepped in front of me and blocked my view of his daughter.

"Thanks for the invite," I replied, shaking his hand and hugging him before he stepped away again so Della could greet me.

"You look wonderful, Della," I told her, kissing her cheeks while keeping my hand safely on her back.

"Thank you, Riggs. No date tonight?" she asked.

"Was I supposed to bring one?"

"No, I was just hoping we'd see you with a woman by your side. You've been single for so long," she said with a pout.

Most of my life, actually. Until now.

"No woman," I replied, looking back at Valley who was walking our way. I had her, and someday it would all come out.

"Hello, Riggs," she greeted, stepping closer to me and placing her hand gently on my chest, then she leaned in to kiss my cheeks the way I did with her stepmother.

"Valley," I replied, our eyes meeting again.

The tension between us was insane, wanting to pick her up and carry her into the back to show her just what she made me feel.

"Valley here got praised by headmaster Thompson last week. She's not only top of her year, but the whole school. She's been studying hard and giving her best," Andrew said proudly, and I raised a brow at Valley.

"I didn't know about that," I said, my voice low, letting her know that I would've appreciated her telling me about her academic achievements.

She's an extremely smart girl, and with that brain she was even able to wrap me around her little finger.

"Congrats," I added.

"Thank you, your brother actually helped me understand a few things in Chemistry which helped me raise my grade. Maybe you can tell Garett—*oh*, I mean Marcus—I said thank you."

She was messing with me, and calling my brother by his fucking screen name just got her a ticket to a hard spanking the next time she came over.

"I will," I muttered with a clenched jaw, pushing my hands back into my pockets before they slipped.

"Let's go sit down. They'll start serving food soon," Della announced.

As the rest of their family followed Andrew and Della into the large dining room overlooking half of the golf course and part of the lake, I stepped closer to Valley to whisper in her ear.

"Don't start," I warned, but the mischievous grin on her lips told me she was going to do the exact opposite tonight.

"I'm just teasing, old man. Don't be so grumpy."

I raised a brow at her, but instead of getting annoyed with her, I placed my hand on her lower back and nodded toward the dining room.

"Go, and stop fucking around."

She laughed softly, and when no one was watching, she placed a kiss to my jaw. "I missed you today," she whispered.

She had left after I prepared breakfast this morning, but before that, we had spent a few hours in bed, cuddled up and not really talking much but instead enjoying our time together.

"Me too," I replied, then nodded toward the dining room again. "Let's go, before people get suspicious," I said, taking one more good look at her dress. "You look beautiful, by the way."

She smiled brightly and squeezed my arm. "Thank you."

***

We sat down at the large, round table in the middle of the room, and of course Valley had to sit right next to me.

Not that it bothered me, I just hoped tonight would pass quickly so I could go home and take off these tight pants and give my dick some space.

Her presence had always had an effect on me, but for some reason, that effect was double tonight.

I also felt as if something was going to happen, not sure if it was a good or bad thing.

Either way, I needed this dinner to be over.

***

Eleven-forty, and we were still sitting at the damn table, this time with dessert on our plates.

Valley was surprisingly calm tonight, not living up to her standards. Instead, she was talking to her cousin, Beatrix, sitting next to her.

I listened in on their conversation, but it was pretty damn boring even with Valley carrying most of it.

Something was up, and it couldn't be possible that she hadn't even touched me underneath the table.

Not even once, so as petty as I was, I took it upon myself to do what I told her not to.

Christ, why was I even mad when she listened for once?

I placed my hand on her thigh, squeezing it while I kept my eyes on Andrew who was telling a story, but when she moved her gaze to me, I turned my head to look at her.

It's been far too many hours since we had properly looked at each other, and our looks mimicked each other's, both filled with need.

I couldn't sit here any longer without touching her, and the longer she stared at me, trying to figure out if she should get up so I could follow her out of the room, the more I wanted her to.

I brushed my thumb along her soft skin, feeling the heat between her legs against my hand.

No panties. Of course not.

I cleared my throat, and as I was about to look back at her father, she pushed the chair back and got up. "Excuse me," she told her parents, and five seconds later she had left the room.

I let a few minutes pass, seeing as the bathrooms were upstairs and would take a while to get to, and when Andrew and Della picked up on their conversations again, I got up as well and walked out of the dining room to get to the large stairs leading to a more private area of the club.

There was a bar upstairs, and the barkeepers were getting ready to serve their guests as soon as they were done eating their desserts.

I walked past the bar to get to the bathrooms, and when I rounded the corner, Valley gripped my tie and pulled me to her, crashing her lips against mine.

"I missed you," she whispered into the kiss, and I pushed her against the wall with my hand wrapped around her throat to immediately take control over her.

"You've been a good girl tonight," I replied, biting her bottom lip and then sucking it into my mouth to show her how much I needed her.

I muffled her soft moans by deepening the kiss, and while I kept her in place with my right hand, I moved my left under her dress to feel how wet she was.

She was wet enough to make her juices drip down her thighs, and I could smell her arousal without having to lift my hand to my nose.

I pushed my tongue into her mouth to taste her, and her hands moved down to my crotch, cupping my dick and squeezing it tightly to show me her needs and wants.

This couldn't go on for too long, but in the few minutes we had left, I wanted to make the best out of it.

I pushed my wet fingers into her pussy after rubbing her clit, and while her legs started to shake, I moved my knee between them to keep her steady on her heels.

She gripped my arms tightly, kissing me back passionately.

As good as she was, not teasing or messing with me, it made me want to fuck her even harder and punish her.

It contradicted everything I stood for, because her being obedient was what every dominant man would want, but it pissed me off more than anything, to be honest.

I wanted her to misbehave, show me her wild side and risk getting caught.

Her tightness squeezed around my two fingers while I moved them faster, and to make her come faster, I rubbed my thumb against her clit, feeling it throb at the touch of it.

"Such a good girl...show me how bad you can be," I challenged. "Come for me, Valley."

Our eyes met again, and I didn't look away and watched closely as pleasure filled hers.

"Come for me," I repeated, my face close to hers as her breath started to hitch.

"Oh...daddy," she cried out.

I kept going until her knees gave in, and when the orgasm hit her, she closed her eyes and threw her head back as I covered her mouth with my hand to make sure not even the bartenders a few feet away heard her.

"That's it, baby. This pussy is mine," I stated, pulling my fingers out and continuing to rub her clit to keep on stimulating her need.

She stopped breathing for a moment, needing a second to collect her strength, then she finally looked at me again.

I lifted my hand while keeping my eyes on hers, holding my fingers to her mouth for her to taste herself.

Her lips wrapped around them, sucking and licking and looking as sexy as ever. "You're gonna get more. As soon as we're outta here," I assured her.

We were both in a trance, only had eyes for each other and forgot for a split second that we weren't alone in this country club.

It was far too late when I heard heels clicking on the marble floor, and when we heard the shocked sigh coming out of Della's mouth, I stepped away from Valley. As if that helped disguise the fact that we've just been all over each other.

"What in God's name are you doing?" she squealed, directing her words to Valley and ignoring me for some reason.

"You are *so* inappropriate, young lady! You're a disgrace!" Della shot toward Valley, and when I turned my head to look at her, there was not a hint of embarrassment on her face.

"Della, let me—"

"How long has she been manipulating you into doing this?" she asked me. "Dear God, Valley! You're eighteen!"

Still no reaction from Valley, which I for some reason was proud of her for not freaking out like Della was.

This could be handled calmly without shouting and attracting the attention from the other guests.

"What is going on?" Andrew asked as he walked up to us and stopped next to his wife.

"I caught your daughter kissing Riggs. That's not how you raised her, Andrew!"

At this point, anything could've been said, but never had I imagined to hear what Andrew said next.

"So what? She's eighteen, and I'm sure she wasn't the only one having a hand in this," he said, looking at me with a raised brow.

Good point, because this wasn't Valley being inappropriate, as Della called it.

This was her and I wanting to be with each other but having to hide it for this exact reason.

"It's not all on her," I told them, not sure how Valley still stood there unfazed.

Guess she had seen this coming.

"It's disgusting! First you do those nasty things with sex toys, and now this? What's next, a porno?"

Jesus fucking Christ, woman.

Though...Valley had been naked on the internet before, so she wasn't that far off.

"That's enough!" Andrew said loudly. "Do you want everyone else to see you like this?"

"I don't care who sees me like this! I don't want a daughter who acts like a slut in public and at home!"

Della calling Valley a slut made my blood boil, even if I called her one too when I fucked her.

It was different though.

"It's on me, Della," I said, trying to get some sense into her. But she didn't wanna hear my side of the story. I've known her long enough, but this was a side of her I'd never met before.

"No, it's not! She's been a brat lately and now she's trying to get back at me."

Valley laughed, crossing her arms over her chest after straightening her dress. "Right," she muttered, rolling her eyes.

"That's enough," Andrew spat. "Don't talk about my daughter like this and stop being such a witch, Della. Let them talk," he told her, then he looked at Valley. "What's going on?"

I turned my gaze to look at her, watching as she clenched her jaw and tried to stay calm and collected.

"Whatever I'm going to say, she's gonna call me names again," Valley said, shooting a glare at Della.

"Because you're not acting like a lady! Is this how I raised you ever since your mother left?"

It wasn't a good idea pulling Valley's biological mom into the mix, and it showed as her brows furrowed and eyes narrowed. "No one asked you to act like my mother," she shot back.

"Well, but I did! And you should be thankful for it. I taught you a lot, and I'm disappointed that you go against everything God stands for!"

Shit, now she threw religion into this conversation.

Not a good idea at all.

"I don't care! Don't force your beliefs on me or anyone for that matter," Valley replied.

"You're going to hell," Della muttered, her disappointment written on her face.

"All right, that's it. You need to calm down," Andrew said, trying to get Della to walk away.

"No, it's not it. Why do you think this is how eighteen-year-olds should behave? You're still a child and not old enough to do such things!"

That was the one sentence that made Valley furious.

My Valley was many things, but her being a child and immature were far from the truth.

"You don't know me! Just because you were raised differently, doesn't mean I have to follow in your footsteps and lose my virginity at thirty!"

Which was literally what happened to Della, but this wasn't about her.

Valley looked at me, silently asking me for help. "Let's go," she whispered, making it sound more like a question.

As much as I hated to leave confrontations open like this, I knew this wasn't going to get resolved anytime soon, especially not with all these people watching the shit show.

I nodded and reached out to her, letting her wrap her hand around mine before passing her parents.

"He's too old for you, Valley. What the hell are you getting out of this?"

Valley stopped, turning to look at Della, ready to answer that question with full determination.

"His love, and he gets mine in return. I'm happy and I'm not gonna let you ruin this for me!"

She turned back around, leaving not only Della, but myself speechless.

"Valley!"

"No, let them go," I heard Andrew say before we walked away.

The stares from all those other people didn't matter, because I had Valley's hand in mine, showing me that no matter what would happen, she'd stand by me and vice versa.

Chapter Thirty-Seven

Valley

Her words hurt.

Not only because she did in fact raise me, but also because she had shown me that she wasn't okay with Riggs and me.

Instead of making it about the both of us, she pushed everything on me to make me feel bad, without giving Riggs and me the chance to explain.

Not that we owed her an explanation, but that would be the only way for her to understand why we were kissing back at the club.

I was sitting on Riggs's couch with a blanket over my legs when he walked back from the kitchen with a cup of tea in his hand.

He sat down next to me, a worried look on his face and a heavy sigh leaving his chest.

"How are you feeling?" he asked, handing me the cup and then brushing back my hair.

I was still wearing the dress, but I had taken off my shoes in his car already, not wanting them to hurt my feet any longer.

I shrugged, looking down at my tea and then up into his eyes. "How are *you* feeling?"

The corners of his mouth curled down, and with a shrug he said, "Only thing bothering me was her calling you all kinds of names. I'm surprised your father didn't throw fists. Thought I'd leave with a bloody nose and on my own."

I smiled, placing my right hand on his cheek while holding the cup with the other. "I'm surprised too. But I'm glad he didn't start a fight."

I caressed his cheek with my thumb, studying his face as he let his eyes wander all over mine.

"Give her some time. I'm sure your father will talk to her to make her calm down, and maybe tomorrow you two will get along again," he told me, but I doubted it.

"Della's gonna be mad for a long time. She's like a little kid who didn't get a toy or candy at the store. She's resentful," I explained.

He grabbed my hand and kissed the palm of it gently, then held it tightly in his lap. "Then give her all the time she needs. But no matter how long that will take, I'm not gonna walk away from you," he promised.

I smiled at him. "Me neither."

"'Course you're not. You said you loved me," he said with a grin.

"I did not say that!"

"Sure did. I might be getting old but I can hear just fine, darling."

I frowned at him as my cheeks turned red. How was I embarrassed when I did and said far worse things in the past?

"You didn't hear correctly," I muttered, taking a sip of my tea and then placing the cup on the coffee table.

"Sure about that?" he challenged, raising a brow at me with a smug grin on his lips.

I shrugged. "I might've said something about love," I muttered, pressing my lips into a thin line and avoiding looking at him.

Riggs chuckled and leaned back with my hand still in his, sliding his fingers through mine and squeezing them tightly.

"I've never seen you like this. Know that I feel the same, Valley. We might've had a rough start...in a good way, and as I told you before, you're mine. And you will be until I take my last damn breath."

Which wouldn't be anytime soon.

Riggs was a healthy man, and working out was only one thing helping him stay healthy.

I stared at him for a while, taking in his words and letting my feelings take over as I moved on top of him to straddle his lap.

Cupping his face with both hands, I leaned in and kissed him gently, showing him my not so wild side for once.

His lips moved against mine, letting me take over and control the kiss while his hands moved to my hips to hold me tight.

My heart was beating fast, making it hard for me to think straight. But when I broke the kiss to look at him again, I smiled before taking a deep, needed breath.

"I love you, Riggs. I don't care how many years there are between us, or who will judge us for being together. You're perfect for me."

His face was serious all of a sudden, and for a split second I was thinking I just made a huge mistake.

Thankfully though, he lifted his hand to cup my own cheek, tilting his head to the side and letting a smile appear on his lips.

"Say that again," he said quietly, his voice rough and deep.

I smiled, biting down on my bottom lip. "I love you," I repeated, knowing that was what he wanted to hear again.

"I love you too, Valley. And I could give less of a fuck about what others think."

Way to make a romantic moment not so romantic.

But that's what I'd have to get used to from now on, and I didn't mind at all.

I leaned in again, kissing him and then wrapping my arms around his neck to hug him tightly.

His arms came around to hold me close as he kissed the crook of my neck and took a deep breath while we held each other.

I closed my eyes to enjoy this moment, but after a few seconds, he loosened his tight hug to look at me again.

"I don't want you to worry too much about Della and her view on this. When she's ready to be confronted about it, we'll do so. But until then, don't let her affect your mood. You're old enough to make your own decisions, and you've shown me that many times."

I nodded, agreeing with him because even if I was only eighteen, that didn't mean I was still a child or had no way of making my own life choices.

And although I wasn't scared of going back home, I hated the thought of Della staring me down and calling me all kinds of things.

"Out of all the things she said to me, I think *immature* was what bothered me the most," I told him.

"Fuck that," he laughed. "You know how normal it was when I was your age to get married or have kids? Della grew up in that era as well, and she knows damn well that age doesn't say shit about your maturity. Hell, I know men my age that are more immature than fifteen-year-olds these days. Push her judgmental self aside. She's the one not able to hold a normal conversation between two adults," he stated.

Fact.

"Do you think I can stay here tonight?" I asked, changing the subject and picking at his tie to then loosen it a little.

"Of course you can."

Before I could say any more, bright headlights shone through the big windows on the front of the house, making us turn our heads.

I got up from his lap and let him get off the couch, and when we walked toward the front door, we saw Dad walking toward the house with a worried look on his face.

"Oh, boy," I muttered, hoping he didn't change his mind about fighting Riggs.

Dad usually wasn't an aggressive person, but I did find it weird how calm he reacted when he found out what happened at the club.

Riggs opened the door before Dad could ring the bell, and when he saw me standing next to my man, he let out a deep sigh, almost as if he was relieved to see me with him.

"Can we talk?" he asked.

Riggs didn't hesitate to let his friend in, but I was still a little skeptical as to why he would show up here after what he saw.

"Hey, sweetheart," Dad said. "You okay?"

I crossed my arms and nodded. "Yeah, I'm okay. Sorry about Della," I told him, but he waved his hand to brush it off.

"She needs some time, that's all. I was unsure if coming here would be a good idea, but

I had to know if you're okay. I just want answers about...this."

I had never seen my father this confused, but it assured me that he wasn't here to hurt Riggs, or call him an asshole for wanting to be with his daughter.

"Let's go sit down," Riggs offered, and we walked back to the living room where we all sat down, Dad on the couch opposite from us.

"I guess I'm here to find out where all this started. You've never talked to me about dating anyone, and now you're with him and I..."

I looked at Dad, understanding his confusion.

Although I knew exactly where this between Riggs and I had started, I couldn't be honest about it.

But I had to be honest about most things, or else this wouldn't make any sense.

"That night he came over for your birthday, that's the first time we actually talked. I guess...from then on it came naturally. I liked him, and the more time I spent with him, the more that grew into something bigger."

"So all those nights you said you were going to see Kennedy you were here?" he asked.

I shrugged. "Most times, and I'm sorry for lying. But I didn't know how you'd react."

Dad moved his gaze to Riggs. "Ever thought about telling me or asking my permission to date my daughter?"

Ugh, shitty question.

"No, I didn't," he told Dad boldly, making me widen my eyes in surprise. "She's got her own mind, and she's not afraid to show what she wants. I didn't talk to you about it because I didn't think you'd take it like this, and to protect her. I don't think either of us knew where this was headed, and if it were only a short-lived fling, I don't think it would've been necessary to tell you."

I did understand Dad, but I also knew what Riggs was saying was important. If this wouldn't have blossomed into an actual relationship, there was no reason for us to tell him we had sex.

"No, that would've been worse," Dad mumbled, rubbing his hands against each other with his elbows propped on his knees.

His eyes move to mine again. "Are you happy?"

"Yes," I replied quickly. "I'm happy, Dad. Riggs makes me happy. And I know it might be weird for you...but I don't want it to be. I don't wanna lose him or you. Or Della."

"I will talk to her when I get back home. Don't worry about it." He took a deep breath and looked at us for a moment before he nodded. "I'm happy if you are. Next time...maybe tell me before Della attracts all the attention of the whole country club."

I smiled and got up from the couch to hug him. "Thank you, Dad. You have no idea how much this means to me."

"I love you, sweetheart. You know I would never stop you from being happy."

"Love you too, Dad." I stepped away from him and smiled, and after he looked at Riggs and gave him a quick nod, we walked him to the front door to say good night.

"I'll see you tomorrow morning."

I nodded, then watched him leave and get back into his car before Riggs closed the door with a relieved sigh. "That went better than expected," he said.

I laughed. "Yeah...still not sure if he's serious or will come back with a gun."

"Let's hope not."

I wrapped my arms around his waist and leaned against him with my head on his chest and my eyes closed.

He kissed the top of my head and put his arms around my shoulders, holding me tightly against him as we both relaxed.

No matter the outcome when I go home tomorrow, I wanted to enjoy tonight with Riggs and not think about what kind of nasty words she had prepared for me next.

***

Everything I hoped for was the total opposite of how she reacted the next day.

She screamed at me, telling me how wrong it was to date a much older man and that I would go to hell for it.

That God didn't appreciate women like me, and how Dad was wrong for defending me.

She had repeated herself about ten times, and while I sat on the couch and listened to her rude and offensive comments, I stared blankly ahead, waiting for her to be done.

Even Dad couldn't get her to calm down, and I wished I hadn't gone home from Riggs's this morning.

I wished I had stayed cuddled up with him in his bed, with his arms around me and our naked skin touching.

But I hoped this would be a normal conversation, seeing as we were both mature adults.

"And in ten years...dear God! Do you really wanna be known as the almost thirty-year-old who's still with a now even older man? Do you really want others to talk behind your back?"

That was a sentence I had to respond to. I sat up straight and looked her dead in the eyes, wanting her full attention.

"I've never cared about what others think, and maybe you should start doing the same. Because the more that comes out of your mouth, the more I realize that this is about you. It's you who can't handle the fact that I'm in love, and you would break with every strange look you'd get, being known as the stepmother whose daughter is dating an older guy. It bothers you and you're scared! But guess what, Della? This isn't about you. This is about me wanting to be with a man who treats me with much respect, and who loves me no matter the circumstances! So I kindly ask you to mind your own business and stop caring about who I wanna be with because no matter how long you'll be angry about this, I won't stop seeing Riggs."

That shut her up, but only for a few minutes.

When I got up from the couch to walk away, she shook her head and laughed. "He won't come here, and for as long as you're still in college, you will not leave the house to go out," she threatened.

I raised my brows at her, then looked at Dad who was rubbing his forehead with his fingers.

"This is still my house, Della. You don't decide who comes and goes. You've done enough talking for today. Go take a bath or something."

I almost laughed because of how annoyed Dad was, but I didn't so she wouldn't get even angrier.

"It's immoral," she spat, and with one last angry look, she headed upstairs.

"I'm sorry for the way she's talking to you, Valley. I wish it were easier. I don't know what to do," he told me.

I sighed and walked over to sit on the arm rest of the couch next to him, wrapping my arm around his shoulder.

"You don't have to apologize. Knowing you accept my relationship with Riggs is enough for me. Even if I never thought you'd be okay with it."

"I've been strict with you all your life, Valley. I think it's time for me to step back a little. You've never gotten into trouble and you're also succeeding in school. You're going to do great things, and I don't wanna hold you back."

"Your words mean the world to me," I told him with a bright smile, hugging him tightly and closing my eyes to make sure not to ever forget this moment.

Chapter Thirty-Eight

Valley

Despite Della still not willing to talk to me, the past few weeks have been incredible.

Riggs and I spent almost every night together at his place, and when Della decided to go out and have dinner with her girlfriends, Dad was nice enough to invite Riggs over.

Dad was back to his usual self, and whenever Riggs was around, I took a few steps back to let them talk about everything they usually talked about without me being in the room.

I mostly left with Riggs on nights like those, so it was all good.

Christmas was coming closer, snow was falling, and although it was getting colder outside, I didn't bother putting on another layer of clothes underneath my uniform to keep me warm.

A coat was enough.

"I didn't see your car in the parking lot this morning. Did Riggs drive you?" Kennedy asked as she stopped next to me by my locker.

"Yes, and he's picking me up again. He's taking me to a little spa retreat up in the mountains," I told her with a bright smile.

I was excited to see him again, and since I've been to that spa once before with Della to have a girl's night out when I was sixteen, I remembered how relaxing that place was.

"The one with the salt water pool?" Kennedy asked, her eyes wide. "Oh, man...I really wanna go there sometime."

"Let Mason know. I'm sure he'll take you. He's been spoiling you since the start," I said.

"I don't wanna ask too much from him. I feel like I can't keep up with him and give back."

"Then you invite him to the spa. It's not always men having to pay for everything," I said with a shrug, placing my books into the locker and closing it.

"You're right. I'll invite him. Makes me feel powerful," she replied, smiling brightly.

"That's how you're supposed to feel. Wanna walk outside with me?" I asked, taking a quick look at my phone to check the time.

It was almost five p.m. and we both had classes all day long, so since it was the end of November, the sun was already setting.

I loved this time of year, when the snow and moon were the only things lighting up the town.

"Of course. I don't wanna miss out on a glance at your hunky man."

I laughed, and together we walked outside to see Riggs already standing there, leaned against his car and his hands pushed deep into his coat's pocket.

"You sure are lucky. Look at the way he's looking at you."

And I looked at him the same way. "I love him," I told her, smiling like a fool at Riggs.

No matter how much had changed in our lives, behind closed doors Riggs and I were still the wildest and dirtiest people in this town.

Our way of expressing ourselves was through sex, but that wasn't possible in public.

Well, it was possible, but I didn't think we'd ever go as far as having sex in public.

"I'm so happy for you. Have a great time tonight. I'll see you on Monday."

I hugged her and said goodbye, then I walked straight to Riggs and let him pull me against him with one arm while I leaned into him and hugged him back.

"Hi," I said, looking up at him and then kissing his jaw before he cupped my face with his other hand to pull me in closer and kiss me.

We'd been out in public before, and even after Della's outburst, people didn't seem to care about us dating, which was definitely how it should've been.

People minded their own business, and there was nothing standing in our way to be happy together.

"Ready?" he asked as he moved back to meet my eyes, and I nodded with excitement, ready to relax and have a great time at the spa.

"Can't wait. I missed you today."

"Getting cheesy again," he grumbled, making me roll my eyes.

"What? Do you want me to take off my clothes right here and tease you until you spank me in front of all these kids?" I challenged.

He knew I would do it at this point. Just to see him mad.

"No. Get in the car," he ordered, his grumpiness shining through again. His moods were like a rollercoaster, which went from being calm and quiet to growly and harsh in a matter of seconds.

That's what I loved so much about him. How unpredictable he was.

"Yes, daddy," I purred, letting my fingers brush along his beard before walking around the car to get inside.

I had packed my bag for the spa last night and brought it with me to his house so he could take it with him before we'd head up there.

Despite me being in college, and him having found a new hobby which was working on a decent sized boat he bought to restore it and prepare it for summer-time next year, we had enough time to be together without worrying about the important things in life.

I was still succeeding in school, even being ahead in some classes and receiving extra credits from teachers.

"You said you've been there before, right?" he asked as he got into the car and turned on the engine.

"Yeah, two years ago with Della. But I know they renovated part of it."

"They did. They added a hot springs pool outside overlooking the whole city," he told me.

"Really? Oh, wow! That sounds incredible."

He pulled out of the parking lot, and I leaned back to enjoy the ride which was only about thirty minutes.

Riggs placed his hand on my thigh while driving, and I placed my hands on his, sighing happily.

"I can't wait," I added, knowing we'd spend all evening at the resort until they'd close around midnight.

***

The hot water felt amazing, and the cold air in my face as we swam over to the border of the pool to look out over the city was a nice contrast to the warmth surrounding my body.

"It's beautiful," I said in awe, taking in the beautiful white scenery in front of us.

Riggs stopped behind me, being able to stand in this deep water pool, and he wrapped his arms around me while pressing himself against my back.

"It is," he said in his usual low voice, his lips close to my ear as he pressed a kiss to the side of my neck.

"We should come here more often. I think this kind of relaxation does both our bodies some good."

Because of all the rough and ruthless sex we had, our bodies reached their limits at times.

"Sounds good to me," he said, his voice low and his lips moving down to my shoulder.

There weren't many people at the spa tonight, and we were the only ones outside at the moment.

I could feel his shaft pressed against my ass getting harder, and since being in public wasn't something holding me back from teasing him, I started to move against him, placing my head on my crossed arms on the border of the pool.

Riggs continued to kiss my neck, and with my hair pulled up in a messy bun, he had easy access to my skin.

His hands moved from my stomach up to my tits, cupping them gently and squeezing while rubbing his fingertips against my hardening nipples.

I closed my eyes and moaned as he continued to massage my tits, sucking and nibbling at my skin.

"I wanna fuck you right here," he growled, moving his left hand down to my pussy and rubbing my clit underneath my bikini.

"Then fuck me," I challenged, wanting to feel more of him.

I've heard about cameras in pools before, but I didn't think there were any in here. And even if...why not risk getting caught?

Wasn't that what this relationship was built upon? Risking things to make it more fun.

I reached back between him and I, placing my hand on his cock and rubbing it through his swim shorts as he continued with his own fingers on my clit.

A moan escaped me, and just as I was about to push his swim shorts down, I heard voices coming from where you could enter the hot springs pool.

I stopped, but Riggs continued, and even with those two people now swimming in the same water as us, Riggs grabbed his cock and pulled it out, brushing his tip against my ass cheek.

"Don't make a sound," he demanded, wrapping his other hand around my throat and squeezing gently.

I nodded and looked straight ahead to the beautiful view, and so it was easier for him, I pulled my bikini bottoms to one side so he has better access.

We had sex in his pool before, but most of our bodies were out of the water, making it far easier for him to thrust in and out of me.

He took his time to get adjusted, and when he finally placed his tip at my entrance, I leaned forward a little more and arched my back so it would be more comfortable for the both of us.

I couldn't stop myself from moaning as he moved deep inside of me, filling me and continuing to rub my clit, while his other hand choked me to keep me from being too loud.

"Don't make a damn sound!" he hissed, and while I held my breath, he started to move his hips, thrusting into me slowly to not cause too many small waves which could attract the other visitors' attention.

They were on the other side of the pool which was round and overlooked a different side of town, yet they weren't far enough away to not hear the water splash against our bodies.

His cock was throbbing, and he pushed harder each time without being bothered by the others.

I didn't think he would mind getting caught, and the thought of it did spark excitement inside of me.

I pushed the thought of being seen while having sex in public aside and enjoyed Riggs's rough fucking.

"So damn tight. This pussy is mine, baby," he growled into my ear.

His finger kept rubbing my clit, making it pulsate as my hips jerked every time he pushed back into me.

I was already close, but lately that had always been the case. It was my attraction to him that could literally make me come by just staring at him, and in situations like these, knowing there might be people watching made everything more intense.

The tingles in my toes moved up my legs, then they spread into my lower belly while I tried to hold back the orgasm.

"Come for me, Valley. Show me how good I make you feel."

I wasn't sure if he wanted to come as well, because as exciting as this was, it wasn't very hygienic if he'd shoot his load in this pool.

Sure, having sex in here wasn't the cleanest thing either, but at least there were no bodily fluids in the water.

Unless kids decided to use this pool as their bathrooms.

"Come," he urged, rubbing his fingers faster as my pussy squeezed around his cock.

"Oh...yes, daddy," I croaked out as quietly as possible, and when my orgasm hit, my body shuddered.

"Perfect, baby...God, you're so fucking beautiful," he praised, keeping his shaft buried deep inside of me while I calmed down.

I was out of breath and it was him doing all the work.

An unpleased grunt came from the man now stepping out of the pool again, and instead of minding my own business and enjoying the feeling after the orgasm, I looked over to see their upset and disgusted faces.

I couldn't help but laugh.

"This is the first time someone caught me having sex in public," I mumbled, turning my head to look back at Riggs.

He smirked, pulling out of me and leaning in to kiss my temple. "And it might not be the last time," he told me, making it sound like a promise.

I turned to face him, my hand immediately reaching for his shaft. "What can I do?" I asked, not wanting him to wait for too long and make him suffer.

He looked at me with a smile, placing his hands on my hips and shaking his head at me. "Nothing right now. Let's enjoy the rest of the night and when we go home, you can show me how much you love my dick in that pretty mouth of yours."

I grinned up at him and nodded. "Can't wait."

He leaned in to kiss me while I pulled his shorts back up to cover him, then I wrapped my arms around his shoulders and kissed him back passionately, secretly wishing we were already home so I could release him as well.

Chapter Thirty-Nine

Riggs

I looked over at Valley who was sitting on the kitchen counter, staring at her phone and frowning.

"Everything okay?" I asked, cleaning the last plate to place it to the side to dry.

"Dad just texted. He said Della started another fight because she won't let you come home with me tomorrow night unless she doesn't attend the party."

"It's their anniversary..." I pointed out, confused as to why Della would miss her own party.

"My point exactly," Valley sighed, setting her phone down and looking at me. "We're going. I don't care if she's there or not. Dad wants you there too, so we're going."

"Didn't say I won't go. I don't think she'll miss her wedding anniversary."

"She's probably gonna ignore us and talk behind our backs," she said.

"Don't care. If she wants to be petty and mad on an important day like that, there's nothing I can do to help it."

Valley nodded. "Besides...she'd act the same even with just me around."

She had a point there.

Della still didn't talk to Valley, barely said hello and goodbye, which really proved the point that even people my age could be immature as shit.

"We'll go tomorrow and see what happens. Can't make her change her mind about our relationship," I told her. "Let's not worry about her. We had a great time last night at the spa, and we spent all day fucking all over the house. There's nothing tearing us apart."

Her smile grew at my words, and when I was done with the dishes, I stepped between her legs and placed my hands on her thighs. "You're stuck with me, and if you ever try to leave, I will remind you what you'll be missing."

"You know I would never leave you," she replied, wrapping her arms around my shoulders and pulling me closer.

I studied her face, wondering if she knew what it meant. Yeah, the age difference didn't bother us, but not even she could deny that when I'm eighty, things most certainly wouldn't be the same.

"Don't you want kids?" I asked, watching as her brows furrowed.

"No. I've never wanted to have kids. I don't think I would be a good mother," she said.

"How come?"

She shrugged. "I have this feeling in my gut. I've never wanted to become a mother...and I've also never wanted to get married. Those are just things that don't sound right. I just...can't imagine myself in certain situations."

I understood, because I've also never wanted to be a dad. Marriage was another thing I didn't think I would wanna go through, as not even relationships were something I was hoping to be in one day.

"And what if you get pregnant? Would you get an abortion?"

"I think that's a difficult topic."

"Why?"

"Because it depends who and where the father would be."

I nodded but wanted to hear more. "Example?"

While she talked, I caressed her thighs with both hands and kept my eyes on hers closely to not miss one single emotion.

"If the father disappears after he hears the news, I don't see a point of raising a child on my own. But if the father stays with me and helps me get through it all...I might change my mind about getting an abortion."

I understood, and before this conversation would turn into a political matter, I leaned in to kiss her cheek gently. "I'm gonna be old in a few years. I'm talking ten, fifteen years. No matter what I say, no matter how often I threaten you to stay with me, I don't want you to feel responsible for me if you don't feel like it. You're going to be in your best years, and if I for some reason start to get health issues, I don't want you to give up everything just because of me."

Valley was shaking her head while I spoke, and once I was finished, she placed her hands on my cheeks with a determined look on her face.

"I don't care what's coming in fifteen years, Riggs. I love you, and if you're lucky enough, I'll still love you in a year."

I laughed, squeezing her thighs and then moving my hands to her hips.

"I want us to live in the moment and not think about the *what ifs*. I'm happy, even without camming. And it's all because of you."

Neither of us were good with expressing our feelings, but Valley just showed me that it was possible if the words coming out were honest and truthful.

I might not have long enough to see her when she's thirty or forty, but until then, I would show her that a man, no matter his age, could do just as much as a guy her age.

Lucky me she preferred older guys anyway.

"Okay, you're right. I'll try my best not to think about the future."

That got another smile out of her, and so I leaned in to kiss her, showing her how much love I was carrying around in my heart for her.

Valley

There had to be someone knocking at our door as we were about to take each other's clothes off.

I sighed as Riggs stepped away from me, a frown between his brows.

"Are you expecting someone?" I asked, looking toward the front door.

I hadn't heard a car pull up, and since the light in the living room was on, it was hard to see who was outside.

"Stay here," he told me, but since I didn't listen much, I followed him to the entrance and waited for him to open the door.

A relieved breath left me as I saw Marcus standing there, his eyes immediately moving to mine.

"You're back," Riggs stated, partly confused and annoyed at his brother's return.

"Yeah, wanted to talk to you," he said, keeping his eyes on mine before he finally tore them off to look at my body.

Marcus looking at me wasn't as creepy when he did it through the web cam, but watching him staring at me with Riggs standing next to me was a bit weird.

"Something important?"

Marcus nodded, taking a quick look at him before moving his gaze back to me.

"I was just wondering...there was this girl I talked to. Very pretty. She never told me her real name, but she was honest and sweet."

Shit.

Did he find out now too? But how?

I crossed my arms and waited for him to continue speaking as Riggs still stood there in front of the door, blocking his brother from coming inside.

"It's weird, you know? I was hoping to talk to her again, but after she texted me that she would be off for a little while because of school, I didn't think she'd be gone for that long."

He knew, and how he knew weirded me out a little bit.

I kept quiet though, because maybe I could act as if I had no idea what he was talking about and turn this whole thing around.

I was uncomfortable, but he wouldn't leave until he had his answers.

Riggs was also still acting like he had no clue what his brother was talking about. "What are you trying to say, Marcus?"

"I'm saying that I didn't realize I had been talking to her, even taught her a few things. And now I also realized that she's fucking my brother."

There it was.

Straight forward and with no warning.

"Strange seeing you without that ski mask, *Dove*."

I couldn't help but roll my eyes at the dramatics he was bringing to the table. This wasn't necessary, and he could've just moved on.

Riggs tensed, and I placed a hand on his back with a heavy sigh. "I'll talk to him," I said, but he didn't feel like letting me discuss this with Marcus.

"What she did on that webcam is in the past, Marcus. There's no reason for you to be here."

"There isn't? Don't you think it would've been appropriate for either of you to let me know? Surely, you knew who I was," he said, staring straight back into my eyes.

So he must've put all the puzzle pieces together. My eyes, maybe even lips, my voice...

"What we did was purely platonic, Marcus, and you know that."

"It isn't anymore," he stated, holding out his hands on his sides. "Not sure how you're okay with this, but doesn't it bother you that I've seen her naked before you ever did?" he asked Riggs who easily towered over his brother.

Still...Marcus wasn't letting go of this.

"You really should go," Riggs replied, already having enough of his bullshit.

"Jesus, how was I so damn blind? Look at you," he laughed, his eyes back on mine. "Had I seen that face while you were fucking yourself with that dildo, I think I would've done far more than just drink my own piss and cum for you."

As frustrated as he was about this, I couldn't say or do anything to stop him from talking and including all those details for Riggs to hear.

"Shit, do you take double as much for him to fuck you in real life?"

That was what pushed Riggs over the edge, and I hadn't even noticed his fists on his sides.

I wasn't a whore who got paid to have sex, no matter what I did on that webcam.

"Leave," Riggs spat.

He wouldn't hurt his brother, and Marcus was lucky Riggs wasn't an aggressive person when it came to conflicts like this.

Yet I was scared it would all turn into a fist fight I couldn't break up.

"I wanna fuck her too. I've been wanting to ever since she showed me that pink pussy on the webcam."

Shivers moved down my spine, making me want to turn around and run away so I couldn't hear him anymore.

"Don't fucking talk about her like that. Leave, Marcus!"

I wrapped my hands around Riggs's upper arm, making sure he wouldn't take a swing at Marcus.

"I bet you talk to her like that, don't you?"

"LEAVE!"

Riggs's roar echoed through the whole neighborhood, and it not only left me shaking, but Marcus as well.

"And don't fucking show your face around here again! Not unless you can talk respectfully to and about my girl!"

His words were clear and finally made Marcus walk away, but as we stared him down, we didn't expect his next move.

It happened so quickly that I could only see what happened when Marcus was already in his car, ready to drive off.

Riggs was bent over with his hand covering his face, blood dripping down his arm.

"Oh, my God!" I cried out, placing both hands on his head to make him look up.

Marcus had bent down to grab a rock on the side of the pathway and threw it at Riggs like an asshole.

Well, that was fucking unnecessary.

"Let me see," I said quietly, and Riggs lifted his head with his hand still covering his nose.

"He could've hit you," he muttered.

As much as I appreciated him worrying about me, I needed to fix his nose because the blood running down his hand was a lot.

"Let's go to the bathroom. I'll clean you up," I told him as I locked the door and helped him down the hallway while I made sure not to make any of the blood drop to the floor.

"I'm gonna kill that fucking bastard. He's sick and needs help."

"Let's worry about him later. Sit," I told him, and he sat down on the small bench in the shower so the blood wouldn't stain the dark gray tiles.

"Keep your head low. Don't want the blood to flow into your head," I advised, and while he let the blood drip, I grabbed a washcloth to wet it and clean up his face.

"He's gonna pay for what he's done," Riggs muttered. "Bastard has been an aggressive piece of shit all his life."

To me, Marcus never seemed like an angry person, but seeing him hurt his own brother changed my mind about him.

It wasn't okay, and luckily Riggs's nose wasn't broken.

"If it helps any...you look pretty badass with that wound across your nose."

His skin was ripped over from one side of his nose, across the bridge and all the way down to his nostril.

Not sure how one single stone could cause such a wound, but it must've been the force Marcus had thrown it with.

Riggs laughed and shook his head as I carefully cleaned the blood off his skin. "At least we got something out of his attack."

I smiled and kissed his forehead, hoping to make it all better. "You won't need stitches. It's not deep, just a horrible part of your face."

"I have band aids somewhere in the cupboards. Strips that will hold a cut together. Just put some of those on and I'm all better."

I nodded, but couldn't refrain from another joke. "You won't be able to give me head tonight."

"Are you sure about that?" he asked, his brow raised high and his eyes serious as ever.

No, I wasn't sure about it. Not anymore.

I pressed my lips together tightly and made him hold on to the washcloth. "I'm gonna look for the band aids," I said quietly, and quickly moved to the sink to look through every cabinet in the bathroom.

Riggs's low chuckle made me shiver in the best way possible, and I hid my burning cheeks while I continued to look for what I was trying to find.

"Check the drawers too," he suggested, and sure enough, I found a pack of band aid strips made especially for cuts.

"Okay, I got them."

I walked back to him and grabbed a clean and dry washcloth to clean him up a little more, then I put the strips over his wound to hopefully hold it together.

"Thank you, baby," he said, placing his hands on the back of my thighs and pulling me closer between his legs.

"Of course. Do you maybe wanna try and calm him? To see if he's okay? As much as I hate him right now, I don't want him to hurt himself."

"He'll be fine. He's gonna crawl back to apologize to both of us sooner or later."

I hoped so, or else we'd both have people in our families who were against our relationship, and truly...one person was enough.

Chapter Forty

Valley

I was talking to Payton while observing Della on the other side of our living room, talking to one of her friends while she looked suspiciously disgusted and annoyed.

Riggs had arrived a few minutes ago, and as he was saying hello to everyone else, it was clear that people had talked about us already, just waiting to see the real thing.

They were waiting for us to greet each other, and since this was me we were talking about, I wouldn't hold back to rub it in their uptight faces that I'm in a relationship with Riggs.

"So us making out really worked, huh? I gotta be honest with you, Val. I did miss you after that night and was hoping you would've called."

I laughed and placed my hand on her upper arm. "I'm sorry I didn't. If my man doesn't have anything against it, I'd love to make out with you again."

"No." Riggs's dark voice made us look up at him, and although I was joking, I loved how jealous he was just hearing me talking about kissing Payton again.

I let out a happy squeal, then turned to him to kiss him in front of everyone.

I didn't care who saw, or what they were thinking, so I deepened the kiss with his hands on my lower back and put on a show before breaking the kiss again.

"Hi," I said, grinning up at him.

"Hey, my love. You look incredible."

Since Della wished for a black and white themed party, I decided to put on my whitest dress with a low cut out in the back.

"Thank you, handsome." He had on a black suit and tie, black shoes and a black shirt, making his white hair pop even more.

I loved it, and it made him so much more attractive. More than ever.

"How's your nose?" I asked, looking at it and seeing his wound was already closing up a little.

"Much better. Still a little swollen, but it doesn't hurt."

I nodded, caressing his cheek before grabbing his hand and turning back to Payton. "This is Payton. Payton, this is my boyfriend Riggs."

They shook each other's hands, and although the kiss between Payton and I didn't mean anything, Riggs didn't seem too happy to see her.

"Sorry for what you saw that night. It was her idea," she said, as if Riggs didn't know I was the mastermind behind our make out.

"Yeah, figured. It's all good," he told her.

"I'll go find my mother. I'll see you around."

I nodded and smiled at her before she left us, and when we were alone, I turned back to Riggs and pointed to the kitchen.

"Wanna go grab something to drink?"

He nodded, and as we walked into the kitchen, Della's eyes followed us until we couldn't be seen anymore.

"She's still not talking," I told him, but that wasn't much of a surprise to him.

"Don't worry about it. If she's still not gonna make a move tonight, it's hopeless. What do you wanna drink?"

I pointed to the glasses of champagne on the kitchen island, and he grabbed one to hand it to me. "Thank you. I think Dad's got a bottle of Gin in the pantry."

"I do. Let me grab it."

I turned to see Dad walk into the kitchen, then he went into the pantry and came back with a bottle of Gin in his hands.

"Saved this for tonight. Ever had this one?" Dad asked.

"No, but I've heard of it. I'll have some."

Dad poured two glasses, and after making a silent toast, we all drank a sip from our drinks.

"You two okay with all these people staring? Must be uncomfortable," he said.

I shrugged and looked at Riggs who didn't seem bothered at all. "I'll get used to it. I don't care what they think."

"Good. But I want you to tell me when someone makes rude remarks. I don't tolerate that, especially not in my house."

I knew that, so I hoped no one would test Dad's limits and get kicked out of here.

"They'll talk behind our backs, but won't say it to our faces. It's all good," Riggs said, looking from my father to me.

I smiled at him and took another sip of the champagne, leaning against the counter.

"Valley told me about what happened with Marcus last night. Sorry to hear. Looks rough," Dad said.

"Doesn't hurt anymore. I'm just waiting on an apology."

"What made him throw that rock?"

I didn't tell the whole story, because no matter how much I trusted Dad with my secrets, I didn't want him to know about the camming.

"Some issue we hadn't cleared yet. Nothing too wild," Riggs said, covering our lies well.

Dad seemed to believe him, and so they continued to talk about things I had no business in while I absently listened and watched our guests enjoy the party.

***

Della had managed to avoid Riggs and me all evening, not even crossing our paths once.

It was impressive, even in a house this big, but when Riggs was the only guest left, Dad told her to sit down on the couch and not run away for once.

It was my idea to get her to listen, no matter if she wanted to or not.

My relationship with Riggs was important to me, and if it meant urging Della to accept it, I would go through with it until it worked.

She's been quiet for too long, and I was sure keeping her anger inside was not good for her own mental health.

When Riggs and I walked into the living room, she straightened her back and looked away, silently cursing Dad for making her sit there.

We sat down on the couch opposite of her and Dad, and after being quiet for a little while, I took a deep breath and started talking.

"It doesn't matter if you sit here and listen or let my words go in one ear and out the other. I hope you'll try to understand, and maybe things can go back to how they were a few months ago." I kept my voice calm, not wanting to anger her or make her think I was doing this out of spite. "I know we don't have the same point of view in many things, but that doesn't mean that we can't get along, or accept each other's choices. We can't always agree with one another, and that's okay. And I hope you will sometime soon see that me being with Riggs isn't wrong."

I needed to take another deep breath. I've said what I needed to say, and now it was up to her to make a choice.

Either she would listen, or she would turn and walk away again.

"It's not fair towards them, Della. Valley said it perfectly. Differences are a big part of life, and I hate seeing you two so distant," Dad said, his usually stern voice softer.

I kept looking at Della, hoping to see some kind of change in her facial expression, but she still didn't look convinced by Dad's and my words.

She also kept looking to the side, not meeting our eyes.

"If it's more time you need, I'm happy to give it to you. But, please...don't act like I don't exist in this house. It's painful enough for me to sit at the table at breakfast or dinner with you giving me the silent treatment, and I can't imagine how painful it must be for Dad."

Because no matter how much her and I suffered, Dad suffered just as much. We were the only two women in his life who loved him like no other, and seeing him all worked up over this was heartbreaking.

Della's body relaxed a little, and I watched her closely as her gaze finally moved. Her eyes met Dad's first, and after a while, she looked at me.

"Can I ask you something?" she asked.

She was talking. That's a good sign...

"Of course. Anything."

"Has he ever forced you to do things you didn't want to?"

At first, that question almost made me laugh out loud, then it made me somewhat angry.

But instead of starting another fight, I stayed calm. "No, he did not. If anything, it was me trying to get his attention. Riggs is a good man, Della, and he would never do anything to hurt me."

Unless I'd ask him to.

Her eyes now moved to Riggs, and I turned my head to look at him and see that his face was relaxed as ever.

Della's words didn't seem to bother him, which was a good thing.

"Why her?"

Riggs was quick to answer. "Because despite all her craziness, she's got a big heart and an insanely smart brain. Even if I would've tried to make her do things she didn't want to, she would've used that brain to send me off running. But like she said...I would never hurt her and I've never had the intention to."

I smiled at his words, reaching for his hand and threading my fingers through his.

"I love her, and I think we made it clear that we don't care much about who talks behind our backs. This is our relationship, and I won't let go of her if this is what she wants."

I was glad to have him right by my side for this conversation, because the more he talked, the more relaxed Della seemed.

"You don't have to change your mind about us right now, but I hope you will sometime soon. We've been friends for so long, and it would be a shame if we'd continue to get out of each other's way."

Even without saying another word, Della seemed to have accepted us as a couple, and I smiled at her happily, silently thanking her.

"I'll still need a few days to process it all. I'm sorry if I made you feel uncomfortable," she said, looking from us to Dad.

He smiled at Della and nodded, rubbing her back to show her that what she just did was the right thing.

"This really means a lot to me, Della. Thank you," I told her, unsure if a hug was too much right now.

I would give her all the time she needed, and to speed up the process, I got up and tugged at Riggs's hand so he would get up as well.

"I'm spending the night at Riggs's. I'm going to school from there and I'll be home afterward," I told my parents.

"Okay. You two have a good night," Dad said, and after hugging him goodbye, I looked back at Della who gave me a quick nod to show me that she wasn't ready for a hug yet.

Fine by me. At least she was rethinking everything she put us through.

Dad walked us to the door where I quickly changed from my heels into my sneakers and grabbed my backpack with my school stuff in it.

"She's gonna sleep on it and be back to her normal self soon. Don't worry," Dad promised.

I hugged him one more time and watched as Riggs did the same, then he opened the door to let us out.

"Have a good night. Call me if you need anything."

"I will. Thank you, Dad."

**

"That went better than expected, huh?" Riggs said as he crawled into bed with me.

"Yeah, well...I hope she does actually get over it. It's not easy for her to get things that bother her out of her mind."

"At least she said she'd try."

I nodded, pulling the covers over our bodies and cuddling up to him. It was late already, and even though seeing him in a suit, looking handsome as ever, I didn't feel like having sex tonight.

We've done some pretty dirty and messed up shit in the past months, pushing each other's limits and showing how much we wanted one another.

Being close and cuddling without the intention of fucking was nice sometimes too, but that didn't mean we wouldn't wake up early tomorrow morning to fuck in the shower before I would head to school.

Riggs kissed my temple and pulled me closer to his body, and I turned my head to look up at him, placing my hand on his chest and caressing his skin softly.

"Have I told you yet how beautiful you are?" he asked, keeping his voice low.

I smiled at him and shrugged. "I wouldn't mind hearing you say it again."

He cupped the back of my head with one hand, his serious eyes flashing with pure love and admiration.

"You're beautiful, and I'm the luckiest motherfucker in the whole damn world," he said, making me laugh at his choice of words.

"I'm just as lucky," I told him in whisper, keeping my eyes on the man I had never known I needed so desperately in my life.

I loved him, and if people lived a second or even third life...I would wanna live mine all over again with him by my side.

No matter what people would think.

And no matter our ages.

Epilogue

Riggs

Six months later

I had thought about this for months now, and I knew it was something Valley wouldn't say no to.

I was waiting for her to come back home after school, pacing the floor in my living room and staring at the door from time to time.

What I had in mind would certainly spice up our relationship, and it would excite her for sure.

There was no way she would decline my offer, and the more I thought about it, the more I wanted to go through with my plan.

The door finally opened, and Valley walked in with her school uniform on, looking incredible as ever.

"Hi," she greeted with the sweetest smile. "I thought you wouldn't be home for another hour or so."

That was what I had thought too, but while I was playing golf with her father and two other friends, I felt the urge to come home early and make her an offer.

"Come here," I demanded, pulling my hands out of my pockets and waiting for her to reach me.

She placed her hands on my shoulders, looking at me with a worried look on her face. "Is everything okay?"

"Yeah, everything's fine. There's something I wanna ask you," I told her, putting both my hands on her hips to pull her closer.

Her eyes widened. "You're not going to propose to me, are you? You know how I feel about that, Riggs."

I chuckled and shook my head. "Stop panicking, baby. You know what I think of marriage. Not my thing."

She looked relieved as I said those words, but the concern still stuck with her. "What is it then?"

I studied her face for a moment, thinking about all the possible things she could say after my offer.

Most of those things were positive ones, so I decide to just spit it out without making her wait too long.

"I know how much you love to be watched," I told her, moving my hands down to her ass and cupping it while giving it a gentle squeeze. "So I was thinking that maybe you could set up your website for just one night and—"

"Oh, my God...you wanna fuck me while someone watches?" Her eyes grew big as her lips parted.

I chuckled. "Yeah, that's what I was thinking," I said. "What do you say?"

"Uh...yes?! Are you for real or are you testing me?"

"I'm for real, Valley."

I knew how much she missed camming, and she was being a good girl for me, not seeing or pleasuring other men.

This was a way of rewarding her, and besides...I would be the one getting to fuck her, not the man watching.

Ever since that night at the spa, I found a new thing I quite enjoyed.

Getting caught or being on the verge of it was exciting, and watching Valley have no shame either was what made me have the thought of fucking in front of a webcam in the first place.

"You're the best! God, I know exactly who'd be into this," she said, already running away from me to get to her laptop.

She was spending every day with me now, but went back home most weekends to see her Dad and Della, who by the way was now our biggest supporter.

It was strange seeing her go from angry about our relationship to defending us whenever one of her friends commented on Valley and me still being a couple.

Valley also had a much better relationship with her stepmother now.

I followed her into my old office which she now used as her own to study and do homework, and while she turned her laptop on, I leaned against the doorframe to observe her.

"Who do you have in mind?" I asked, unsure if I really wanted to know the guy's name.

"His name is Garett," she said, and I raised a brow at her.

"Stop fucking with me," I muttered.

She laughed, thinking it was funny pulling my brother into this. After throwing that damn rock, he apologized sometime around Christmas but I hadn't heard from him ever since.

I knew he found a woman as crazy as he was, and that they were trying to get pregnant and all that.

As long as he wouldn't come back here asking for help, I didn't mind being an uncle.

"His name is Jared. Nice guy, but very lonely. At least he was when I was still frequently camming."

I kept watching her as she set up everything, and with only one text, she somehow managed to get into contact with Jared who was immediately up for it.

"Where do you wanna fuck me, daddy?" she asked, her eyes filled with excitement and so much fucking naughtiness.

I looked at the laptop, knowing she still had to turn on her webcam before we could be seen or heard.

"In my bedroom," I ordered.

Without hesitating, she grabbed her laptop off the desk and walked past me to get to my bedroom, and once we were inside, I pointed to the bed where she placed her laptop.

"Put on your ski mask," I demanded, not wanting Jared to see her face.

I didn't need one, as my head would be out of frame anyway. Besides...it wouldn't matter if he'd see my face. At almost fifty-seven, I started to give less fucks about certain things.

Valley had brought all her toys over to my place as she spent most of her time here anyway, and when she pulled the mask over her head, I reached for her hand to pull her to me, placing my right hand on her throat and kissing her while I still had her to myself.

"You gonna be obedient?" I asked into the kiss.

"Yes," she responded.

"Yes, what?"

"Yes, Daddy."

Good girl.

"Turn the web cam on," I demanded, and while she did, I took off my shirt and placed it on the chair in the corner.

"Hello, Jared," Valley said, making me look at the screen of her laptop.

The man was about my age, maybe a little younger, and he was already naked and rubbing his dick.

Other men didn't bother me, as long as they weren't here in real life to touch my girl.

He could watch and make himself come while I fucked Valley, but nothing more.

"Hey, Dove. It's been so long."

"I know, but I'm here now. I fell in love, you know?"

Hearing her say that still made my heart flutter, because with every day that passed, I still couldn't believe she was mine.

"That's wonderful to hear, Dove. It's gonna be exciting to see him fuck you. He looks handsome from what I can see from here."

Valley turned around and grinned at me, mouthing the word *bisexual* before turning back to the screen.

Got it.

So Jared wouldn't just be staring at my girl, but also at me which was somehow making this whole thing better and also flattering me.

"He's very handsome," Valley agreed, then she stepped away from the laptop to walk over to me.

I gripped a fistful of her hair through the ski mask at the back of her head, then pulled her to me and kissed her again while her hands moved directly to my crotch.

She unbuttoned my pants and pushed them down my hips as I deepened the kiss with my tongue in her mouth, dancing with hers.

Soft moans sounded from her mouth, and before she could get rid of my boxer briefs, I pulled away and pushed her down on her knees with my hand still gripping her hair.

She loved looking at herself on the screen, but this time, she wasn't alone in her room, pleasuring herself while those men watched her.

"Eyes on me," I ordered, making her tear her eyes off the screen.

I pushed my boxer briefs down my legs, then stepped out of them so they wouldn't be in the way, and with my hand wrapped around the base of my shaft, I rubbed my tip along her lips, watching her closely and focusing on her rather than the man watching.

I could see out of the corner of my eye that he was stroking his own dick, but it didn't bother me one bit.

Good thing he didn't speak, or else it would ruin my whole mood.

"Open up, baby. Show me how far down your throat you can take my dick."

Her lips wrapped around the tip of it, and she slowly started to work her way down to the base, slowly but so fucking sensually.

She wasn't just teasing me, but also the man watching, but I had the pleasure to be here with her. I would've gone crazy if I were in his position.

I pushed myself into her mouth deeper, hitting the back of her throat with my tip and now holding on to her head with both hands to keep her right there and take control over her.

"You're a good little slut," I praised, starting to ignore the fact of being watched fully.

I loved watching her do things she put heart and soul into, and for me to have taken away something she was so passionate about was wrong.

I realized that now, and I was starting to have a feeling that this wouldn't be the last time we'd fuck in front of other people.

Only over a webcam, though.

Valley was the love of my life, and with her beauty and smart mind came all the naughtiness stored up inside her.

So who was I to stop her from being herself?

Valley

Jared and I weren't the only ones enjoying ourselves tonight, and once he disappeared from my screen, I looked up at Riggs who had just come inside of me for the second time tonight.

It took me a moment to recollect myself, and once I had the strength to tell Jared goodbye, who was breathing just as heavily at Riggs and I were, I made Riggs lay down on the bed with me, both sweaty and dirty.

"I love you so much for this," I told him, finally getting to be Dove again.

At least for this one time.

I missed her, and although she never left me, I could only show her whenever Riggs wanted me to.

Dove needed a webcam to be her true self, and tonight, Riggs let me be her.

He pulled me close and wrapped his arms around my body, kissing my forehead and then placing his hand on my pussy to cover it, trying to make the aching stop.

"You were incredible tonight. As always," he told me. "And I wanna see you like this again."

I frowned at him, unsure of how to interpret his words.

"What are you saying exactly?" I asked, observing him.

"I'm saying that I wanna see you like this more often. You're different when Dove shines through, and I don't mind fucking you in front of other guys. I thought I wouldn't enjoy it as much...but seeing you like this changed my mind."

He had no idea how much that meant to me, and I pushed myself up on my elbows to lean over him.

"And you're not joking, are you?"

I needed reassurance, because I had dreamed about this day before.

"Do I look like I'm joking?" he asked with a raised brow.

I smiled brightly, shaking my head and leaning in to kiss him. "Thank you, thank you, thank you!"

It was a weird thing to be excited about, seeing as most couples restrained from fucking on camera unless they were in need of some good money.

I didn't do it for the money, not really, and knowing that Riggs found a liking in this made it all so much better.

"You're the best," I told him, kissing him once again before he started chuckling at my clinginess.

"Keep that shit up and I will change my mind in seconds," he muttered.

I rolled my eyes at his words.

"Those are just empty threats and you know it."

He let out a laugh. "Try me."

***

"When will you be home?" Della asked, her voice coming through my car's speakers as I couldn't hold my phone while driving.

"Tomorrow. I'm headed to Riggs's. Didn't Dad tell you I won't be home for dinner tonight?"

"No, guess he forgot. Have fun then. And tell Riggs I said hi."

"Will do. Bye, Della."

We were back to our usual selves, talking daily and telling each other about this and that without holding back details.

Della opened up after that night of their anniversary, and I was happy she accepted my relationship with Riggs now.

It seemed more and more people started to show their support, but one who had always had my back was Kennedy, whose name lit up on the touchscreen right after Della hung up.

I pressed the green button, smiling and focusing on the street. "Hey, girl," I greeted.

"Hi! Does tonight still stand? Mason's excited, and I can't wait either," she said, her voice filled with excitement.

We decided to go out on a double date, and after many hours of trying to convince Riggs, he finally agreed.

"Of course it's still on. Did you pick out your prettiest dress?" I asked.

"Sure did! I'm wearing it right now, and I can't wait for you to see it. I think I'll look better than you tonight, and that's hard to beat even when you're wearing sweatpants," she joked.

I laughed and shook my head. "I know you'll look incredible. I can't wait. I'll text you when we leave, and I'll see you later, okay?"

"Sounds good. See you later!"

I arrived at Riggs's house and quickly got out to walk to his front door, pushing it open without knocking as this place felt like home anyway.

"It's me!" I called out, closing the door behind me before walking down the hall.

"Bathroom!" he replied, and when I entered his bedroom, I already saw him standing there with a towel wrapped around his hips, his hair damp, and a beard trimmer in his right hand while he leaned over the sink with his left hand pressed against the mirror.

"You're not ready yet?" I asked, placing my clutch on his bed and walking over to the bathroom door to get a better look at him.

"I just got back from golfing with your father," he stated, keeping his eyes on his beard as he trimmed it just a little.

"Well, we gotta hurry. The restaurant is thirty minutes away and I don't wanna make Kennedy and Mason wait."

"Why do we have to go that far out of town anyway?" he asked, now looking at me for the first time ever since I arrived.

His eyes wandered down my deep red, velvet dress which matched my lipstick. "You look beautiful, baby. As always."

I smiled at him, then I turned back to the conversation we were having. "Kennedy wants to avoid people she might know. Her relationship with Mason isn't public yet, and she's still trying to figure out how to tell her parents about him."

"Sounds a little like you when we first dated," he said, smirking.

"Yeah, but it's different. Her parents are insanely strict, and they wouldn't be okay with Mason. Or any other guy for that matter."

Riggs nodded, and once he was done trimming his beard, he walked over to me and placed his hands on my hips. "Guess we're lucky in a way. Your parents finding out could've ended far worse," he said.

"Yeah, it could've. I'm glad we're where we are now though. And I wouldn't change it for the world."

I reached up to wrap my arms around his shoulders, smiling up at my handsome man. "What's wrong? You look like you want to tell me something. Is everything okay?" I asked, caressing the back of his head and wrapping his wavy hair around my fingers.

He kept looking at me, studying me closely until he finally spoke.

"Move in with me."

I frowned. "I already live here, Riggs. Half of my clothes are here."

"I'm not really giving you a choice here, Valley. Move in with me."

He was dead serious, but how on earth could I move into his house?

"I'm literally here almost every single night. Besides...I don't think—"

"As smart as you are, I want you to stop thinking for once. I want you here every day. Every night. I want to be able to come home and see your face. I wanna watch you do your homework and study, and later on I'll fuck you so you can relax your brain. I want to go do all the shit couples do together. Groceries, shop for new furniture, change up a whole guest bedroom just for fun. I want you here, Valley. So move in with me."

This side of him only shone through when he was desperate for something, and knowing him, that wasn't often the case.

He really wanted me to live with him, share this house with him.

How could I ever say no to him when he was passively begging me, making it sound like an order?

I kept my eyes on his the whole time, making him suffer through my silence but I finally gave in.

"Okay," I whispered. "But you have to promise me one thing..."

"Anything," he replied, a smile already spreading across his face.

I leaned in closer, my lips brushing against his while my eyes closed. "Promise to love me forever."

He chuckled, pressing my body against him with his hands on my lower back. "You should know I will by now, Valley. I've shown you every day how much I love you, and I will continue to do so."

"Good, because no matter what...you'll always be my man."

And he could never get rid of me.

Not in five, ten, nor fifteen years.

Follow Seven

Instagram
@sevenrue

Reader's Groups on Facebook
Seven Rue's Taboo
Extremely Taboo, Shockingly Sick and Twisted
2.0

Subscribe to my newsletter!
www.authorsevenrue.com/newsletter

SCAN THIS CODE FOR MORE SEVEN RUE BOOKS

Made in the USA
Monee, IL
22 May 2023